GLENN ROLFE

Encyclopocalypse Publications

www.encyclopocalypse.com

For my rock n roll splatterpunks out there.

VOLUME I

NIGHT SWIM

Edward Young stroked through the warm water of the beautiful, new hotel swimming pool–his heart rate steady, his muscles in full swing–thinking about one thing: Paula. He found her in the local newspaper in the classifieds under "companionship." Paula was a hooker. No ifs ands or buts. For two hundred dollars, she let him in any hole he wanted to enter; sweet deal for this area, especially considering she wasn't a complete swamp donkey. Besides her crooked teeth and pointy nose, Paula was pretty. He promised he'd call her again tonight. Three nights in a row, that was a new record.

He reached the center of the pool on his sixth lap when he swam into a cold spot, sharp and out of place. The ice pocket sent his nerves on end. He'd gone swimming in the northern Atlantic Ocean off the coast of Maine during a late May visit to Old Orchard Beach–this stark coolness, completely out of the realm of possibilities for the pool's eighty-two-degree water, had that same unexpected bite. The bitter cold passed. He collected his thoughts, caught his breath, and finished his last lap. Walking up the pool steps, he sensed a presence. Something else was here and he had the goose bumps to prove it. The room was freezing. Not normally a man so easily spooked, Edward grabbed his towel from the plastic chair he'd left it on and made for the door.

Stepping into the long, empty corridor, he could see his own breath. The icy presence had followed him. Even the maroon carpet which ran all the way down to the inn's lobby was cool beneath his bare feet. The immense chill permeated every available space around him, freezing every door handle in sight, and sparking to life an intense fear in him. He broke into a run, heading for the nearest restroom.

Edward reached for the silver lever, his mind two thoughts away from setting his axis permanently out of whack, and, despite the icy cold beneath his palm, shoved open the door. He spun around to the other side shutting out the cooling hallway of the Bruton Inn.

Something followed me.

Standing in the men's room, clad in nothing but his swim trunks and a tiny pool towel that wouldn't fit a child, he waited. He was shivering, his teeth chattering, heart pounding. He could feel the wooden door at his back growing colder by the second. The small pool of water puddled beneath his bare feet began to freeze before his eyes. He stepped out of the slick space his wet body had created, and stood before the mirror, face to face with himself, intent on talking some sense into the man looking back at him.

"This isn't happening. This isn't fucking happening. Get a hold of yourself, you stupid asshole," he said through quivering blue lips.

A series of cracking noises stole his attention. He gazed back at the door. The floor beneath it began freezing over, the ice reaching out and to where he stood.

"What the *hell?*"

He turned to face himself and found his reflection blurred behind the frost settling over the mirror.

Another form began taking shape in the icy glass. He closed his eyes, took three deep breaths and tried to wrap his head around the insanity of this moment.

I fell asleep, I'm still in my room, this is just a bad fucking dream. I'm okay, I'm okay.

Forcing a smile, he opened his eyes. His gaze settled upon the girl now standing behind him.

Her cold breath prickled the back of his neck. Despite her beauty, he was more frightened than he'd ever been in his life. His lips quivered, pathetically mumbling out a prayer for help. Her frozen hand caressed his cheek, silencing the prayer and stealing his breath.

"I, I..." he said.

A shushing sound, like a mother comforting her stirring infant, reached his ears, yet in the mirror, the girl's lips did not move. Her dark brown eyes, mesmerizing and powerful, held him. Long autumn curls hung over her pale shoulders like a collection of coiled snakes waiting to strike. She was beautiful, and though her full lips refused to part, he began to hear a whisper, so small and sweet. The message floated between his ears. He caught fragments of sentences:

"Watch...", "...this way...", "...with me."

He tried again to speak, but his mouth betrayed him. He could no longer move. Ice encompassed him from his stomach to the floor.

How did I not notice this happening?

"Watch this," the voice spoke to him.

His eyes returned to his reflection in the frosty mirror. He he could still feel her breath on his neck and her hand on his face, but he could no longer see her.

The cold touch on his cheek lifted, the skin beneath it pulled until he felt it tear free. He screamed through his frozen jaw in absolute pain and horror watching his own flesh rip from his face. The chunk of skin and blood hovered in the palm of the invisible ice queen behind him. His terrified eyes, shaking in their sockets, followed its decent. The torn flesh hit the ice covered tiles at his feet with a sickly *plop*.

The entity caressed his chin.

He began whimpering a preemptive cry as he felt the invisible hand begin pulling away from his face, the flesh of his stubble-covered jaw line ripping up and away with its cold, dead touch. A deep ache beginning somewhere in the dark tunnels behind his eyes pulled him deeper into this horror show. Tears dribbled down his cheeks as the cool hand released another chunk of him to the frozen floor.

The deathly touch landed upon his forehead returning for another pound of flesh.

"No...no..."

He tried his prayer again, even managing to get out, "Please God," before his own voice became unrecognizable. The invisible demon tore the flesh of his forehead free from the top of his face. Blood rained down from the burning wound and into his eyes.

Let me out, let me out, let me out!

The cold presence landed over his right ear. Its icy touch penetrated his ear canal, funneled inside, and filled his head with a deep freeze that numbed his fearful mind.

In the mirror, his brain registered the condensation from his final breath as it made its escape past his blue lips. Seconds later, as his heart froze within his chest and the blood in his veins congealed to a halt, his pale blue eyes, reflecting in the mirror before them, frosted over.

The ice queen reappeared behind the body of Edward Young. She spared no smile, only a cold glance over the shoulder of the frozen soul before her. She slipped away, back to her place beneath the inn's heated pool.

***

Jeff Braun fought to keep his eyes open. A born night owl, working third shift at the hotel was normally a cakewalk. He immersed himself in book after book and graphic novel after graphic novel, scoured the internet for naked beauties or chat room-ready clowns to aggravate, and once in a while, snuck in a movie in the back office. Occasionally, like tonight, working the audit became a battle of wills. Sitting on his stool behind the front desk, eyes closed, his head jerked.

An incessant beeping startled him from his fugue state. He rubbed his sandpaper eyes, closed the graphic novel sitting on the desk, and walked into the back office to find out which alarm was going off.

"Where are you?" he said.

The fire alarm box in the entry way was silent. The busy chirp was coming from around the corner. He stepped to the other side of the partition and saw a flashing gold light on the settings box marked "Pool Room." The temperature monitor read fifty-eight degrees.

"What the fuck?"

The pool was supposed to stay at eighty-two degrees. Second shift had scribbled a note in the log book about an alarm going off earlier this evening, he hadn't really read it.

Jeff put up the *be right back* sign and headed down to the pool room.

He unlocked the door with his key and froze.

"Oh shit."

A bluish body floated face down in the pool.

CHAPTER ONE

Timothy Laymon, speeding twice the posted limit of 35 miles per hour, watched the October-altered foliage blur past his window as he cruised down the desolate back road labeled Route 5. His destiny was in the arms of the secluded sanctuary otherwise known as the Bruton Inn. The cool stream of wind from the slightly opened window of his Ford Mustang let in just enough crisp freshness from the chilled Maine morning to keep him alert. The man and woman on the radio, who were under the assumption that they were somehow funny, spoke of a brothel in some small town that had disguised itself as an exercise studio before getting busted.

Sexercise, I could really use a workout.

It was a silly thought, juvenile even, but true. He hadn't been with a woman since Beth Marston, and that had been over two years ago. *Blue balls* was a term he had learned to live with. He'd learned to live with a number of things beyond his control over the last few years. Losing Beth had caused him pain, sure, but the loss of his hair somehow cut deeper. He woke up one morning back in March ready to attack the internet with a can of Red Bull, and a couple of quick and easy book reviews for his paid blog, *Timothy's Horror Corner*, when he noticed his hairline running for the hills, casting his large, greasy expanse for the world (and all the pretty little girls) to see. He'd since shaved it all off, going with the cue ball look. The clean scalp had been awkward for the first few days, but he'd acclimated to it just fine by the time the hundred degree mid-July days came rolling in.

He ran the palm of his hand over his baby smooth scalp, and smiled a crooked toothed grin at his reflection in the Ford's rearview mirror—the dead girl in his backseat smiled back.

The Mustang swerved, crossing the yellow line over and over again until he slammed on the brakes, screeching to a halt in the middle of the deserted street.

Cold droplets of sweat busted out over his brow and down the length of his back. The gas station cheeseburger he'd ingested from a 2 AM pit stop, stirred in his suddenly nerve-racked stomach. He stared at his clenched fists in their white-knuckled death grip on the steering wheel. He was afraid to look again, afraid to confirm what he thought he'd seen.

"I'm real," she whispered in his ear.

He spun to face the impossibility behind him. *She was gone.*

"Fuck," he gasped out loud. "Holy fuck."

The overnight drive must have worn him out more than he'd thought. He sat facing forward behind the wheel of the powerful car, rubbing his tired eyes, taking a few more seconds to reset. Once he got a handle on himself, he eased the car forward, gradually getting it back up to speed. He wanted to convince himself that the vision had been the work of his exhausted mind and tired eyes, but could not stop glancing in the rearview mirror, certain the girl would reappear. She did not. He passed a sign that read:

The Bruton Inn- "Better Beds, Better Service, Better Stay."

5 miles

***

Somewhere beneath the heated indoor pool of the Bruton Inn, Sarah smiled, patiently awaiting the arrival of the unsuspecting harmony to her dark melody.

Chapter Two

"I don't know what to tell you. I stepped into the room and the light wasn't on. That weirded me out enough, but I could see my breath. It was cold, like winter cold."

"You heard what they said happened here, didn't you?" Shannon said.

"Something about a guy having a heart attack in the pool?" Jenna said.

Rhiannon stood just inside the door to the laundry room after using the employee bathroom. Jenna and Shannon's conversation about shadows and cold spots–a bunch of nonsense some of the housekeeping staff indulged their wild imaginations in–caught her attention. Being the new front desk girl, and admittedly not the most social butterfly amongst the female employees, most of whom talked about drinking and fucking and what happened last night on Teen Mom, Rhiannon had to eavesdrop for any gossip not pertaining to the aforementioned backwoods slut talk. She didn't believe in ghosts, but this was at least halfway interesting.

"Well, yeah, but you know why he had a heart attack?"

"He was outta shape?"

"I don't know about that, but I overheard Carla telling Pauline she thought it was the ghost."

"Fuck you, Shan. You're just trying to freak me out."

"No shit. Carla said she'd felt it too. She said she'd been cleaning rooms and had to step out because it got cold all of a sudden, and that sometimes she thinks somebody's watching her."

"Oh yeah? And what did Pauline say to that?"

"She told her not to be so superstitious. That the hotel isn't haunted."

"Well, there you go."

Rhiannon heard the door to the laundry room open with a loud clack. She quickly stepped back into the bathroom, flushed the toilet and walked back out pretending she'd been in there the entire time. Carla was giving the gossip girls the business.

"You two in here just jibber-jabberin'?"

"No we were just–"

"You get all the rooms down here finished already?"

"No, we still have a few–"

"I didn't think so. Now get your butts back out here and hurry it up. We got a full house tonight."

Rhiannon stepped around the corner and past the two girls with ugly faces.

"Hey there, Rhiannon, how are you doin' today?" Carla said.

"Pretty good. We've already had some people checking in early though."

Jenna walked between them, followed by Shannon. Shannon shot her a nasty "thanks for piling it on" look. Rhiannon smiled back. She wasn't really friends with any of the females outside of Pauline the general manager and Carla. She mostly talked to Kurt, who worked second shift, and the overnight guy, Jeff. Keeping company with the boys rather than the catty girls didn't do much for her reputation here either, but she didn't really give a shit.

"Well, we'll get the rest of those rooms ready for ya then. Back to the grind."

Rhiannon followed the wider woman out the door and into the hallway. Normally Carla could be heard swishing down the hall singing some oldies tune or another. Today, she was all business and that's what the girls were getting an earful of on their way back to their duties.

Back at the front desk, Rhiannon sipped her coffee (no cream, one sugar) clicked through some Facebook messages from her friend Angela who had left for college in New York this week, and waited for Kurt to arrive. He was due in half an hour. They had started at the hotel together two months before right after the body was found in the brand new swimming pool. She thought for sure that Kurt was going to ask her out, but so far that hadn't happened. She was independent and forward with most things, but something she'd never shaken was the idea that a guy should make the first move. It sounded stupid even in her head, but it's one of those, maybe the only, old-fashion things that she chose to cling to.

Kurt was sweet and cute. He played in a band and was constantly talking music. He was really into the sugary, bubble-gummy power pop stuff, bands like the Pick-up Sticks and The Connection. She preferred her music with more teeth, edgier punk/ alterative stuff like L7, The Explosion, or the Sex Pistols. But Kurt's love for all things rock 'n' roll was infectious. She could listen to him wax poetic on everyone from Elvis Costello to the Beatles to Green Day. He had an amazing smile and a cool fro-like hairdo that seemed to fit his personality perfectly. and with Angela gone, Kurt was the closest thing she had to a best friend here.

Her parents lived in Farmington, where they tried to convince her to go to school. Instead, she and Angela migrated toward Hollis Oakes, a slightly bigger city than Farmington, yet still smaller than Portland or Bangor. Their two bedroom apartment already seemed filled with shadows where Angela's stuff had been. Mr. Mittens, Rhiannon's black tabby, was the only comfort she had left. She planned on going to school at some point, but she wasn't feeling it just yet. She really dug her job at the Bruton Inn and would have been lying if she said Kurt had nothing to do with her decision to hang around a while longer.

Right on cue, he came through the front lobby doors snapping his fingers.

"Heeey Rhiannon, what's up?"

"Not much. Just a shit ton of arrivals tonight."

"Oh hey, I have something for you." She watched him reach inside his jean jacket pocket and pull out a cassette tape. "I thought I remembered you saying you still had a Walkman?"

"Yep." She'd shared that nugget of nostalgic info in their very first conversation during a lunch break. He was going on about classic albums on vinyl; she confessed her own precious caveman device, a waterproof, yellow Sony Walkman. She'd started collecting cassette tapes, two for a dollar, at a local music store called, Bullmoose Music.

"Here." Kurt's cheeks reddened as he handed her a mixtape. Her heart fluttered. The tape was labeled on the spine, "Rhiannon's Cool Kicks." She ran down the track list and found tons of stuff she loved: Joan Jett and the Blackhearts, The Ramones, Fugazi, and even some Dylan and Beatles.

"Aw, thanks, Kurt." She felt her face flush with warmth and tucked a long strand of dark hair behind her ear. "This is so cool. I can't wait to check it out. First thing I'm gonna do when I get home."

"Cool, I've been taking mental notes in our conversations. I hope I got most of your favorites on there."

"Yeah, definitely. What's that?" He held some magazines under one of his arms.

"Oh, I brought in the new Rolling Stone, new Q, and a cool KISS comic I found at Vintage Hannah's for Jeff."

"You boys and your comics."

"Well, I picked it up more because it's KISS, but they had two copies, so I snatched one for me, one for him." He set them down beside the front desk computer. "I'm gonna go get changed."

Rhiannon watched him bebop down the hallway. She looked at the cassette again. It'd been a while, maybe since sophomore year, since a boy had made her a mixtape. She was surprised to feel the same love-buzz course through her at the mere thought of it. The phone rang. She put the TDK-labeled plastic relic down next to her computer and answered it.

The rest of the night was full of check-ins and phone calls. She and Kurt were right out straight until 9 PM, then with all but two guests in, things died down. She confessed being tired and Kurt told her she could head out an hour early. As much as she wanted to hang with him, she really was worn out from the hectic night—plus, she wanted to listen to his tape.

She cranked a new CD as she drove the back roads into town. She wished her car had a tape deck, but she had no idea how to install one. It took her twenty minutes to get to her place. The apartment sat in darkness. She usually left the light over the kitchen sink on, but must have flicked it off when she did the dishes that afternoon before heading to work.

"The light wasn't on, which weirded me out enough... it was cold, like winter cold."

"Carla thought it was the ghost..."

Goose bumps broke over Rhiannon's arms as Shannon and Jenna's dumb ghost conversation replayed in her head.

She pushed past her irrational fear, pulled out her keys, and opened the door. A quick flip of the switch by the wall and light flooded the room. Mr. Mittens mewled at her and ran over to rub against her legs.

"Hello, Mr. Mittens." She picked up the cat and closed the door. The apartment was far from cold. The heat from the day clung to each of the apartment's small rooms. She walked down to her bedroom, turned the light on, and cranked the box fan by her bed. She set Mr. Mittens on her comforter and crossed the room to the yellow Walkman atop her burrow.

Slipping out of her work pants, she folded them and placed them back in the bottom drawer, grabbed some cotton pajama bottoms from the next drawer up and slipped into a large worn-in Patriots t-shirt she'd stolen from her dad. After dropping the mixtape and the Walkman on the bed next to Mr. Mittens, who was already curled up and sleeping, Rhiannon went out to the kitchen, grabbed a glass of water and shut the house down for the night.

Tucked in bed, headphones on, Mr. Mittens by her side and the fan blowing full steam at her, she hit play and let Kurt's Rhiannon-ready playlist sing her to sleep.

She dreamt of the cold pool room and a girl with curly hair.

Chapter Three

"Thank you so very much for all that you've done for us." Ms. Caroline Philips looked from Lee's eyes to her three cohorts, Ester, Lizzy, and Linda who sat nodding from their regular perches on the porch to The East Wind House.

"Ah, Ms. Philips, it's my pleasure. I'm just happy to help you ladies get some peace and quiet at this gorgeous property." Lee gleamed his charm toward her and her flock and graciously accepted her check for three thousand dollars. Her "evil spirits" were cast back to the dark side. The inn was clear and ready for business again. The "spirits" that brought such stress and fright to the little old lady brigade had been nothing more than creaks and moans of an old place combined with a healthy dose of too much TV and Lee suspected a confusion of medications on the part of at least two of the four women. He'd seen it before and couldn't wait to see it again. Easy money.

"Where are you off to next?" Ester asked from the little wicker couch next to the screen door.

"Heading inland to do a couple of book signings. I think a city called Hollis Oaks is next on the list."

"Oh, that's a nice little town. You have a safe journey, Mr. Buhl. And thank you from each and every one of us."

"Thanks, Ester."

"Are you sure you don't want to stay with us for another evening? It's a good little haul from here to Hollis Oaks?" Caroline said.

"Quite certain, Ms. Philips. It has been a pleasure, as I said, but I have a pretty tight schedule to keep and I always like to get settled into my next hotel the day before an event. Good to get in and do a nice spiritual cleansing before starting a new adventure."

"Oh, of course, dear."

Lee nodded to each of the ladies, kissed the back of Ms. Philips's hand, and made his way down the porch steps and to his car. They bid him farewell from the breathtaking white, wrap-around porch. The check in his pocket was all the appreciation he needed.

He climbed into his Mazda Shinari and waved as he drove away. He'd been taking on clients as an Urban Shaman for the last four-and-a-half years. The "cleansings" brought in a good chunk of change, but it was the series of books, *Paranormal Experiences through the Eyes of the Urban Shaman*, written about those jobs that really filled the bank. The East Wind House would fit lovely in his current book: *Paranormal Experiences through the Eyes of the Urban Shaman: Ghosts by the Sea*. He had already begun Ms. Philips's entry last night, being sure to add a plethora of sinister voices and ghastly shadows trying to shoo him away. The piece could be finished tonight if he got into town early enough. Hollis Oakes was about an hour and twenty minutes inland. He could make it in half that. Lee turned up the classic rock station on the radio and pressed the pedal toward the floor.

Less than a minute down the road, blue lights shined in his rearview mirror.

He pulled the car over to the shoulder and waited for the State Trooper to come say hello. Lee grabbed a couple copies of the latest in his Urban Shaman series, *Deep Woods*, and set them on his lap.

"Evening, sir," the officer said. "License and registration."

"Hello, Officer. Let me grab the registration for you." He picked up the books and placed them on the dash and watched the trooper eyeing them. "Here you go." Lee handed him the requested credentials.

Officer Betts checked out the license and then motioned to the dash. "You write those books?"

"Yes, sir. I'm actually on my way inland to do a signing tonight. Running a bit behind. I got caught up at the East Wind House doing some research for the next one."

The trooper handed him his information. "Be much obliged if you'd sign a copy of one of those for me. The wife loves a good ghost story. Stephen King's her favorite."

"I'm sure he is. I'd be more than happy to extend a free copy to you and..."

"Bethany." The trooper said.

"Absolutely." Lee pulled his pen from his shirt pocket and flipped inside the front cover: To Bethany, Happy Hauntings!–Lee

"Here you go."

"Thank you, Mr. Buhl. Now you just try and keep it under seventy, okay? I'm sure you've got fans who'd like to see you arrive in one piece tonight."

"I'm sure. Thank you, Officer."

"You have a good day." Officer Betts tipped his hat to Lee and patted the book in his hands. Worked every time. Lee nodded in return and pulled back onto the road. He'd make up the lost time once Officer Betts was long gone.

Forty minutes later, he passed the *Welcome to Hollis Oakes* sign. The big green billboard featured two wolves on a mountain top howling at a full, yellow moon. Wolves always made Lee think about his grandparents; wolves were their spirit animals. His grandparents had introduced him to Shamanism and were responsible for the path he'd chosen in life. Well, sort of. They probably wouldn't be overly thrilled about the way he used his spiritual inheritance, but he figured they'd at least appreciate the success it granted him. The spoiled-milk feeling in his guts disagreed with that assessment, but he did his best to push past that and focus on the little city he was driving into.

The Motel 6 came up on his right. He pulled next to a dirty maroon minivan and killed the engine. A far cry from the East Wind, but they had indeed left the light on for him and he knew he'd be able to grab a smoking room. He got out, stretched his arms like a bird in flight and pulled out a cigarette. The zippo refused to spark. He'd filled it not more than two weeks ago. He gave it a shake. It lit up. He sparked the smoke to life. His last drag was accompanied by a shiver. He recognized it for what it was: a sign. There was something here for him. Too early to tell what exactly, but a real spirit had said hello.

CHAPTER FOUR

November, 1983.

"Christina, you get your ass back here right fucking now!"

"No," she cried. Her mother had finally pushed her too far.

"I said get back here. Maria!"

Christina LaRoza, with tears streaming down her reddened cheeks, ran along Woodlawn Street as hard and fast as she could, refusing to look back as her mother screamed out for her at the end of their driveway. *Her* driveway. *Not mine, not anymore.* She rounded the corner and made for the tree line of Brenner's Woods. She didn't want to be on the road. She did not want to be seen. The last thing she needed was for the cops to see her hauling ass down the road looking like this. She could taste the blood from her split lip, and knew she had at least one black eye. Not to mention she thought she might have a broken knuckle.

Her mom had never been much of a parent. Her father died when she was three, and in her thirteen years of existence since, her mother had been with more men than she could count, and had staggered through more inebriated days than sober ones. Their relationship consisted of Christina doing pretty much all of the cooking, all of the household chores, which of course entailed cleaning up after her drunken mother's shamble of a life: vomit from the carpets, tending to Mother's cuts and bruises (as well as her own), from one scumbag boyfriend or another, and most of the driving even though she had neither a license or a driver's permit.

Somewhere over the last couple of months, their relationship had managed to sour further. Most of the time, Christina no longer wanted to be at home. She believed her mother, sensing this, began trying to put her foot down. A missed dinner was met with a slap. Any and all back talk was met with a barrage of the scrawny woman's bony fists. And if Christina dared stay out for the night, she would be ducking empty bottles and random, crappy ceramic trinkets purchased from her mother's weekly pilgrimages to Packard's Flea Market. This afternoon's full-out brawl was the last straw.

Now, as she hurdled through the densest part of Brenner's Woods, pine tree branches whipped her sore face, stung, scratched, and clawed at her, but she wasn't about to let anything slow her down. She knew where the trails started out here, and understood that the path to her future waited on the far side of Berry's field. She would run to the field, and then catch her breath. It was a plan, and so far, outside of leaving, it was the only one she had. It would have to do.

Present day

"Hey Jeff," Kurt said, grinning from ear to ear.

Jeff Braun walked behind the front desk carrying his messenger bag filled with graphic novels, mostly *The Walking Dead* series, and the first few books of *30 Days of Night*. He was short, with floppy brown hair, and was often mistaken for a high school student by guests, even though he was thirty-five. His eyes were a near-permanent bloodshot from lack of sleep, and his shoulders were constantly slumped forward–a look worn more often by awkward pre-teen girls and Wal-Mart employees.

"Hey, man. What the hell are you all smiles about?" Jeff asked, placing his bag upon the waist-high side counter.

"I did it, man. I finally did it," Kurt said.

"Okay, I give. Did what?"

"Guess who's taking Rhiannon to see the new Quentin Tarantino movie?"

Jeff cocked his head as he rubbed at his stubble-covered chin, feigning a look of deep consideration before answering, "Kenneth McGowan, in 219?"

"What? No, dude. Me. I'm taking Rhiannon to see *Django Unchained*. Can you believe it?"

"Good for you," Jeff said, "'bout time you stop living this romance in your mind, and actually put yourself out there."

"Yup, but I gotta run, man. I think I have a new tune brewing in my head." Kurt grabbed his turquoise sunglasses off from the desk and threw them on.

"All right, Rock Star, go write your dream girl another song," Jeff said as he set to logging in on the front desk computer. "And you might wanna use your high beams if you're gonna be wearin' those shades–it tends to be pretty dark after midnight."

"Haven't you ever heard that Cory Hart song?" Kurt said. Backing toward the lobby doors, he sang out, *"I wear my sunglasses at night, so I can, so I can…"*. Before Jeff could answer, Kurt was on his way out the door and into the night.

Without averting his eyes from the log in screen before him, Jeff said, "Goodnight, Rock Star."

He scanned the in-house list looking for any of the usual suspects. The Bruton Inn only had a few regulars, but he liked to check, regardless. It was an old habit developed from his years working the front desk at the Hampton Inn in Augusta. He'd worked there for five and a half years–three on the four-to-midnight shift, the last two and a half doing the overnight audit. He liked the audit, preferred it—more time to read. The apartment he rented with his old college buddy, lovingly referred to as Scotty Pluto for all the time he spent smoking pot, was in a constant state of chaos. Scotty's gaming buddies and co-workers were constantly getting high and shouting at each other (or their online competitors) in the small living room next to his bedroom. It was too loud most of the time to concentrate. He now did most of his reading at work, or at the *Barnes and Noble* in Hollis Oaks.

Scanning the in-house list, Jeff found that the inn was almost full. It was late summer. August in Maine could be sweltering, especially with the humidity, and The Bruton Inn was within driving distance of Emerson Lake. Maybe there was something going on in town he hadn't heard about. Whatever the case, he only recognized two names from the list: the aforementioned Kenneth McGowan in 219, and Meghan Murphy.

Kenneth McGowan was the kid of some rich family in Avalon who appeared to be afraid of his own shadow. According to his license, he was twenty-four, but he looked and acted more like a twelve-year-old. He'd been staying at the inn since late July courtesy of his parents and called at least every other night with some crazy complaint, or another. Usually he griped in his meek, nasally voice about hearing people in the next room "making it," or whispering obscenities that were directed at him from the hallway. The funny thing was that he rarely had anyone in the room next to him. The room next to his was a handicap accessible room, the only one on property. Only some old Vietnam vet, named Roger, or Roland, Jeff couldn't quite remember which, had stayed there at the beginning of the month, and then again for a couple days last week. That guy had been in a wheel chair, so he was not "making it" with anyone in any room. Kenneth McGowan was a weirdo, and a nut-job. Meghan Murphy on the other hand was something else altogether.

She checked in last night shortly after 1 am, smiling behind gorgeous brown eyes, her long dark hair pulled back, wearing a knee-length pleather skirt and an Alkaline Trio t-shirt. He wasn't Brad

Pitt by any stretch, but he had, from time to time, been able to use his affable charm and vast knowledge of books to counter his lack of strong-jawed good looks.

He and Meghan had seamlessly slipped into a conversion about things that go bump in the night. Jeff had been somewhat amazed and eternally grateful when she decided to grab a cup of the inn's complimentary coffee and stick around to continue their discussion on all things horror. Turned out she was a big fan of the *30 Days of Night* series, as well as Joe Hill's *Locke and Key*. She didn't care much for zombies, telling him that she preferred ghosts and goblins. After twenty minutes and another cup of coffee, she finished her drink, wished him a good night, and had disappeared off to her room.

Now, staring at her name on the screen before him, he found himself praying she would make an appearance on his shift tonight. He was also elated to find she had extended her stay from the two nights he had put her in for, to twice that.

Ring, Ring, Ring.

"Front Desk."

"Hello, this is Kenneth McGowan in room 219."

"Hi, Mr. McGowan, what can I do for you tonight?" he said, managing to keep the annoyance out of his voice.

"There's someone that keeps talking to me from the room next door."

Jeff rolled his eyes, pulling up his Facebook page. "Are they bothering you, Mr. McGowan? Are they keeping you awake?"

"They–" Kenneth started.

The line went dead.

"Hello?" Jeff asked. "Mr. McGowan?"

Nothing.

"Fucking weirdo," Jeff spoke aloud to the empty lobby.

Kenneth was certainly the strangest resident at the inn. He would probably fit in a little better at an asylum. After a few minutes of checking his Facebook updates, Jeff moved on to his actual duties.

While he was finishing up the rest of his nightly checklist, Meghan Murphy showed up at the coffee station by the desk, barely registering his existence. All he got was a simple nod as she averted her eyes, crossed the lobby and took her coffee into the guest computer room. No hello, no smile. He was confused and disappointed with the 180 in her behavior. He thought they'd hit it off last night, maybe he was wrong. He'd never been great at reading women–Stephen King was much more his speed. Maybe it was something else altogether. Maybe she just woke up, or maybe she just didn't want to give him the wrong idea. Still, whatever magic he thought had been there last night seemed smothered by the cold blanket of rejection.

A tall guy with short dark hair stepped up to the desk.

"Hey, sorry to bug you. I locked myself outta my room. Any chance I can get another key?"

"Sure. Happens all the time. What's the last name on the room?"

"It's under Gentry or Curren."

"Yep, got it."

Jeff punched in a new key and handed it over. "Nice *Evil Dead* shirt. You see the re-make?"

"Cool, thanks. Yeah, I thought it was pretty rad. Wish Bruce Campbell would've been in there somewhere, but it was still okay."

"I agree. Ash should have made a cameo."

"Well, thanks, man. Have a good night."

"You, too."

Jeff waited until the tall guy disappeared down the hallway and then, doing his best to shrug off Meghan's withdrawal, dug the latest Ronald Malfi novel from his bag and returned to a warmer, more comforting place of refuge.

CHAPTER FIVE

*K*nock-knock

Kenneth McGowan stood frozen, gooseflesh dressing his skin as he stood clinging to the door frame of the hotel room's bathroom. In the darkness, he sat in perfect silence listening to the first of the thing's little visits.

No doubt about it, The Bruton Inn was haunted. But it was not nearly as haunted as his family. The voices, the sounds, the little visits presented by whatever was hanging around this place were all preferable to the alternative. Shivering, despite the eighty plus degree reading on the room's thermometer, his mind faded away from the knocking in this present time to a few months ago at his step-father's estate...

"*Kenny*, it's me. It's Uncle Wes."

The door to his bedroom creaked like Dracula's casket as the large shadowy figure of his "Uncle" entered (*invaded*) his room. Kenneth awaited his fate. The nightly intrusions from "Uncle" Wes had been occurring like clockwork since the odd man's arrival last winter. He would knock twice, very quietly, announce his presence, then slip in, close the door behind him, and lock it. He stood six-foot-four, the physique of a professional wrestler. Kenneth had tried to fend him off in the beginning, to attempt to dissuade the man from doing his dirty deeds, but it was no use. Kenneth was much too small to physically protect himself, and the verbal threats Uncle Wes whispered in his ear were enough to scare him into total obedience.

The first couple of weeks, it was just some kissing and light rubbing, but the abuse quickly escalated to oral sex, and then, to the inevitable. He had been raped by the man nearly every night for five months before his mother shipped him off to the inn, hiding him away like *he* had done something wrong.

His step-father was a liar, a cheat, a pedophile, and a known rapist, but he was also the richest man in Avalon. He practically owned the town. And Uncle Wes wasn't the only rotten soul in his stable, either. Luckily, Kenneth hadn't been exposed to any of Reni, Tobias, or Hunter's fun and games. They preferred little girls, namely his cousins Deidre and Holly–their screams could be heard at various times any given day or night. Kenneth watched them both meander through their daily chores, like lifeless pretty things.

His step-father and the man's collection of Avalon trash, was about a hundred times more frightening and harmful than whatever was living at the Bruton Inn.

As the icy voice began whispering its foul offerings from the other side of the hotel room door, he slouched down on the bathroom floor atop a quilt his grandmother had made for him when he was younger, and shut his eyes tight as if Uncle Wes were with him. The flashbacks struck his consciousness like a wet towel, the shivering intensified as his still recovering rectum clenched in sharp jolts at the phantom memories.

He reached up to the lip of the bath tub, grabbing the little baggy of purple pills he'd appropriated from his mother's medicine cabinet. He dry swallowed two of them before lying back down and curling into a fetal position.

As the comforting wave of soft blackness enveloped him, the flashbacks dispersed like worms retreating into the earth. The whispers by his door carried on, but he no longer heard the awful things that they said.

***

At the end of the otherwise empty corridor, Eric Gentry crept back to his room, new room key in hand, hoping not awaken his roommate, Jimmy. He slipped the magnetic keycard into the reader, and paused. He thought he heard crying. Placing his ear to the door, the crying ceased. He backed away and listened, glancing down the well-lit hallway decorated with portraits of old steam engine boats from the early 1900s and black and whites of prominent Maine figures. The depiction closest to him resembled Abraham Lincoln sans beard. The name read: *Alfred Greaves Jr.* There was something menacing in the man's eyes. Unsettling.

There was a tingling in his solar plexus that often accompanied feelings of dread. Being a comic book nerd, he liked to refer to it as his *spidey-sense.* He hadn't felt it since the night he came home to find his apartment back home in Sausalito, California broken into. Standing six-six and weighing in at a good two hundred and fifty pounds, Eric was big enough to take care of himself in most troublesome situations.

He hadn't been afraid that night, just uneasy, but ready. This was different.

Butterflies swarmed in his stomach as he left the door to his room and crept down the hall, listening for the cries. Three doors down, he heard the whimpering. He looked at the room number– 211. He placed his hands on the frame and as stealthily as he could, easing his ear to the door. As if aware of his presence, the whimpering slowed. He took a step back. His *spidey-sense* was screaming at him to move on, to go back to his room and lock the door. Against those better senses, he returned his ear to the barrier, this time with more urgency, compelled, having to hear the cries again.

What he heard on the other side was not crying, but a quiet cackle. His chest began thundering so hard he thought he might be having a heart attack at thirty-one. Then he heard her speak:

"Come in, Eric. I've been waiting for you," the icy voice of his new mistress welcomed him. Before he could decide his next course of action the door flung open. He was wrenched inward by a force that snagged his entire frame as if it were that of a ten-year-old.

Behind the door to room 211, Eric Gentry's screams were snuffed out. His eyes rolled into the back of his head at the sight of *her* true form.

***

"Guest services, Jeff speaking. How can I help you?"

"Yeah, this is Ben and Gale Thompson in 213. I don't know what the hell's going on next door, but it sounds like someone is getting killed over there."

Jeff's skin attempted to physically crawl from his body. "Which room did you say?"

He was met with irritation from the other end.

"There's something fucked up going on next door. Listen, my wife and I are paying good money to stay here. This is fucking ridiculous–Gale, Gale. Get back here."

"Sir," Jeff started, "I'm going to ask that you and your wife both stay in your room. I'll go check on–"

Further from the receiver Jeff heard the man calling to his wife. "Gale, where the hell are you going? Let them take care of this. Gale!"

Jeff hung up the phone and slipped the brass knuckles from his messenger bag into his pants pocket.

As he rounded the corner of the desk, his eyes met Meghan Murphy's beautiful deep browns. She sat behind the glass window of the computer room, smiling at him, but her eyes looked different, *darker*. He broke her gaze and jogged toward the elevator at the end of the hall.

CHAPTER SIX

November 14, 1983

Two days after running away from home, Christina met her new best friend, Sarah Ford. Late that night, with seven dollars left in her pocket, Christina hitched up Route 5. Tired, weary, and nearly ready to cave in and call her mom to bring her home, she was picked up, literally and emotionally, by Sarah Ford in her sugar daddy-rented red Pontiac Firebird.

Since running away from home, Sarah had been living with her boyfriend in a shitty apartment in Denver. Something bad had happened. Some sort of fight or physical altercation between them, she hadn't really wanted to talk about it. She'd taken a Greyhound from Denver to Boston. There, she said she met another guy, this one from Maine. He played in a band and brought her home with him after a show. According to Sarah, that relationship lasted for three months before she was forced to leave him. She wound up shacking up with a married man in Farmington. He stashed his new teen squeeze at the Bruton Inn, supplying her with ample cash and a rental car.

"So this guy just pays for your room, and that really cool car?" Christina said. The sweating bottle of Schlitz in her hand and the warm buzz the alcohol was delivering to her exhausted body felt like paradise.

"Well, I mean, it's not like it's for nothing," Sarah began. "I have to fuck the guy like three nights a week, and suck his dick about twice that." She paused to light a Marlboro. "He isn't even good-looking, but he's fucking loaded."

"Wow. What about his wife?" Christina reached for the pack of cigarettes lying on the bed between them.

Sarah exhaled, handing her the pink Bic, "What about her?"

Christina lit the cigarette, took a drag, and asked, "Have you met her? Does he talk about her?"

"What do I give a fuck?"

"Do you want him to leave her?"

"No fuckin' way." Sarah said, rising up from the bed. She was dressed in a Van Halen t-shirt, and a pair of cut-off blue jeans, and with her long dark curls and perfect ass, she loosely resembled Daisy Duke from *The Dukes of Hazzard*. She was beautiful. No wonder she had a married man wrapped around her finger. Christina envied her.

Sarah went to the mini fridge by the television, grabbed two more beers and continued, "Tina, just look at this. This is fucking perfect. I get this rad room, money, beer and cigarettes, and that fucking car, and I don't have to live with this guy or all of his fucking problems." She handed Christina one of the brown bottles. "If he leaves this cunt, I'll have to live with him and put up with his small dick every night. No thanks."

Right off the bat, Sarah had taken to calling her Tina. It was not the first time her name had been shortened. Her Algebra teacher, Ms. Dalton, had also called her Tina. Christina liked her name just fine, but was cool with whatever anyone else liked, especially Sarah. She was in awe of this girl. Sarah had it all; looks, grit, coolness, and she had the attitude to make it all work. Christina couldn't remember ever seeing a woman so strong, so sure of herself, so in control.

"What will you do if he tells you he wants to leave her?" she asked, scooting her bottom up against the headboard.

Sarah's eyes narrowed, her expression like a junkyard dog; mean, and nasty. "Let's just hope for his sake, he isn't that fucking dumb."

The look didn't quite fit her beauty; it was too dark, too heavy. Christina didn't like it. Sarah Ford was something all right, but Christina wasn't sure what.

Present Day

The second floor hallway was different, yet the same. It took Jeff a minute to figure it out. The light at the opposite end went out, and he realized what it was—the portraits lining the corridor walls were all upside down.

Approaching room 211, the second light from the end went out, then the next, and then the next. He stopped.

"They won't stop screaming."

Jeff turned to find Gale Thompson standing directly behind him. He hadn't heard the tall blonde creep up on him, and found it unnerving. Her ice cold blue eyes stared beyond him. Turning to see what she was looking at, he was terror-stricken by the two people approaching from the shadowy end of the hallway.

The tall guy from room 213 and a beautiful dark-haired girl he had never seen before stalked in their direction. The big guy, wearing a blood-covered grin, carried something in his hand that was dripping all over the plush maroon hallway carpet. The severed head of Ben Thompson. The dark-haired girl's long, sky blue gown was also splattered with blood. Black orbs stared out from their skulls in place of eyes. Depthless, yet infinite—no white, no color, just perfect darkness.

Jeff tried to retreat, backing into the tall blonde whose husband's head was in this monster's hands, but she didn't budge. He turned backed to her and found her blue irises had also gone cold. She unleashed a heart-stopping scream as the blood began to seep from the corners of black eyes.

Jeff Braun woke up screaming and sat bolt upright in his hotel bed. Sweat, exuding from every pour, slicked his bare chest and back. He frantically searched for the lamp on the night stand, knocking the alarm clock to the floor. The little black box landed with a soft thud. He found the switch, and with a trembling hand, turned the bedside light on.

He swung his legs out of from under the heavy covers and placed his feet on the plush carpeting feeling the full fibers between his toes. Bending over, he buried his face in his sweaty palms, trying to rub the nightmare away. His right leg was shaking up a storm, a nervous tick he'd had since he was a kid. He saw the dark pools that served eyes of the people from his dream flash across his mind.

He jumped up from the bed. "Fuck."

He was in room 109. On average, he slept at the hotel about once a week, usually when he hadn't gotten much sleep the day before, or if he was just in need of a break from his roommate. Last night's odd trio of events had sunk in a little deeper than he had thought.

He made his way into the bathroom, filled the Dixie cup with cold water, and guzzled it down. He put it on the counter, and picked up his cheap brown wristwatch lying next to a blue and white bottle of toothpaste.

9:38

He'd slept the entire day away. It wasn't that strange considering he had been up most of the day before and worked until seven this morning, but he usually rose well before sunset when he stayed at the inn. As comfortable as the king-sized beds were, he still had a tendency to wake up after only five or six hours of shut-eye like he did whenever he'd stayed at a friend's house, or on the floor after a party somewhere he'd never been before; there was an anxiousness that set off his internal alarm clock so as not to overextend his welcome. He chocked it up to the dream.

What a fucking dream, he thought, starting the shower. Letting the water's heat seep into his skin, washing the perspiration and the nightmare away, he thought of the odd couple in room 213, replaying last night's peculiar events:

After receiving the phone call from the Thompson's in 213 about the noise coming from 211, he rushed up to the second floor. Unhappy guests usually get a full refund– Bruton Inn policy. Upon exiting the elevator, he turned the corner to find Mrs. Thompson and her husband, Ben, standing in the hallway staring at the door of the room next to theirs.

"Hi, I'm so sorry about this," he started.

"Shhhh, don't you hear that," Mrs. Thompson said, placing her ear to the door.

Jeff couldn't hear a thing, but made an effort to extend his guests the courtesy of being interested. "I don't hear anything," he said, before turning to Mr. Thompson. "Did you say that they were screaming?"

Ben Thompson, dressed in blue-and-white-striped pajamas, grabbed his wife by the wrist and pulled her away from the door, pushing his way past Jeff without saying a word. His wife just smiled, staring at Jeff with eyes that danced like a witch at a séance.

Without another word, they returned to their room and shut the door. Jeff never heard from them again. Perplexed by the overall strangeness of the moment, he decided to take another listen, this time placing *his* ear to the door to room 211, not sure what, if anything, to expect.

There was nothing, and then–he thought he heard a giggle, like a small child playing hide and go seek. Trying not to give themselves away, but unable to hold back their excitement. It sent a chill spiraling down his spine. He wanted to back away, but could not. There was movement behind him.

He spun around, startled by the presence. It was Meghan Murphy

"What the hell are you doing?" he whispered, embarrassed by his fear.

"I was about to ask you the same thing," she whispered back. Her brown eyes looked at him playfully. "I hope you haven't been eavesdropping on me, too."

Her devilish grin erased his resonating dread, along with the unwarranted hurt he'd felt at her for ignoring him earlier. All was forgiven.

"Of course not, I am a gentleman. I would never stoop to the levels of lesser men." They moved away from 211, heading back down the hall in the direction of the elevator.

"Good," she said, looking ahead. "I wouldn't want you hearing what I do to myself in the privacy of my own room."

The bizarre statement swam between them, awkward and out of place. Nonetheless, he blushed imagining her masturbating. *This girl can't be for real.*

"Sorry we couldn't hang out tonight. I had some work to catch up on."

"Aw, that's all right. I had some business to take care of, too." He nodded in the direction of room 211.

"I'll make it up to you tomorrow night, okay?" She bit her bottom lip, and placed a hand on his forearm.

His flesh tingled under her touch. A rush of warmth flooded his face, but he remained cool. "Yeah, that's fine. I'll be here."

"Good night." She leaned in and planted a kiss on his lips.

Fireworks went off in his mind, accompanied by a sense of light-headedness. He smelled and tasted the cherry flavored Chap Stick on her lips. She kept her soft mouth pressed to his for an extra couple of seconds. He tried to say goodnight, but was speechless.

She smiled, and disappeared behind the door.

"Good night," he whispered, swimming deep in the love buzz.

His thoughts were only of her for the rest of the night; the odd couple from 213, and the disturbing giggle behind the door of room 211, all but forgotten.

Now, standing in the shower in his room, he remembered the taste of Meghan Murphy's lips, and thought of her pleasuring herself in the privacy of her room. He imagined what tonight might have to offer, while doing a little pleasuring of his own.

Chapter Seven

In room 211, Eric Gentry opened his new eyes and saw red. *She* had spoken to him. *She* had caressed him. *She* had changed him. He brought his hands up before his face; the red luminous outline faded fast returning the pinkish skin back to the more flesh-toned covering he was accustomed to. They looked the same, but beneath the surface, he knew they were not. Eric was no longer what he appeared to be. He wasn't sure *what* he had become, but whatever it was felt strong, far stronger than he had been before his transformation at the hands of the icy apparition.

He rose to his feet, t-shirt covered in blood. He moved through the spacious suite, knowing she was gone, but seeking her nonetheless. He was alone. He stepped into the bathroom to gaze upon his new eyes. Blackness stared back.

A voice inside gave him his first initiative.

"I will."

Without a moment's hesitation, Eric Gentry went to the door, exited room 211, and headed back to his room.

"What the fuck..." Jimmy Curran managed groggily. He heard the door open, and through squinting, adjusting eyes, saw the silhouette of his large roommate dressed in the pale hallway light. "What time is it, man?" Jimmy gazed at the red LED's of the alarm clock next to his head.

3:33

"Shit, dude. Did you get lucky, or something?"

Eric moved to his bedside, looming like Frankenstein.

"What are you doing?" Jimmy fumbled for the lamp behind the alarm clock.

"I wouldn't do that if I were you." Eric said.

Before Jimmy could ask why, Eric locked his fingers into Jimmy's curly brown locks, effortlessly lifting him up off the full-sized bed and tossing him across the room into the TV stand.

Jimmy felt his ribs snap as he crashed against the large piece of oak furniture. A cry escaped his lips. He pulled his knees up under him, and reached out in the dark toward the shape coming for him. "Jesus Christ, Eric, what the fuck's wrong with you?"

Eric's size 12 boot smashed square into his face, exploding Jimmy's nose in a bloody mess and sending him flat on his back.

Gagging on two of his front teeth as they hit the back of his throat, the pain from his cracked ribs was a distant memory in comparison to the abrupt rearrangement of his face. Jimmy's thoughts tumbled over one another in his befuddled mind, swimming through a mix of fear, confusion, and pain. Through tears, coughing up the blood now pooling in his throat, Jimmy Curran made one last attempt to make sense of this sudden whirlwind of chaos. "Why are you doing this?" He stared up at his dark friend. The crack of light, suffusing through the partially open door, gave him the first glimpse of the thing before him, and its black orbs. "Y-your eyes. What the hell's wrong with your–"

Eric Gentry slammed the heel of his army surplus combat boot through the mess of his friend's face; the impact making a sickly crack, pop, and squelching sound. A mix of blood, other fluids, and bits of brain matter sprayed a splattered pattern of gore from where he planted his foot through the last terrified expression of his roommate's face.

The voice within was pleased.

November 19, 1983

"Bring her in. She can watch." Gordon Kilpatrick licked his lips as he gaped at his naked teen beauty as she picked up the receiver by the desk. He couldn't believe she had a friend who wanted to join them. He was one lucky son of a bitch.

Sarah had to dial down to the lobby where Christina was killing time during Gordon's visit.

"He wants to meet you…No, Tina, its fine. You don't have to do anything. Just come up while we finish, okay?" There was a pause on the other end of the line. Sarah lit a smoke as she waited. "Okay, I promise, cross my heart and hope to die. Just get up here already."

She hung up the receiver and moved to the fridge for another beer.

"Well? Is your little friend coming up to play?" Gordon said. He lay naked, propped up on his right elbow, still sweating from their last fuck.

Sarah was disgusted by the look of excitement and anticipation upon his ugly mug. Her disdain for him was furthered by the thin black mustache sitting above even thinner pale lips, and the sweaty tangle of graying chest fur that extended down to his thick patch of pubic hair. His giddiness was getting on her nerves, but she had a plan.

The door opened. Christina crept in wearing dark sunglasses, a light blue Incredible Hulk t-shirt, and a red skirt she'd borrowed from Sarah.

"Hi Sugar, what's your name?" Gordon said.

"Her name's none of your goddamn business." Sarah stalked across the room, and smacked him hard across his twitching face.

He sat in shock for a split second before exploding in a rage, grabbing her by the breasts and pushing her into the wall beside the bed.

As she gasped for air, he landed a right cross to her jaw, dropping her to the floor. He then turned his attention to Tina.

Christina circled around the room trying to avoid him. She glanced around the disheveled desk, searching for anything that could be used to fend this asshole off. She settled for a beer bottle.

"You wanna hit me with that? Huh? Come on sweet tits, take your best shot." He offered up his chin.

"Fuck you." She hauled the bottle back behind her head ready to strike down with everything she had, but never got the chance.

He dove for her, driving her to the floor with all 170 pounds of his nakedness.

She could feel his hard-on stabbing at her thighs as he reached up and swatted the bottle out of her hands. Pinning her arms above her head with one hand, and reaching beneath her skirt with the other, Sarah's sugar daddy tore Christina's panties off with one violent tug.

"Sorry, sweetheart. I *won't* be gentle, but I'll make up for it with a strong effort." He squeezed a knee between her legs, prying them apart, leaned in close, and lapped at the tears streaming down her face.

Christina shut her eyes against him, and prayed for help.

Gordon suddenly whaled like a banshee in the night, releasing her throat and grabbing at his back. Tina screamed, pounding at his face with her boney knuckles. She managed to squirm her way away from the prong he had been trying to stick her with. His blood was everywhere as he started shouting, "You bitch. You ungrateful little bitch."

Sarah pulled a knife out of his back, producing another scream from him.

Christina watched as dark clouds pulled back over Sarah's pretty features just before the incredible, raging girl propelled forward and straddled her sugar daddy's bleeding back. She raised the long blade above her head before plunging it into the back of the man's neck.

Sarah left the blade buried within him as she sat up, naked and panting like a wild animal. She turned her gaze on Christina, the dark look holding for a second longer before dissipating into a look of determination.

"We need to hide him, and quick," Sarah said. "There might not be a lot of people at the hotel right now, but chances are, someone heard that. They're gonna call the front desk, or come banging on our door to find out what the hell's going on."

Christina sat trembling in the corner of the room where she had planted herself after her near-rape. Her eyes unfocused, her knees knocking together like the time after her mom spun them out driving too fast on an icy road last Christmas on their way to her grandmothers.

Sarah slid from the bleeding body, scrunched her naked form down in front of her, and slapped her hard across the face. "I said fucking help me. Jesus, Tina, do you wanna put us both in jail?"

Christina shook her head erratically, taking Sarah's outstretched hand.

No one called. No one came to check on them. They had the dead body wrapped up in the thick comforter of the bed and stuffed in the back of the large walk-in closet.

Sarah, who had put on a clean flannel shirt and jeans, lit another cigarette as she watched her timid friend staring out the large hotel window at the setting sun. Tina was a nice kid, too nice maybe. But there would be time to deal with that later. "We'll have to get him out of here tonight or he'll stink up the place. I have his credit cards and his wallet. We can cruise to the K-Mart in Hollis Oaks and get some clean sheets. We should have enough cash to stick around here straight through to Christmas, at least. I always made him bring me cash."

Sarah didn't like the look Tina threw her. "You act like you've done this before," Tina said.

"Yeah, well, guys are pieces of shit." Sarah answered, taking a long drag from her cigarette.

"I, I can't believe you." Tina stood up and shook her hands in the direction of the closet. "You act like this is nothing?"

"I can't believe *you*. This fucking asshole, scumbag-fuck, just tried to rape you," Sarah said. "And I stopped him."

"You brought me up here. You're the one who put me in that position," Tina said.

Sarah's eyes narrowed. She stepped up to Tina's face and stared the smaller, weaker girl down. She grabbed her beer off the desk next to her and flipped the television on. Jack Tripper was ogling a nice blonde down at the Regal Beagle. "You'll go down at 3:30 and distract the old man that works the desk at night while I move that dead bastard out through the back entrance."

Sarah went back to laughing at *Three's Company*.

Present Day

In his room, Kenneth McGowan stared through a Thorazine haze out at the multicolored forest behind the Bruton Inn. Perched before the large window, his eyes drifted over patches of green, yellow, and auburn as they danced playfully in a soft breeze under the rays of a late October sun. His mind was on a holiday. Sitting motionless, barely breathing, he hid in the blurred-out corners of his mind from the beautiful girl with the hollow eyes sitting on the bed behind him.

Down the hall, after a refreshingly quiet night, Jeff Braun jerked and twisted, serving guests from a nightmare version of his hotel. He was talking in his deep, suffocating sleep. The words were prayers, each one colored in desperation.

Chapter Eight

A day off from work meant Rhiannon could catch up on some much needed shopping. First up was the Goodwill. She managed to pick up a couple of cool new vintage t-shirts and scored a rare find: a purple pair of Chuck Taylors. Next up, she grabbed a sandwich at Subway, then headed to Barnes and Noble to hit up the only Starbucks in forty miles and grab a couple of new magazines to read at work.

A poster for an in-store signing this afternoon hung by the stack of "New Arrivals." An author named Lee Buhl. She'd never heard of him or the series of books next to his picture. He was pretty cute, but had that smug writer look: condescending eyes over a cheap perfect, white smile. A lavender button-up shirt opened so you could see a wooden Indian pendent hung over his fit chest, and more rings on his fingers than any man should be allowed. Okay, maybe the "condescension" in his eyes was her projecting upon the guy, but she'd met enough uppity jerks at the hotel to recognize the type. Lee Buhl may be the sweetest guy in the world, but she had her doubts.

She grabbed the new *Entertainment Weekly* and the new *Fangoria*. She wasn't a huge horror fanatic, but Jeff would probably appreciate it, and she enjoyed bringing in rags that her buddies could flip through as well. Her generosity ended at *Maxim*. She stepped in line and couldn't help but notice the man who walked through the front doors. It was the author from the poster. He stopped just inside, reached in his shirt pocket and threw on a pair of sunglasses. *Yep. Definitely a schmuck.*

She laughed to herself and decided between the magazines and this jerk, she had enough reason to swing by the hotel and see Kurt.

***

Lee Buhl liked to get a feel for a book store and its customers prior to his autograph sessions. Some towns, like Dalton, Ohio, were over-run by scummy trailer trash. Others, like Portland, Maine featured a nice mix of wealth and character. Hollis Oaks seemed to be one of those in-betweens–not too ugly, not too pretty, just a bunch of regular folk. Plain was his preference. They were just happy to have a pseudo-celebrity in their midst. Their smiles were sincere and their requests were humble–a quick picture here, a "with love" there. In a place like Dalton, their smiles seethed with jealousy, in the bigger, hipper cities, the crazy fans or wanna-be writers were out in droves.

Lee smiled at a couple of blondes by the Nooks next to his poster, and then made his way to grab a shot of caffeine. The blondes strafed along behind him. No doubt recognizing him from the mini-bill-board. He watched them from behind his shades as they whispered to one another, eying him. Dressed in tight jeans and t-shirts that left little to the imagination, the two girls looked dangerously young. They waited until he had his iced Frappuccino in hand before making their move.

He signed copies of his book they grabbed from the "New Arrival" table. One of them asked him to sign it to Sexy Lexi. He did. Before they moved along, he produced his business card and scribbled his cell number on the back for "Sexy" Lexi. Nine out of ten times, they chickened out from making the call. He figured her a bit young to have the balls, but you never know. Young girls these days are full of surprises.

Another shiver danced through him. This time, he was pretty sure it was from the cold drink, but he'd been wrong before. He needed to find out if there was really something special in this town. He made a mental note to meditate on it when he got back to the motel.

CHAPTER NINE

Timothy Laymon pulled his purring blue 2012 Ford Mustang into the back lot of the Bruton Inn. In the two days since checking in he could not find one thing to complain about. Everything had been perfect. The breakfast was terrific (bacon and eggs). The indoor pool was 9-feet-deep, had a diving board and two Jacuzzi's to boot. The inn, which seemed empty when he arrived on Thursday morning, was now crawling with beautiful college girls, and unfortunately, their parents. According to the cute young girl at the front desk, this was a parent's weekend for the nearby college. The sights around the pool the night before were unbelievable. Blondes, brunettes, red heads, and even a punker girl with blue hair, all hanging out around the crystal clear water, wet from head to toe and showing off their nubile bodies in bikinis and hot shorts. He couldn't believe his luck. Timing is everything.

He strode into the lobby clad in a midnight blue dress shirt, a Henry Jacobson black and white striped tie, and a pair of skinny jeans, armed with a case of Maine's best beer, Shipyard Summer Ale. There were two dark-haired girls who could have passed as sisters watching him. He smiled behind his shades. They smiled back, the taller one on the left giving him a quick wave. *This is going to be a great weekend.*

He got into his room, unloaded the beers in his fridge, and flipped on HBO.

There had been one girl last night at the pool with long, dark curly hair, swimming around in a silver two piece bikini that was barely big enough to hold her in place. She'd made eye contact with him numerous times, but seemed to stay in the pool forever. By the time he finally gathered the balls to get into the pool and talk to her, she was gone. He hadn't seen her leave, but figured she must have slipped away while he was busy gawking at the plethora of other beauties. Still, she was all he'd been able to think about since. Something about her seemed familiar, but he couldn't quite figure that one out. Whether it was that she looked like someone else, maybe a celebrity or something, or whatever, he felt drawn to her.

Timothy sat back, killing time watching a showing of *The Departed* while he waited for the evening to come on. Hope whispered in his mind of getting another crack at the beautiful mermaid from the pool.

CHAPTER TEN

Kurt Costello watched the elderly couple from room 106 pouring themselves tea at the coffee station off to the right of the front desk. Something about them seemed off to him. He couldn't really explain why he thought this. Maybe he was just projecting his own state of disenchantment. His date last night with Rhiannon had not gone as well as he'd hoped. The movie had been great, but she had been distant, just out of his reach the whole evening. He couldn't shake the feeling that their date would be a one-time gig. Sure enough, she called out of work today, leaving him flying solo for the Saturday afternoon shift. Jeff, the night audit guy, was sleeping upstairs. He'd told Kurt to call his room if it got too busy. Things were quiet at the moment, but there was a strange currency flowing through the fading rays of the sun-brightened lobby.

Stepping out from behind the front desk, Kurt watched the elderly couple shuffle back down the first floor corridor. As their cup-free hands reached for each other, a small bit of warmth penetrated Kurt's somber vibe at this ancient display of affection. He watched as they came to a sudden halt halfway down the hall. The old woman with the long gray pony tail hanging down over her worn-out pink cotton sweater turned her face back in his direction. He could sense, more than see, a blackness reaching out for him from behind her eyes. His stomach tensed. Bile rose in his throat, making its way to his mouth. Engulfed by a sick flash of terror, he cupped a hand to his lips and rushed to the employee restroom in the back office.

The little old lady's wicked smile faded. She wasn't sure why she had stopped here. Their room was two doors down. She glanced past her husband, Harold, through the glass door of the pool area. Standing there, like an angel from a dream, stood a young woman with the eyes of the devil. Millie Kafka dropped her steaming cup of tea, and clenched the little gold cross hanging around her wrinkled neck. There was evil here. She had never been so sure of anything in her long life.

Harold began coughing, his hot cup of lemon tea joining Millie's on the maroon carpet. After a few more body shuddering barks, he brought his rough and wrinkled hands away from his face. His palms were full of blood.

"Harold, Harold? Oh my, oh my, Harold? Someone help!" Millie cried as her husband collapsed to the floor. She glanced back up at the girl in the pool room. The she-devil with the features of a beauty queen, smiled behind the blackest eyes Millie Kafka had ever seen.

Kurt, his sudden illness past, heard the woman's pleas for help as he came out from the back office. He grabbed the portable phone from the desk, and dialing 911, rushed down the corridor to where the woman stood staring across from where her husband lie convulsing on the floor.

"Yes, yes, I work at the Bruton Inn out on Route 5. We n-need an ambulance. Oh my God, oh my God, there's a man having a heart attack or something," Kurt said. "Yes, I don't know, I don't know. He needs help, please hurry." The line went dead. "Hello? Hello?"

Kurt reached the elderly couple, and tossed the phone on the floor. He knelt next to the quivering body of the old man. There was blood all over the guy's mouth, neck, and hands. Kurt looked up at the wife for help, finding her still gazing across the hall, clenching her necklace and quietly chanting something he couldn't understand. He turned to see what could be more important than tending to her dying husband. There was nothing–just the door to the pool room.

Despite the inn being at ninety percent capacity, the hallway remained eerily vacant, cold even. The man's body stopped its convulsions and lay perfectly still. He was gone.

Millie Kafka prayed against the demon. The demon that looked like a pretty young girl and smiled like an arsonist watching their work go up in the brightest, most wondrous conflagration. The devil's eyes dissolved into black hollows, her skin draining of color, leaving her epidermis ashen in its wake. Millie watched in horror, oblivious to the young man kneeling at her dying husband's side trying to speak with her, ignorant of the blood running from her palm that clenched the gold cross her granddaughter, Abby, had given her for Christmas last year–the thing before her continued to change, revealing its true self.

The grey skin tightened, highlighting every bone in the body of the ghastly creature behind the glass. Millie watched the long flowing brown curls surrounding the skull-faced demon turn from a dark auburn to a flat white. Pain, blossoming to life in her right arm and chest, whispered of her fate.

The succubus passed through the pool room door, and spoke empty promises to Millie Kafka's ears. It made good on only one–the demon swallowed the elderly woman's last breath. In a final, vulgar display of power, the creature surged forward, disappearing in a flash of invisible energy, blowing the brittle body of the old lady off her feet, and slamming her into the wall at her back.

An impossible chill permeated the hallway. Kurt stared at the elderly woman crumpled on the floor. The black-and-white framed photo of the Maine capital building lay shattered at her feet. He stared into her dead eyes, holding her husband in his arms, slipping into a state of shock himself. The doors at the entrance flew open. Two paramedics came rushing down the hall. Kurt's mind swayed. His skin tingled, prompting a rash of goose bumps. He could no longer feel the deceased man in his arms or the emotions that had swam through his mind like a school of fish darting from one direction to the next. He turned to face the man with the white mustache speaking at him, but didn't hear a word. The corridor went dark as he collapsed to the floor next to the old man's lifeless body.

***

In room 211, Eric Gentry was reunited with the thing that changed him.

VOLUME II

SPELLBOUND MOMENTS

There is a magic in these haunted halls. She knew the moment she set foot within its confines, all those years ago, that she could make this place something *more*. She was referred to, more in her victim's thoughts than actually spoken aloud, as the Mermaid, the Dark-haired Devil, the *Ice Queen*, but somewhere, lost in a pool of sorrow and rage, this lonely young girl once known as Sarah, waits. This powerful *thing* waits. For those who open themselves up to its glorious crimson charms, to its blood soaked memories, to its spellbound moments of desire–there is a dark promise waiting to be fulfilled.

After years of lying dormant, silently preparing, her little tribe of breathing ghosts has finally started to come together. Each one of those chosen and blessed with her wonderful talents holds within their fragile psyches their own unique potential. Eric–big, strong, and obedient–is the ultimate weapon. She feels his rage, his love of death, and his compulsion to please. Watching him immerse himself in his work at her whim is something truly invigorating. And then there is poor, broken Kenneth. Sodomized by a friend of the family, and banished to this out of the way inn, left to rot and *to remember*. So small, lost, and frail–*even in his dreams*. Through her gifts he shall ascend to a level of depravity and usefulness he has never known. There's also the pretty girl, Meghan, so easily possessed. Sarah shall play her with delicate precision, like the most dark and beautiful of classical pieces—a dramatic Chopin. There is a special plan for her...soon enough. For now, it is sufficient to toy with her, using her loveliness to play with the little overnight clerk, Jeffrey, and his romantic reveries. His fun is just beginning.

Of course, there is one other not yet mentioned, for he is not fully aware of their connection. Oh, their eyes met, briefly, her presence already working its way within him. His secrets can hear her whispers, for they speak the same tongue, they dance to the same rhythm, bleed the same song, and share the same vocation.

Soon, my sweet Timothy, soon.

The Ice Queen's much anticipated gathering would not be rushed. Not a single decadent moment. Not now, not when it is all so close at hand. On the contrary, her intentions are to bathe in every act of wicked defilement, every splattered droplet of blood, and every ounce of pleasure and pain. She waits with desires unbound; as they were in the flesh, so are they now in death. All will be attainable soon enough—once her path of wicked wonders is leveled, once this collection is complete, she will be free to roam these haunted halls.

Before she could rest, Sarah, the *Ice Queen*, had a few more enchantments to cast.

CHAPTER ONE

"Wake up," the voice whispered in the dark.

Somewhere in his opiate-induced slumber, Kenneth McGowan shuddered. His dreams were no longer the wonderland of adventurous, childlike imaginings they had once been. In those happier dreams, he had watched himself climb mountains made of Legos; he had ridden an elephant through a city where the streets were crammed with characters from *Mary Poppins*, *Star Wars*, and *The Never Ending Story*; he had played Cowboys and Indians with childhood friends he'd never had. Once, the dreams were his friends, but not anymore. In the time between when his mother abandoned him here in July and this cold October evening, something sour had burrowed its way into the lone solace he had known from his real world of shame. The dreams, no longer holding his hand, had begun filling with vile scenes of overdoses, rape, and death.

In tonight's little vision, the attack from Uncle Wes had been relatively easy and expedited. After the act was finished, Uncle Wes exited Kenneth's hotel room. Then, the most beautiful girl he had ever seen brought him a small wooden TV tray of pretty turquoise pills and a bottle of water. Unable to make eye contact, even in his own dreams, he thanked the girl, taking the pills and bottle of water from the tray she had left while watching her saunter away into the bathroom. He threw the pretty blue-green capsules into his mouth, unscrewed the cap from the water, and closed his eyes as he washed the remedy down. He pulled the plastic bottle from his lips and sucked in a mouth full of warm saline water. His squinty eyes burst open to find that he was submerged in the hotel pool. Panicked, he thrashed his scrawny limbs, helplessly reaching for the surface above, only to descend further from the light and the promise of oxygen; there was something, or *someone* pulling him. He looked down to find the gorgeous pill delivery girl naked, her breasts jiggling as he attempted to jerk his legs from her grasp. His lungs, taking in more of the warm, salty water, threatened to cave in upon themselves. Ready to quit and give in to death, he found the cold dark eyes of the beautiful dark-haired devil at the pool's concrete floor. As his lungs quit and his heart slowed, he heard her soft voice, whispering to him from somewhere in the depths.

"Wake up."

Kenneth opened his eyes surprised to find it was still daylight; the constant pill-popping had made a mess of his body's internal clock and its ability to keep track of time. She was standing at his bedside, calling him from his sleep, from his nightmares.

"Hello, Kenneth," the angel said.

He opened his eyes to find the gorgeous pool creature from the dream standing before him. Dark curls hung down over a body that belonged in one of his cousin Jarod's girly magazines. He thought he was still asleep.

"Who are you?"

"I am anyone you want me to be."

As if to show that she was speaking the truth, he watched in awe as her long brown curls straightened, changing color before his eyes, turning from a dusky earth tone to dirty blonde; the small pale lips of her mouth curled downward at the corners, giving her a permanent melancholy look. Cold blue eyes welcomed him home.

He reached his hand out to her. "Mother?"

"Yes, dear," she said in the soothing voice he remembered from his youth, as opposed to the smoker's rasp she had developed in the years since. "If that is who you desire, that is who I am."

He took her hand, gently at first, like that of a tender child in need of the slightest reassurance that she was there with him in a room full of strangers. A change broke over him, his grip on the over-tanned hand tightened. Something more mature passed through his drug-hazed contemplations.

The angelic girl with the long brown curls hanging over her bare breasts, returned. He stared hungrily at the delicious fullness and wicked promise of her grin. Her dark eyes, now gazing into his, were in a constant state of transference, seemingly changing in easy fluid waves from brown, to black, to something darker, and back again. This impossible display was mesmerizing. The angel pulled his salivating mouth to her chest. He was *hers*.

***

Somewhere in the fog that had settled in beyond the hotel lobby's front doors, a phone rang on and on like a broken record inviting Jeff Braun to come out and set it straight. He wasn't sure what else was hidden within the thick ground cloud that seemed to be alive. So many awful things had already emerged from the endless dispenser of oddities; a seven-foot-tall blond bombshell dressed in a skintight red latex suit; a boy that didn't speak, but barked—and Jeff understood every word; a centaur whose human half was a large-breasted pregnant woman with lactating nipples—the droplets of mother's milk still lay glistening before him on the front desk. There were others as well; a teenage girl with a terrific body wrapped up in a form fitting white dress that looked as though it belonged on some Hollywood red carpet—her face pockmarked and oozing a yellowy puss from several pulsating cysts. The parade of bizarre characters had him on the edge of sanity. And now, that incessant ringing–almost as if it were the fog itself calling to him.

Jeff Braun opened his eyes, the fog-dream of idiosyncrasies collapsing and fading from his half-awake mind; the phone next to his head was ringing. He reached out for it, remembering he had stayed at the hotel. "Hello?"

"Jeff? Sorry to wake you, but we have an issue down here." It took him a few seconds to recognize the voice of his co-worker, Rhiannon. Jeff looked at the alarm clock beside the phone.

7:02

"Yeah, what is it," he yawned. "I'm not in until Midnight. What's going on?" He got up from the bed, stretching out of his sleep.

"Kurt had to be taken to the hospital."

"*What?*"

"Kurt's on his way to the hospital. Get down here–there's more and I don't wanna talk about it on the phone."

Within a few minutes, Jeff was dressed, and at the front desk.

"So what the hell happened?" He followed Rhiannon into the back office and closed the door behind them.

She looked shaken as she paced back and forth. "I was coming to see Kurt, and you know, apologize for our strange date last night. And as I came in through the front doors, I see him down the hall, sitting on the floor with this person in his arms. There's this old lady standing next to him, and she goes flying back into the wall, like she's been shoved or something. I started running toward them, and that's when I see Kurt just crumble to the floor." She brought a sleeve-covered hand up to her eyes. "Kurt wouldn't answer when I called out his name, and when I got down there, he-he didn't look good. I was getting up to call 911, when the EMT's came rushing in past me."

"Holy shit, is he okay?" Jeff plopped down in the chair in front of her.

"They said they didn't know. They couldn't tell what was wrong with him."

Rhiannon stood and took her red pea coat from the swivel chair beside him as she wiped more tears away from her eyes.

"I'm going to drive over to the hospital and see how he's doing. Sorry I had to wake you up," she said.

"No, no, don't worry about that."

Rhiannon swung her coat on, passing him on her way to the office door. She opened it, and without so much as a glance back in his direction, started for the lobby exit.

"Rhiannon," he said. He watched her turn back looking like she was on the verge of devastation. Stepping around the front desk, peering down the hallway, Jeff said, "Where are the two guests Kurt was helping. Are they okay?"

"The paramedics said they were both dead."

A chill ran down Jeff's spine. His thoughts drifted back to June when they had found the body of one of their guests floating in the pool. Management had said the guy drowned–plain and simple.

"I-I gotta go," Rhiannon said.

"Of course, yeah, call me when you get there. Let me know how he's doing."

She disappeared out the doors. Jeff glanced down the hall wondering what the hell had happened.

CHAPTER TWO

Christmas week, 1983

The disposal of Sarah's sugar daddy had gone just as she said it would. Christina had helped her load the bloody body of Gordon Kilpatrick onto a mobile luggage cart before heading downstairs and successfully distracting the old guy at the hotel's front desk. Sarah never told her what she did with the body; Christina never cared to ask. In the days and weeks that followed, she was amazed, and somewhat frightened at how quickly things seemed to return to normal. She had been certain her sleep would be forever haunted by the killing, but the dreams never came. In fact, she thought of that violent day less and less; the passing days had a neat way of making the details fade.

Since then, things had been somewhat calm, almost *normal*. The two girls were getting along famously and having a blast running wild throughout the hotel. They would go for late night swims, inviting cute boys to sneak out of their rooms after their parents had gone to bed and join them well after the pool was supposed to be closed. They spent mornings sleeping until noon, and then made their way down to the fitness room where they would get the married men all hot and bothered. That's where she met Jason.

Jason Perry was a short, stocky but handsome man in his early thirties. He told her he was on vacation from his job at the fire department back in Dorchester, Massachusetts. He was staying at the hotel with his wife and two little boys. Christina and Jason flirted with each other for most of the week; in the fitness room, down at the pool and now, here at breakfast. He confided in her that part of him wished he had come alone. The admission sent her blushing all the way over to her table in the back corner of the dining room. Sarah, who had been watching them all week, started in as soon as her paper plate hit the tabletop.

"Tina, you should get that hunk to come upstairs. He's totally into you."

"Ah, I don't know. That feels...*weird*," she said.

"Come on, don't tell me you wouldn't like to get those muscly arms wrapped around you. I mean, just look at him."

And she did. Even watching him from across the room playing with his two adorable little boys made him that much more attractive. Christina knew it was wrong, the guy was married, but she couldn't deny that she was crushing on him pretty hard. Against her better senses, serving her own desire for affection, she waited for him to refill his coffee cup, and shied toward him.

"Hey," she said, saddling up next to him at the coffee station.

"Hey," he said.

"I was wondering. If you aren't tied up all night with the family, maybe you could stop by my room. You know, just to hang out for a bit before you guys head home." She read the nervousness in his eyes. "I mean, if you wanted to, maybe you could say you needed to come downstairs to work out or go to the store for something." She couldn't believe she was actually doing this, but after initiating the offer, the last thing she wanted was to be rejected.

She watched him glance over her shoulder toward where his family was seated. "Yeah, yeah I think I'd like that. What time should I stop by?"

"Honestly, whenever. Whatever works for you." Christina couldn't stop the smile from spreading across her face.

"There it is," he said, grinning in return.

"There what is?"

Jason lowered his voice, leaned in closer and said, "That gorgeous smile. How can I say no?"

Christina, getting momentarily lost in his beautiful hazel eyes, felt the heat flooding her rosy cheeks.

"It would have to be later though, like eight or nine," he said.

"Sure."

She watched his eyes light up as Sarah strode up on the other side of him and whispered something in his ear. A mix of jealousy and fear wrestled within Christina's guts as she watched her roommate stare at Jason like a starving wolf eyeing a piece of fresh meat. She was certain that she had just made a huge mistake.

Just after 9 pm, there was a knock at the door.

Sarah charged past Christina to get to the door. Christina's bad feeling about where this would lead crawled over her fading excitement like a spider over a sleeping baby.

She watched Sarah step aside to let the nervous looking man in. He was already wiping the sweat from his palms on the thighs of his blue jeans. He gave Christina a modest nod. "Hey Christina, Hi Sarah."

"So did you go with the workout, or are you at the store right now?" Christina jumped up next to Sarah.

"Actually, I'm meeting an old friend." A handsome sparkle gleamed behind his gleaming eyes.

Christina started to say something else as Sarah stepped in front of her. She watched as Sarah stripped off her t-shirt and jumped on Jason like some horny slut from a porn flick. It happened so fast, she didn't have time to process what was going on.

Tits hanging out, Sarah wrapped her long legs around Jason who made only the feeblest attempts to pull his face away before quickly giving in, melting like butter as Sarah shoved her tongue down his throat. She only stopped to turn and bark at Christina, "Jesus Tina, get out of the way."

Christina retreated in defeat, flooded with an awful sense of déjà vu watching the salacious act unfold before her. Jason's face was flushed pink, but his once nervous eyes were now hungry flames desperate to be stoked into full roar. Sarah undid his jeans and slipped them down to the floor, crawling back up to take his exposed manhood in her mouth.

"Oh my God," he said.

After a minute of getting him worked up, Sarah rose, and then hauled Jason down on the bed with her, spreading her legs for him. "Give it to me," she said, tearing at his broad back.

Sarah slipped a hand under the pillow by her head and produced something shiny. Christina snapped out of her dead end daydream. Jason's thick, muscled back tensed. His *ohs and yeahs* came faster. Sarah swung her arm up; Christina blinked at the flash of light reflected from the object in her hand. Jason's roar of ecstasy was interrupted–Sarah slid the straight razor across his throat. Blood gushed from the split skin like water from a spilled paper cup. Jason's face went pale. He sat up, gurgled out in an incoherent sentence and dropped back down atop Sarah lurching and twitching until he fell still.

"What the hell are you doing? Why? Why?" Christina rushed to the bedside, already in tears.

Sarah slithered out from beneath the man, her face and chest covered in blood, murder weapon in hand, and hellfire burning in her eyes. "Stop right fucking there. I swear to hell, I will gut you next." The threat hung between the two girls as Sarah smiled under a mask of blood.

Christina bolted for the bathroom, slamming the door behind her. She wanted to purge the gut-wrenching feeling and the guilt that accompanied it to the porcelain god. She wanted to get the sickness that was Sarah Ford out of her system before it set in and took hold. In between her heaving, she cried for what she had done. She cried for the life she had just helped to destroy. She mourned for the wife that was now widowed, and the children now fatherless. Her moment of depthless sorrow was cut short by the horrific series of sick wet thuds—like the sound of mud slapping blacktop—coming from the room beyond the closed door.

She rose to her feet, wiping vomit and saliva from her mouth with the bottom of her t-shirt creeping toward the sickening sounds. Placing her hand on the bronze knob, unaware that she was holding her breath, she pulled the door open wide just as Sarah buried something shiny into the bloody mess on the floor. Blood splatter rained down over Christina's bare feet. A scream worked its way up from the bottom of her eternally damned soul, tearing through the room like a the wail of a chainsaw.

Before she could stop, she was tackled off her feet by the psychotic girl with the meat cleaver in her hand. They landed hard on the floor. Christina's breath shot from her lungs halting the scream—the back of her head smacked the solid tub behind her. Stars danced before her horrified eyes as she fell back into oblivion.

When she came to, Christina found herself lying on the bed. Fresh blankets, the second set Sarah had now bought at K-Mart, now covered the scene of the crime. Sarah sat at the end of the bed smoking a cigarette, watching another episode of *Three's Company*. Christina wondered if it had all been some sort of bad dream. She tried sitting up, but was hit by a wave of light headedness and nausea that dropped her back onto the fluffy pillow behind her.

"I wouldn't try to go anywhere if I were you," Sarah said. "You've probably got a concussion." Sarah turned her corrupt eyes toward her. "And don't worry about your admirer—I disposed of him myself. *Every last bit of him.*"

The psychotic look in the girl's eyes confirmed Christina's worst fear–she was stuck in an unholy union with this devil in the land of blood and murder. She knew what she had to do.

Present Day

Dressed more for a party than a man heading for a dip, Timothy Laymon strutted down the hallway like he was Brad *Fucking* Pitt. He wasn't sure where his newfound confidence was coming from, but he liked the way it fit. He stepped up to the elevator and hit the down arrow before turning to check his look one last time in the floor length mirror on the wall across from the elevator doors. Dressed in a dark blue button up shirt, and a pair of black jeans, he double-checked his freshly shaven scalp. There were already fresh sprouts of hair growing where such a thing shouldn't be possible. The elevator arrived with a *bing*. He finished tying his canvas shoes and stepped in.

The interior of the elevator, although quite warm and a bit too stuffy, was a very appealing blend of stainless steel and mahogany–it was beautiful. Before the doors slid shut, a large hand appeared in the dying crack of light. Timothy stepped back, allowing room for the guest to enter as the stainless steel door slid open. This man stood well over six feet tall and must have weighed around two hundred and fifty pounds. He was dressed in plain black shorts, a black t-shirt, and bare feet. It wasn't just his size that was intimidating, it was his eyes. There was darkness in them. Darkness that made Timothy drop his own nervous gaze down to the maroon carpeting sporadically patterned with gold lobsters. He dared a glance out of the corner of his eye, and wished that he hadn't. The towering figure flashed a crooked grin.

The elevator descended to the ground floor, and the *bing* sounded again. Timothy felt swallowed by the dark shadow cast, both figuratively and literally, by his companion. He stepped out of the too-cramped space, alleviating the heaviness of the moment then headed left, toward the pool area. His new shadow followed.

CHAPTER THREE

"**D**o you like what you see?"

Kurt tried to open his eyes to match the face with the sultry voice, but was greeted with blinding light and black dots. It felt like he was lying on a sheet of cool metal. His head weighed a thousand pounds and he couldn't stop shivering. "I-I...I can't see anything," he said. "W-w-where am I?" An icy cold hand clasped his bare shoulder.

"Don't worry that pretty little head of yours," she said.

He could feel the cool touch move through his body as the fingers ran through his hair. "What...what are you doing? W-wh-what's happening to me?"

She gripped her fingers into his hair, pulling so hard he was sure she would rip the follicles out. He cried out then tried to move his arms to protect himself, and couldn't. The woman continued to pull on his hair. His scalp was threatening to rip. He tried lifting his arms once more, straining with all the force he could muster in his weakened state, and was met with intense white heat where his right arm ripped free. His screams filled the small room. "What are you d-d-doing to m-m-me?"

"I'm going to let you in on a secret," she said. Her cold breath spread over his mouth like a second skin. "You're dead."

***

Rhiannon drove her Ford Escort into the parking lot of the Hollis Oaks General Hospital. She didn't like hospitals; they reminded her of sickness, of death. Her Grammy Lilly had passed from cancer last fall in this very building. Rhiannon had gone to see her three times a week until the very end. Even now, looking at the large building, she could sense the ghost of the monster with no cure hanging around, waiting for its next victim. She hoped Kurt was all right.

She had taken a liking to Kurt their first day at the hotel. Two people had quit at the start of the busy summer season–something about a guest drowning in the pool. Some of the employees were convinced the death had been somehow *supernatural*. Rhiannon figured that the middle-aged quitters had seen one too many "reality" ghost shows. She, for one, did not cater to such nonsense, and as it turned out, neither did Kurt. He was shy and nervous around her, but also very funny, very charming in his own way. If he had asked her out that very first day, she would have said yes. She hadn't felt this way about a guy since junior high. Back then, it had been a stupid thirteen-year-old's ill-conceived idea of love that sent her jumping from one boy to the next. Any boy who showed interest in her. Once she got into high school, things changed. She discovered women who were loud and in your face. Her idols became Brody Dahl from the Distillers and Kim Gordon of Sonic Youth. She established a truer sense of self-worth and developed a natural edginess, slipping into a skin that fit like a record needle to a groove.

She considered herself tough, callous and cool, but sitting in her car, taking the last drag off her third straight cigarette, Rhiannon wondered if there was more than a little of that desperate and sappy seventh grader left in her than she liked to admit. She tossed the filter out of her window and stepped out into the cool evening.

At the emergency room entrance, she pushed the door open, and approached the receptionist's desk. A frazzled looking woman with dark hair and black-rimmed glasses, whose name tag read Marci, looked up at her.

"May I help you?"

"Yes, I'm looking for a friend of mine that was brought in from the Bruton Inn, Kurt Costello," Rhiannon said

"Are you family?"

"Well, no. I'm his girlfriend," she said, chewing her nails as she watched the receptionist tap the keys before her.

"It looks like he was brought up to the third floor. They want to keep him overnight for observation."

"Can I see him?"

Marci looked back over her shoulder at the clock on the wall. "Visiting hours go until 9 pm. You have about an hour."

"Thank you." Rhiannon turned and headed straight for the elevators.

The silver doors opened, releasing an elderly gentleman with his arm in a sling. The man paused to look at her, watching her with a cataract eye. Rhiannon diverted her attention from the milky, glazed-over orb as she stepped past him. She was turning to select the third floor when the man spun around and placed his good arm on the elevator doors, preventing them from closing.

"She's got him, you know," he said.

Rhiannon took a step back. "Excuse me?"

"You're too late, you little bitch."

Rhiannon watched in stunned horror as the glossed-over eye cleared, like a frosted windshield in a warming vehicle. A gray-blue eye stared back at her, looking more lost and confused than sinister. The bewildered man pulled his arm back and turned around without another word.

What the fuck?

The doors slid closed. The elevator began its ascent to the third floor.

***

Kurt Costello could feel the girl, *the thing*, whatever she was, and her breath against the flesh of his ear. A river of terror flooded his dizzying mind; all of his thoughts becoming a jumble of memories, unfulfilled dreams, and regrets. The thing behind the sultry voice placed a frozen palm flat upon on his chest. A deep, penetrating sensation beyond the most frigid Maine morning seeped from the deathly hand. All he could manage from his shivering body was a whimper as the cold encompassed his slowing heart. Frost formed on the hairs of his nostrils. His blue lips drained of any sense of their former life. The black dots that reappeared behind his closed lids began to pool together and spread until there was nothing but a perfect blackness.

"Shh, shh, shh. You have a higher purpose. I promise," she said.

Kurt's last fragment of life wheezed from his open mouth and into the white sterile room in a cloud of vapor.

***

Rhiannon walked into Kurt's icebox of a hospital room, and screamed.

CHAPTER FOUR

Christmas Eve, 1983

On Christmas Eve, sitting in a darkened movie theater with her psychotic roommate lost in Tony Montana's drug-crazed bloodbath in *Scarface*, Christina was mentally preparing to do what had to be done. If she was going to get away from this wicked girl, she was going to have to lower herself to the bitch's level.

After the three-hour movie came to its ultimately depressing climax, they walked arm in arm to the little powder-blue Volkswagen Bug that Sarah had acquired. As they drove the 40 minutes back to the hotel, the local rock station played an array of new songs that she normally would have enjoyed. But under the circumstances, Def Leppard could just as well be the Carpenters.

As far as she knew, Sarah didn't have a clue about her true feelings. Since the night of Jason's death, Christina had shoved the burning rage and complete hatred for her down deep. She had tried her best to appear as the desperate friend she'd been when they met. She knew she'd have to catch Sarah off guard.

They pulled into the near-empty lot of the Bruton Inn and headed in through the back entrance.

"I think I'm gonna go for a swim."

"Cool," Sarah said.

Christina was certain Sarah would find her way down once she got bored with the TV. Sarah Ford may have had a tough and confident exterior, but it was one predicated on having to project it upon someone.

Minutes later, Christina entered the large pool room. It was empty, as it should be–pool hours were posted stating a firm ten o'clock closing time. Christina and Sarah had yet to adhere to this rule, even after being caught by the old pervert at the desk that ran the night shift. He could care less. They let him watch them swim, which made Christina's skin crawl, but it afforded the girls the freedom to do whatever they wanted within the hotel walls.

She didn't bother using the changing room, deciding to drop her clothes in a pile at her feet, baring her naked body to the empty room that smelled of chlorine. At the moment, the odor also represented the smell of something else–her impending freedom. Slipping into the navy blue one-piece that Sarah had picked out for her, she stepped to the pool's edge and dove in. She slid through the water, skimming mere inches above the pool's concrete floor, before heading back up toward the light and air above. She broke the surface, bringing her hands up to clear the water from her eyes, and nearly jumped out of her gooseflesh skin under Sarah's heavy sparkling gaze.

CHAPTER FIVE

Timothy's new shadow tailed him. Whether the big guy with the fucked up grin was actually following him or just had the same plans for the evening was still up in the air. Paranoia had always been a Timothy-staple.

He made his way down the first floor hall feeling eyes upon him the whole way, but he wasn't about to let the weaknesses of his past ruin the promise of this night. He reached the pool room, grabbed the door handle and turned–the big guy was no longer there.

Where the hell did he go?

He stepped into the pool area, his dress shoes slapping against the granite tile, and was reminded of a study he read about how confined spaces with high humidity were perfect breeding grounds for bacteria and disease. This thought evaporated as Timothy took in the primal scene set out before him. Beautiful young ladies jiggled about everywhere. They filled the pool, they relaxed or texted in lounge chairs. They drank, they giggled, and at least a few of them were looking in his direction.

Two scantily clad blondes in matching red and white-striped bikinis approached him. They smiled and offered him a Bud Light. He accepted the ice cold beverage–despite the fact that he thought the stuff tasted like Alka Seltzer–and smiled back at them.

"Cheers," he said.

The one on the right replied, "You're welcome, handsome."

He tipped the beer bottle in response and continued forward. A few feet past the edge of the pool, a couple of steps led up to a second tier. He had never seen anything like it in another hotel. Two hot tubs bookended a row of very modern-looking pool furniture. He found a free seat, and planted himself between the two Jacuzzis.

"Hi."

A cute redhead in a plaid bikini top leaned over the edge of the hot tub to his left.

"My name's Janey," she said. "What's yours?"

"Tim."

"Hello, Tim." Janey rested her chin on her folded arms. "Are you going swimming or did you just come down here to stare at all the pretty girls."

"A little of both, actually," he said.

"You should come have a seat in here with me."

He looked down at his pants, then back at her. "In these?"

"I bet you have some cute boxers on under there," she said, grinning from ear to ear.

He looked out over the crowd of wet, young bodies, "I think I need to finish my drink and get a good feel for the atmosphere before I join in on any of the activities."

"Whatever." She rolled her eyes, sat up, and turned her back to him.

He assumed they were playing "the game." Oh well, he had already decided he wasn't chasing anyone this weekend. There were plenty of cute little fish in this sea. If this girl was playing hard to get, she was going to be waiting a while.

He lifted the cold bottle of crappy beer to his lips when someone in the pool caught his attention. It was *her*–the girl from the backseat of his car, or at least a damn near perfect look-a-like.

***

The Ice Queen stared at the object of her desire. This time, she would show him all the dirty things he thought he had buried deep down where no one would find them. But first, she wanted to have a little fun.

***

It had been over an hour since Rhiannon left for the hospital. Jeff was gnawing through his fingernails at an alarming rate waiting to hear about Kurt's condition. It didn't help his anxiety that the enigmatic and thus far elusive Meghan Murphy had called down and renewed his hope of getting to spend a few good hours in her company. She was fucking up his head. One night they hit it off, the next she acts like he's invisible, then they kiss, and then she disappears. He could not figure her out. With the whole situation around Kurt today, he was grateful to have something to keep his mind from giving itself over to the girl of empty promises.

Jeff decided he would just call Rhiannon's cell. He found her number on the emergency call list by the phone at the desk, and dialed—it went straight to voicemail.

"Hey, this is Rhiannon. Leave me a message and–" Rhiannon's voice was interrupted by another girl's: "You'll be lucky if you ever see this little bitch again." Jeff's neck hairs were standing on end as Rhiannon's voice came back through "–maybe I'll get back to you."

Beep. Beep. Click.

Unsure what he had just heard, he tried the number again. Nothing–not even the voicemail. He Googled the number of the Hollis Oaks General Hospital, found it, and dialed.

"Hollis Oaks General. Marci speaking, how may I direct your call?"

"Hi, I'm looking for a friend of mine that was brought in earlier from the Bruton Inn. His name is Kurt, Kurt Costello."

The sound of Marci's keyboard clicking chattered in the receiver.

"Are you any relation to Mr. Costello?"

"Yes, I'm his brother."

"He's in the ICU. I'm not supposed to transfer calls up there after nine pm..."

"Please, ma'am, I just have to know that he's okay."

"Okay, sir. Since you are family," she said. "But I'm only transferring you one time. If the call comes back–"

"Thank you, Marci,"

"Okay, I'm putting you through."

The phone rang twice before someone picked up. It was the other voice from Rhiannon's voicemail.

"Hello, Jeffrey. Looking for your friend?"

Jeff's blood froze.

"You shouldn't worry about him. He's going to be quite all right. You might even get to see him again."

"Who is this?"

"Why don't you go check on the girls in the pool?"

Jeff pictured her on the other end, smiling behind the eyes of some famous serial killer–*Dahmer* or *Bundy*. The temperature in the lobby dropped; goose bumps, like boiling water, bubbled up to the surface of his skin. Before he could respond, the line went dead.

"What. The. Fuck?" he said a lot louder than he should have. The preppy couple at the coffee station shot him a set of matching dirty looks.

"Sorry," he said.

Jeff grabbed the "Be right back" sign from under the desk, placed it up for guests to see, and started down the hall, heading toward the pool. The fucked up voice reverberating in his head, followed him down.

CHAPTER SIX

Eric watched Timothy talking with the red-haired girl across the room. All around him he heard the whispered promises of one impish little girl or another. He watched them frolicking in the pool; young men and women, women and women, men and men, rubbing up against one another and not one of the so-called parents to be found.

The short brunette, who had been taking him in with her eyes since he slipped into the room, placed a hand on his thigh. He turned to her with his dark eyes and crooked grin, grabbed hold of her wrist, rose to his feet, and led her into the changing room. She followed along.

On the other side of the changing room door, they found a couple finishing up from their own private moment. The boy and the chubby blonde, who was working hard at stuffing her ample breasts back into the black one piece she wore, dropped their half-smiling faces to the floor, excusing themselves from the room.

"Well, you got me in here, now what are you going to do," the little brunette said. □

He reached past her, clicking the lock on the door. Stepping in close to her until her breasts were pressed up against stomach, he lightly rubbed her bare shoulders while looking her over.

"Oh, I think I like where this is going." She placed her hands on his hips.

"I wouldn't be so sure of that," he said, slowly raising his hands to her neck .His eyes turned from natural deep brown to pitch black. Her playful grin died upon her face.

"Shhhh," he whispered in her ear. "If you want to cry for help, you can whisper your useless little prayers to me." The smile returned to his face as he stifled her screams by clenching his hands around her neck. She jerked and kicked, her spastic, terrified eyes bulging within a face that was turning blue. He could have had a little fun with her, but Kenneth–*her* newest follower–was outside in the night, waiting for another body to dump.

The brunette's flailing body gave in to the sweet kiss of death. Eric threw her over his shoulder and walked to the small rectangle-shaped window beyond the last stall. He reached up and opened the window; the sun from the day had given way to the promise of a darker pledge. The smell of ozone in the cooling breeze rolling into the otherwise warm and sweaty changing room spoke of the coming storm.

As he lifted the body of the dead girl to the opening, Kenneth McGowan's dirt-covered hands reached through from outside, took hold of her, and pulled the corpse into the darkness. Eric watched her bare feet disappear through the opening before returning to the pool room.

***

Outside, Kenneth scurried as quick as he could, dragging the dead girl's body across the freshly paved blacktop of the deserted rear parking lot and down the small decline in the back corner of the lot. He heaved and grunted, hauling the dead weight through the copse of trees just past the lot. The disposal was hard work, but for *her*, it was worth it.

Kenneth got the body through the thickest area of forest, stopping short of the pit he spent the day digging with his bare hands. Soon this hole would match the two beside it. The bodies of two former hotel guests had already been taken care of, presumably by the big guy. Kenneth pushed the corpse into the earth and began returning the dirt to its former place of rest. Thunder boomed overhead. He barely had the body covered with a layer of soil when the first drops of rain began to tap the ground.

***

Meghan sat hunched over the edge of her hotel bed, her pounding head between her knees. Since arriving at the hotel, she'd been having blackouts. One minute, she would be watching television or reading a book, the next a wave of exhaustion would sweep over her like the late Thanksgiving effects of a heavy dose of tryptophan. She was lucky if she made it to the bed before she was out cold. She had woken up on the floor twice already, clueless to how she'd wound up there.

During these "blackouts" she had the most horrible dreams. In them, she was always acting like a complete slut, dancing up on men she had never met before, grinding against them and letting them paw at her. Then, there was the big guy. He was close to twice her height and had the darkest eyes; to look into them was to look into the epitome of death. Yet, despite his awful gaze, she found herself *longing* for him, *needing* him, knowing that she was to go to him. She would wake up from these dreams woozy and missing large chunks of time.

Now, sitting on the plush bed, feeling the impending lethargic wave coming in from the shores of her mind, she decided to fight it, whatever it was. The last time she tried, she wound up in the dirty dream before waking up on the bathroom floor, but tonight, she felt stronger.

CHAPTER SEVEN

Christmas Eve, 1983

"Holy shit, Tina, you act like we just went and saw *Poltergeist*," Sarah said, behind a curious grin.

Christina couldn't ignore the sick feeling squirming through her stomach like maggots through a torn trash bag. She put on her best *I could give a fuck* mask and swam over to the pool's edge to meet her. Sarah looked great dressed in her silver two-piece barely big enough to contain her perfect breasts. The stirring of envy bellied up within Christina again. She squashed the jealous feeling under her recently self-initiated directive to stop putting this cold bitch up on a pedestal. "I just didn't hear you come in. Water's warm." She dipped back under, disappearing into the quiet waters before reemerging at the other end (farthest from Sarah) of the pool.

"You're ass looks nice in that suit," Sarah said.

"Thanks. You comin' in, or you just gonna stand there with your tits hangin' out?"

"Mee-ow. Listen to you. Wherever did you learn to talk like such a bitch?" Sarah said, reaching her slim arms up behind her neck, undoing the knot that held the tight silver top in place. "How about I up the ante around here?" She brought her arms down to her hips, letting her top fall to the floor, her breasts out for the world to see. "Skinny dipping? Or as the French would say-*plongement maigre*?"

Christina, in spite of her best attempts not to, blushed like a school girl going in for her first kiss. She cursed herself for not being able to stifle the natural reaction. She watched as Sarah's bikini bottoms landed next to the silver top. Sarah stood naked as the day she was born. "Well, you gonna strip? Or are you still too shy?"

Christina quelled the urge to spit hell-fire at the bitch and her stupid attempt to control the situation. Sarah had issues, and this time, Christina decided she wasn't playing her dumb little games. "I think I'm good. You go ahead and play naked mermaid without me." She watched Sarah closely, trying to gauge her response. Sarah's nostrils flared. Her brow furrowed, and then the grin slid back into place.

"Fine. Be a baby all your life." Sarah said. She raised both hands over her head, placing one palm over the other in a diver's stance, and propelled herself into the water with precision, barely the hint of a splash.

She watched as Sarah closed the distance between them, cutting through the water like an eel. She broke the surface too close for comfort. Face to face with Sarah, her effort to respond was preempted by a kiss. Sarah placed an open mouth to her own—a tongue slithered its way past her lips. Stunned, both from the act itself and the surprising sense of arousal birthing from the lip-lock, she found herself kissing this devil back.

She felt Sarah press her nakedness up against her. Christina, as if in a sexual trance, found herself touching her, exploring the amazing body pressed tightly to her own. She snapped out of it at the fingers pressing between her legs. "Whoa, what are you doing?" she said, breaking the embrace and swimming back toward the side of the pool.

Sarah smiled wide following after her. "I think you mean what are *we* doing?" Sarah came forward again, but was met with a hard slap across the face. Christina, shocked at her own brazen move, watched as the meanness took over her pursuer's features. Storm clouds funneled within Sarah's brown eyes.

Like a caged lioness unleashed, Sarah roared, grabbed Christina around the neck with both hands, and squeezed her throat, causing her sight to fill with a mix of stars and spots. Forced beneath the water, certain that she was next on Sarah Ford's kill list, one thought passed through Christina's clouding mind: *I made a huge mistake.*

Present Day

Timothy rubbed his eyes, hardly believing who he was seeing. The gorgeous woman in the center of the pool seemed to hover in place, her gaze locked on his own. There was a connection, more mental than tangible. He rose from his seat, unbuttoned his dress shirt, dropped his slacks to the floor, and propelled himself into the pool, splashing into its lukewarm depths. Coming up somewhere in the middle, close to the spot where he'd seen the woman, he emerged from the water, only she was nowhere to be found. He wiped the water from his eyes, spinning around, scanning the pool, then the room, for the beautiful creature.

"Where do you think you're going?"

He twisted around, expecting to find the pool beauty, but instead, came face to face with Janey. *How did she...* his thought was hit by Kryptonite—she had the most wondrous emerald eyes. He could not break her gaze as she swam up closer to him; her hands suddenly appeared on his hips as she got up into his face, bit her bottom lip, and reached between his legs. "Isn't this supposed to shrink when you're in the water?"

"I, uh...I was looking for someone," he said

"I'm someone," Janey said, putting her hands into the front of his boxers, gripping him tight. "Do you want to go up to my room with me?" She put her lips to his ear and whispered, "I'll make it worth your while."

His breathing grew heavy as she began to move the hand wrapped around his penis back and forth. He turned to look around and see if anyone else in the largely populated room was paying attention. No one was. They all appeared to be caught up in their own microbursts of seduction. He turned back to respond to her request and came eye-to-eye with the dark-haired beauty he had originally been chasing.

"Surprise," she said.

His head felt like a top, spiraling aimlessly. He wasn't sure what the hell was going on or how the two girls had switched; he was still being tugged on below the water's surface.

"How h-how did you–" he said, but before he could spit out the rest, his body quivered as he ejaculated.

"Mmm," she moaned in his ear. She pulled her hand free from his underwear and swam in a circle around him, leaving him euphoric and dazed.

He looked up to see the blue-eyed blonde he had passed by the ice bucket of beers smiling at him. His face warmed as he turned to follow the dark-haired sex queen who had just made his night—hell—who had just made his year. But she had disappeared, again.

CHAPTER EIGHT

Jeff reached the inn's pool area, and froze at the impossible sights behind the glass. There were at least twice as many people in the pool room than there should be. Some were dancing, some were laughing, but most of them were tangled like lovers at a swinger's party. Underneath the hip hop music bumping bass-pounding beats from within, he could hear moaning. He spotted couples in the pool rocking back and forth, another couple intertwined against the far wall, and a group of three girls having their own make-out session. Jeff knew he should step in and put a stop to all of this. Standing and staring at the whole decadent scene, his mouth dry, and his heartbeat accelerating, he found his hand resting weakly on the door handle, unable to turn the knob and open the door.

***

Eric had watched the man named Timothy flirt like a fool with the ginger across the room, then watched him drop his fancy clothes and plunge into the pool in pursuit of *her*. He had stood gritting his teeth as she had her way with the weak, baldheaded buffoon. The smirk returned to his stone face after she left the pool and returned to his side.

"I need you to go to the girl for me," she said. She stood, dripping wet, her eyes looking deeply into his.

"As you wish," he said. "What about him?" Eric nodded at the lost looking man treading water in the center of the pool.

"I'm just getting started with him," she said. "I trust young Kenneth is finished playing in the rain?"

"He should be. Should I go find out?"

"No, no, no. I'm sure he'll be fine." Turning back to him, she said, "You better get upstairs. Ms. Murphy is ripe for the taking."

Eric nodded, and headed for the door.

***

Jeff was still wrestling with himself to end the orgy going on in his pool area when the door handle twisted beneath his palm. He let go as the big guy from room 231 stepped out of the heated room, knocking him out of the way. He watched the mountain of a man turn the corner and disappear.

He was still trying to shake off the goose bumps covering his skin when he stepped into the now half-empty pool room. The music was blaring from a set of portable speakers by the Jacuzzis, but all of the adult situations had dissolved into a collection of scenes much more PG.

I must be losing my fucking mind.

He took a walk around the pool, scanning the corners for anything that resembled what had been happening before, but saw nothing out of the ordinary. He shook his head and made his way back toward the door.

Jeff thought of Meghan as he headed back to his nightly post. He had brought in his entire *Tales from the Crypt* graphic novel collection in hopes of rekindling their conversational magic. He hoped she would at least show up, whether she ignored him, or enjoyed his company. He just wanted to see her again.

CHAPTER NINE

Meghan Murphy felt like she was going to faint. Stars were dancing before her eyes like the celebrities from that terrible contest show her mother used to watch; tumbling and crashing into moons from an impossible galaxy. She stumbled into the darkened bathroom intent on splashing some cold water on her flush face. Her bare feet went numb on contact with the tiled floor as cold as a cracked blacktop in the middle of February. She high-stepped out of the re-frigerated room as if crossing over hot coals.

Something caught her eye as she glanced into the chilled lavatory. Even without the lights on she could read the frost-covered mirror. Two words were sketched into the frozen glaze:

He's coming.

***

As the metallic door slid open, Eric stalked out into the hallway; the light's all dimmed in his presence. He passed room 231. Beyond its door, the blood and brain matter from Jimmy Curran still dressed the carpeting and wall beside the broken entertainment stand. Eric was wrenching his large mitts together in anticipation of his next directive. His gait was that of a machine–decisive and steady. The new beast beneath his flesh was starving.

"Eric, Eric."

He turned to find the rain-drenched form of Kenneth McGowan shuffling up from the stairwell behind him, covered from head to foot in mud and filth. Combined with the wet strands of brown hair slapped across his elongated face, he looked like a sewer rat.

"What is it?" Eric said, trying to mask his irritation. *She* had deemed this sorry mess of a man worthy of her gift, all Eric saw was someone pathetic and weak.

"The storm, the storm is making a mess of my holes," Kenneth said.

A door opened farther down from where the two incongruous men stood, and a middle-aged gentleman and his son stepped into the dimmed corridor. The boy, dressed in a Red Sox rain slicker and a tall pair of goulashes, moved behind his father at the sight of the two awkward characters down the hall.

"It's okay, Joey. They're just staying at the hotel, like you and me," the man with the tan Carhartt jacket and shoulder-length dark hair said to his son.

"Come on," Eric said. He pushed the wet rat back toward the room still registered to Jimmy Curran. As they stepped inside, he slammed the door behind them.

"Did you see the way those two were looking at us?" Kenneth said.

Eric grabbed his giddy accomplice by the collar of his store bought army jacket, yanking him up off the ground until they were nose to nose. "You mention our business out in the open again, before she tells us it's time–you're going in the dirt next."

***

Down the hall, the door to room 209 opened. Meghan stumbled out into the hallway. Driven by the compulsion to get away from her cooling room as quick as she could, she made her way to the stairs, taking the steps two at a time. She was nearly to the bottom when a phantom shape appeared before her. Looking into the black eyes within its skeletal face–she fell. Her head slapped the concrete with a loud smack, sending Meghan into the arms of her vision.

****

The lock to room 209 flashed green, and then clicked. The door smashed against the rubber doorstopper on the wall behind it as Eric Gentry charged his six-foot-six frame into the cold room. Kenneth the rat filed in behind him.

"Where the hell is she?" Kenneth said.

Eric turned, shoved the rat into the wall by the door, and headed back into the hallway. "She's gone."

Chapter Ten

Rhiannon was still screaming as a group of doctors and nurses pushed past her into Kurt's hospital room. Urgent voices filled the suddenly cramped space of the cold hospital room. No one looked in her direction. Through her tears she saw someone standing in the back of the room. *A girl.* She watched the figure with the long brown spiral locks slowly maneuver around the hectic scene of medics–none of whom seemed to notice her–as she began to make her way across the room. Their eyes met, Rhiannon's body went cold–she was nauseous. There was something heavy, something evil in this girl.

She bolted down the fluorescent-lit hall, feeling her life hanging in the balance, like whatever had gotten Kurt wanted her next. It was crazy, but something inside told her it was right. She ran past the elevators, to the stairwell, and began her descent; a cold chill pulling at the fine hairs on the nape of her neck the entire way down.

CHAPTER ELEVEN

Christmas Eve, 1983

"You ungrateful little cunt, how dare you fucking put your hands on me," Sarah's muffled voice seethed with hatred above the water's surface. Below and out of breath, Christina tried to focus her flailing mind on one thing–survival. She brought her hands up to the backs of her death dealer's arms and sunk her lengthy fingernails into the taught flesh.

"Ahh! You fucking bitch!"

Free from Sarah's grip, Christina popped above the surface gasping for the air she thought she'd never breathe again. Her victory was short lived as Sarah dove at her, taking her back under mid-breath, causing her to take in a mouthful of pool water. The two girls, completely submerged and entangled, scratched and clawed, kicked and pulled at one another as their combined weight moved them to the pool's floor.

In a last ditch attempt to not have these be her final living moments, Christina flung her body backwards pulling Sarah with her, managing to knee her in the solar plexus. She felt the hands at her throat loosen as air bubbles flumed from the girl's mouth. Christina swam toward the surface. Sarah's hand caught her ankle and yanked her back down. Face to face with her insane roommate, Christina screamed out into the water as she spun and struck her palm up into the more aggressive girl's nose. Blood, spread from the wound—as if Jaws had just taken a chunk out of another careless swimmer—and contaminated the pool. Sarah's arms and legs floated like seaweeds–a subtle dance propelled by the motion of the water and nothing more.

Christina tried willing her way upward, but the life was draining from her body at a breakneck speed. The lights above calling her home, taunted her as the black border surrounding her blurry vision drew inward. Her arms quit first, her legs followed. Two strokes from life, the darkness closed in–complete and eternal.

Present Day

Lee Buhl, having just finished up his book signing event, made his way over to the Hollis Oaks public library. Initially, he'd only planned on doing some research but the tremors that had been shuddering through his body since he arrived here demanded he stop fucking around. Over the years, this ritual had yielded a good many tales for his books. Although he was only about one-fifth Native American, and that was being generous, Lee Buhl embraced the tribal part of his heritage and turned it into a great money-maker. He made a good living from his books and from performing shaman ceremonies at the "haunted" sites he wrote about.

As the heavy rain pounded the large glass panes of the recently renovated Hollis Oaks Public Library, Lee was glad he'd decided to drive over from the Barnes and Noble rather than walk. The intensity of the weather kept him digging around through the library longer than usual. The added time spent investigating uncovered an interesting piece of history from a nearby town. For a property relatively new, having been built in 1977, The Bruton Inn had a bit of an enigmatic history. Back in the eighties two young woman were found dead in the hotel's indoor swimming pool. The article he found in a local paper,

The Coral County Sentinel, went on to say "the two young women were said to have been staying together in a room rented to a local man, Gordon Kilpatrick, who himself has been missing for two months." There were also quotes from past workers who claimed the place was haunted. The whispers of ghosts appeared to dry up over the nineties and early 2000's. Lee couldn't find a single related blurb. Then, he came across a piece the paper had run this past summer about a man named Edward Young who was found drowned in the Bruton Inn's new swimming pool. This is what was pulling at him. He was certain. The wheels of Lee Buhl's always ready and open mind began to churn. He scribbled down the address of the out of the way inn and placed the little black notebook in his messenger bag.

A pretty little brunette with short spikey hair, chewing on the tip of a pen, caught his attention. She looked maybe eighteen, more likely sixteen. He flashed a smile her way causing her to redden as she bit her pen and looked at him the same way "Sexy" Lexi had just a couple days ago. Turned out Lexi was eighteen and *ballsy*. Her phone call led to a nice night of fun for them both. This one across the way looked ready to play, as well.

Not tonight, Lee.

Still, he couldn't resist walking past the pretty young thing as he made his exit, dropping one of his business cards next to her biology book.

The strange currency flowed through his stomach again as he stepped out into the storm. His instincts–or the spirits, as he often referred to them before his hosts–often brought him to grounds fertile with supernatural possibilities. After shutting out the heavy rain pounding down from the heavens, Lee started his car and heard a voice. *A fan, from the book signing?* He looked around the lot, but had trouble believing anyone would be waiting out in this crazy weather.

Lee sat behind the wheel of his Shinari staring at a puddle being riddled with a black rain. He thought of the Bruton Inn and its indoor swimming pool. A deep chill sunk into his marrow. He drove out of the library's parking lot thinking of mermaids and devils.

VOLUME III

A Change Has Come

She delighted in the hurricane of chaos and devastation sweeping through the hallways of the Bruton Inn. The malevolent creature, formerly known as Sarah Ford, smiled. It was a long time coming. She was nearly at full strength and ready for her resurrection. The autumn chill, and a magnificent rainstorm punishing the earth, set the evening up for a crescendo that would bring an end to a very successful chain of events, and birth a new beginning.

Her boys, Eric and Kenneth, were playing their parts like a couple of seasoned pros. Eric, *brutal Eric*, was intimidating and stifling the life from various guests, while little Kenneth discarded the bodies that aided in feeding her power. Meghan, only slightly stronger than she had originally given her credit for, was running, but her avoidance would only make her transformation that much more satisfying.

The two hotel clerks, Jeffrey and Rhiannon, providing a great many opportunities for her to flex her awakening abilities, were in for a reckoning of sorts.

Her final game piece was ready to be moved; Timothy Laymon's haunted past was about to bring him home... *to her*. She recalled lyrics to a more than fitting rock n roll song by one of her favorite bands. *"It's down to me... a change has come..."*

CHAPTER ONE

Rhiannon emerged from the side exit of the Hollis Oakes General Hospital. Her heart hammering a Gods of Metal theme within her chest, her body trembling in collusion with her mind, threatening to break her temple. She stumbled onto the cold concrete sidewalk under the moonlit night trying not to scream; she failed to stifle the whimpers flowing at will.

What's wrong, little girl? A voice that was not her own whispered from inside her mind, sending chills spiraling down the staircase of her spine.

"No," Rhiannon screamed into the night, clamping her violently shaking hands over her ears. She spun around, certain the girl giving chase would be standing behind her. There was nothing. She started backing away from the door, unable to stop the tears from falling.

"Hey you."

The male voice startled her. She turned toward the front entrance to the hospital. It was the old man from the elevator with the milky eye and wounded arm, standing, staring, and calling after her.

"I told you. I told you she got him. I told you she got him." He began to laugh.

The inappropriate cackle prickled her goose bumps to rise. Flooded with nausea, Rhiannon doubled over.

"She got him–" his voice was still a good hundred feet away. "–Now she's got you." He said, suddenly inches from her ear.

She could smell his musky aftershave, the same kind her grandpa used to wear. She spun around and unleashed a blood curdling scream. There was nothing, no one–just her, the moon, and the shadows of the night. She glanced back to where the man had been taunting her. He was gone.

I'm losing it, I'm fucking losing it.

She stayed kneeled in the grass just off the sidewalk, her arms lying like two dead branches hanging at her sides, the limp hands at their ends–lifeless in the grass. The towering pine tree at her back, casting a malevolent shadow over her, rustled with the chilled wind. She began crying and laughing hysterically.

She dared a glance upward. From behind the semi-frosted window above, a grinning face disappeared.

"Ma'am, are you okay?"

Rhiannon wiped the tears from her face as a well-dressed man stepped toward her. She noticed, despite the concern in his voice, he had not stepped from the security of the entrance lights.

"Miss?"

Rhiannon climbed to her feet, dusted off her dirt-covered knee, and ran for the parking lot. She had to get to her car and get the hell away from this place. *Kurt's dead.* The thought brought a fresh set of tears to her burning eyes. She tried to push away the sight of that hospital room. His body, cold and lifeless–so unlike the man she had worked with over the last half a year. She had adored him. And in spite of this and a lack of close friends, she'd kept him at a distance. She cursed herself for not making more of their time together. More glimpses of that desperate seventh grader cracked through her defenses. She crossed into the Emergency Room parking lot, wiped away the tears, and made her way to the little red Escort. She fumbled the car key out of her jacket pocket and worked it into the slot beside the door handle.

"Leaving so soon?"

Rhiannon froze. She raised her eyes above the car's dented roof and saw the strange girl from Kurt's hospital room standing four cars away.

This can't be real, this can't be real.

She opened the car door and climbed in not bothering to check the other girl's position. She turned the engine over and slammed the Escort into reverse. Checking her rearview mirror, the red brake lights illuminated the odd girl behind her in a vision of demonic glee. The devil in the mirror was smiling at her as she drove away.

The car fishtailed onto Jefferson Drive, straightening out as she headed toward downtown Hollis Oakes. She wanted to call Jeff at the hotel. There was no one else who would understand. She had to tell somebody what was happening. She reached into the small space beneath the car's radio and ashtray, and found her cell phone.

A Subaru Outback followed her onto the road, pulling up in the lane next to her. The driver turned toward her, his milky, white eye reaching out for her, looking into her. The girl from Kurt's hospital room was riding shotgun.

Rhiannon, keeping an eye on the road before her, tried dialing her work number.

Kkkrrrrrr.

The Outback slammed into the side of the car, causing her to swerve across the yellow line and drop her phone. She screamed as the car came in for another swipe.

"Leave me alone," she screamed, the tears falling again.

Honnnnk.

Rhiannon veered back toward the green Subaru to avoid hitting an oncoming SUV and saw the set of traffic lights up ahead.

"Why are you doing this?" She looked from the intersection to the Subaru and back–there was no way they were making the green light. The old man behind the wheel began convulsing; the bitch at his side continued to smile. Rhiannon stamped both feet on the brake pedal and screamed. Her tires screeched into the night.

The Subaru flew into the crossing traffic–a moth to a flame–and collided in an explosion of plastic, metal, rubber, and flesh.

Chapter Two

Jeff Braun felt like his brain was hanging upside down. No sooner had the disconcerting phone call with someone screaming been disconnected than he heard a loud commotion to the left of the front desk, like someone had fallen down the stairs. He hurried to the stairwell shocked to find Meghan Murphy sprawled out on the concrete floor.

"Meghan," he said. "C'mon, are you okay?" He reached down and put a hand under her head–there was a large egg-shaped bump, but no blood. "Meghan, Meghan. Can you hear me?"

Her eyes fluttered open.

"Hey." Jeff helped her up. She was unsteady, but otherwise seemed okay. "C'mon." He led her through the door to the lobby, around the front desk, and into the back office.

"Are you okay?" Jeff said, holding Meghan's hand. She sat next to the stack of magazines that always occupied on end of the black futon.

"I, I saw someone," she said. He followed her glare over his shoulder.

"What do you mean? Who'd you see?" Jeff pulled her forward as he sifted his fingers through her black hair looking to see if she had suffered more damage than he had thought. She was lucky she hadn't cracked her skull on the concrete floor.

"Do you have any water?" she said.

"Yeah, sure. Hold on." Jeff got up and went through another door to the right of the futon. He returned with a bottle of water, a couple of pills, and an ice pack. "Here, put this on your head."

"Thanks," she said.

"And take these. They won't touch the headache you're probably gonna have, but it's better than nothing." Jeff handed her two Tylenol. He watched her toss the pills back, and guzzle down the cold water. She replaced the cap, set the bottle on the floor between her bare feet, and returned the ice pack to her head.

"I probably look like an idiot, huh?" Meghan said.

"No. I don't think you could look like an idiot if you tried," he said, blushing, but not breaking his gaze.

"I'm sorry I've been so...weird. I haven't felt like myself these last few days," she said.

He felt her grip tighten on his hand. His heart revved up. He worried his hands were going to start sweating.

"I'm not sure how much longer I'll be here, but–" Meghan began, sitting up straight, looking him in the eyes, "–I hope we get to spend some time together."

Before he could respond, she leaned in and kissed him. The taste of her cherry chap stick, the smell of her hair–something fruity, definitely not the hotel shampoo–she was intoxicating. Their mouths opened, allowing the sweet kiss to reach its full potential; it was soft, slow, and perfect. He placed his right hand on the small of her back and pulled her closer.

Ring, ring, ring.

Jeff made like he was going to get up. She gripped him tighter, kissed him harder, and slid a hand to the thigh of his dress slacks. He gave up any notion of answering the phone, and fell further into their moment.

***

Ring, ring, ring.

"Come on, Jeff. Fucking pick up," Rhiannon said. She had pulled into the parking lot of the 7-11 over by the traffic light the green Subaru went sailing into. Three cop cars and two ambulances arrived on the scene to tend to the unfortunate. She watched the Subaru with the intensity of a sniper waiting for his mark, having to know if the old man and the strange girl had survived. She watched as the EMT's pulled the old man out, his face was a mask of blood–he did not move. Neither the EMT's nor the officers on the scene had gone near the passenger door.

Rhiannon hung up the cell phone, slid it in the pocket of her red pea coat, and headed toward the accident. She approached the closest officer whose badge read: Gilmatt.

"Excuse me, Officer Gilmatt," she said.

"Ma'am, I'm going to need you to step away, please. This–" Gilmatt started.

"I saw it happen," she said. "I saw the whole thing happen. I was coming down the road right behind that green car." She pointed to the mangled Subaru at the center of the four-car mess.

"You witnessed the accident occur?" he said, suddenly appearing interested in what she had to say.

"Yes, that green car went flying past me. I was slowing up for the light, but that car went flying by like a maniac. I don't know if he thought he was going to make the light, or if he lost his brakes, or what."

Officer Gilmatt produced a notepad from his breast pocket and scratched down some notes.

"Is the driver...dead?" she said.

"I'm afraid so. An elderly gentleman. It looks like he may have suffered a heart attack or a stroke, which would explain why you didn't see him slow down."

"What about the girl?" Rhiannon said.

"*The girl?*" the officer said, raising an eyebrow.

"Yes, I, I saw a girl in the passenger seat when they went past me."

"There was no one else in the vehicle, ma'am, just the gentleman."

Rhiannon shook her head. "No, no. That's not right. She was in there," Rhiannon said. She stepped off the sidewalk and rushed over to where the battered Subaru sat tangled with a blue Blazer.

"Ma'am! Ma'am!"

"No, no...this can't be," Rhiannon said, stopping before the scene.

Officer Gilmatt grabbed her by the arms and directed her back toward the parking lot of the 7-11. "Ma'am, I'm going to need some more information from you–"

Rhiannon pulled herself free and made a beeline for her car. She climbed in, threw the key into the ignition, and backed out without looking, nearly causing a collision of her own with a silver pickup pulling in.

"Hey! Watch where the fuck you're goin'," yelled the man behind the wheel of the pickup.

She only half heard him as she threw the car into drive and hooked a right down Champlain Street. She slipped her phone from her pocket and tried the hotel again.

***

"I can't do this, I can't," Jeff said.

Meghan sat back, crossed her arms, and looked away.

"I want to, believe me I want to, but my manager could come walking in through that door any moment." It was true, however unlikely. He had called his front office manager after Rhiannon left for the hospital, but had been unable to get through to her. He left a message about what happened with Kurt and the elderly couple, but as far as he knew she had yet to return the call.

"I'm sorry," Meghan said, wiping at the tears rolling down her cheeks.

Ring, ring, ring.

"I have to get that," he said.

Meghan sniffled and nodded as she reached for the discarded ice pack.

Jeff stepped out the door, and behind the desk. His attention was stolen by the two gentlemen sitting at a table in the lobby. One was Kenneth McGowan . The other was the big guy from room 231. They were both staring at him. He wasn't sure why, but he had a bad feeling that they were after something.

He picked up the phone on the seventh ring.

"Thank you for calling the Bruton Inn, this is Jeff speaking. How can I help you?"

"Jeff," Rhiannon said.

"Rhiannon? Where are you? Are you okay?" he said.

"He's dead," she cried.

"What? How? Wait–where are you?"

"He–" she tried. "He's...."

"Are you on the road right now?" Jeff said.

"Yes."

"Do your parents live up this way?

"No, they live in Portland."

"What about friends?" he said.

"My friend Michele is gone away to school in Oswego."

"Okay. That's all right. I'm here. Pull over if you need to collect yourself, all right?"

"I already have–twice," she said.

"That's good. We don't need to lose you, too," he said. "Listen, I was thinking about staying the night again here, you're on tomorrow, why don't you just come back here if you don't want to stay by yourself, we can get a room with two beds," he said. Jeff couldn't help but wonder if Kenneth and his new friend were eavesdropping on his conversation. They were whispering to one another and grinning like they knew something no one else did.

"Yeah, I think I'd prefer that to my empty apartment," Rhiannon said, sniffling on the other end of the line. "I'm not too far out. I should be there in a little while. I'll talk to you when I get there."

"Okay, be safe. See you in a bit." Jeff hung up the phone, locking eyes with the big guy accompanying Kenneth. Uncomfortable in the presence of the dynamic duo in the lobby, he stepped out from behind the desk, glanced down the hallway, then toward the front doors. Satisfied that he was not needed, he returned to the back office.

Chapter Three

After a minute to clear his thoughts, Timothy Laymon swam back toward the diving board and climbed out of the pool. He stood up and looked back to the spot in the water where the two beautiful women had just played with him. Scanning the room for either, he came up empty. He returned to his seat between the two Jacuzzis and found his pants were missing.

"Great," he said.

All of the girls that smiled at him when he arrived earlier were now shooting daggers his way instead.

"What the fuck are you looking at?" said a brunette stepping into the hot tub.

"Nothing, I was just leaving. Sorry."

He walked down the two steps to the first level of the room, making his way to the front corner where the towels were kept, and picked one up. The thing looked like a little kid's towel. He used it to wipe down his body, giving up on his original plan to wear it to his room for fear of his junk hanging out, and deposited it in the used towel bin by the door.

"You're up," said the blonde in the bikini that had handed him the Bud Light.

"What was that?" he asked.

"Excuse me?" the blonde said.

"You just said something to me."

"In your wet dreams maybe." She laughed as she walked back to a big, square-jawed guy with spiked black hair.

Timothy turned, leaving the warmth of the pool room behind him.

He was shocked by the coolness of the hallway. He shivered as goose pimples busted out on the backs of his arms. Then he noticed the sight at the end of the corridor. The amazing dark-haired girl from the pool stood, waiting. She was down by the stairwell on the east end of the building holding his pants–a devilish smile playing across her full lips.

"Missing something, handsome?"

"Ah, yeah. I could probably use those. How did–"

"Come and get 'em." She waved them out to her side like a matador.

Timothy started down the hall. The beautiful girl darted up the stairs. He broke into a run, chasing after her.

He climbed the stairs, listening for her footsteps, but heard nothing. He rounded the corner toward the second floor hallway, and there she was. She slammed him to the wall behind the door and put her mouth to his with the intensity of a rocket set to explode. He gave himself over to her. She pressed her perfect body up against his; his wet underwear poking at her nether regions.

"Come with me," she said between kisses.

He moved his lips to her soft neck, kissing and nibbling her flesh.

She grabbed him by the waistband of his underwear and pulled him around the corner and down the hallway.

A man passing by in the opposite direction wearing a dress shirt and slacks gawked at the girl as they passed. Timothy grinned. The slender woman next to the man was not so impressed.

"Nice, Kevin. Looking at other women on our anniversary," the woman said.

"Honey, what? No..."

"What's your name," Timothy said to this beautiful mystery girl. She stopped them outside the door to room 211.

"Shhh." She opened the door and pushed him inside. "I want you to fuck me, Timothy."

"Huh? Uh...yeah, yeah. Hell yeah, I can do that," he said. He grabbed the straps of her swimsuit and peeled the wet fabric off, exposing her naked perfection.

She grabbed his hair and pulled his mouth back to hers before sliding down his body, grabbing his waistband with her teeth, and dragging his boxers to the floor. She slithered back up to his erection taking him into her mouth.

Timothy was as high as a kite in a flawless summer sky. This unbelievable woman had chosen him over all the douchebag frat boys down at the pool. He laughed at the thought even as the beauty blowing him brought him closer to ecstasy.

She finished him off sucking down every bit of his seed. Rising back up, she wrapped her arms around his neck. "My name is Sarah."

"Well, Sarah, thank you for that."

"I know you," Sarah said.

"Oh yeah? Where from?"

She turned her back and pressed her ass against him. "I knew Shannon."

Timothy backed away from her, fear and anger pooling together in his clouded mind. *How could she? No way, nobody knows about that.*

Sarah sat down on the edge of the bed and twirled a finger through her bouncy brown curls. "I know *all* about that," she said, as if he had spoken aloud.

"Fuck you." He looked around the room for his pants.

"Oh, we'll get to that, but first, I want to talk about Shannon."

"I don't know who the hell you are, or what the fuck you think you know, but I think I need to leave." He reached down for his boxers, and felt her tongue in his ear.

"She deserved it. She was, after all, the one who fucked somebody else," Sarah whispered. Her voice played through his head like the song of the pied piper; his fear and anger being led away. "She was the one who fucked that mustached loser. You had every right to smash her head in."

"Yes," he said, barely hearing himself.

"She even brought him home to your bed."

"Yes."

"We're the same, you and I," she whispered.

He looked at her, feeling desperate and alone.

"Oh yes, I used to know lots of guys who would tell me they loved me, then turn around and nail the first thing that smiled at them. And my father was the worst of them all."

"I would never do that to you," Timothy said.

"I know, I know. That's why I chose you. We're the same."

"Yes," he said.

Sarah guided him to the bed and pulled him down on top of her. "Fuck me, Timothy. Let's help each other feel good again."

He felt himself grow hard and slipped inside of her.

Chapter Four

Rhiannon drove like a mother rushing her child to the emergency room–on edge, yet determined. She had no idea what was happening tonight. Who was the strange girl at the hospital? What was she doing in Kurt's room? Had she really been in the car with the old man? What the hell did it all mean? All these questions riddled through her mind at warp speed and then cycled back unanswered as if the train of queries was an endless loop.

She raced down Route 5, heading back to the hotel. She considered going home, but she was too frazzled to sleep, and her TV and Mr. Mittens, her cat with the extra thumbs, wouldn't listen. She desperately needed to talk to someone. Jeff had offered to be there, and at the moment, he was really all she had. She wasn't sure how or why, but she just knew he would believe her when she told him about the crazy shit-storm she'd just been through.

***

"I don't want to be alone right now. Come upstairs with me," Meghan said. Her eyes danced between brown and black.

"I can't," Jeff said, denying the change in eye color. "I'm the only one on right now. I'm waiting for someone–" he paused, realizing he hadn't mentioned what happened to Kurt.

Meghan pulled herself from his arms. If looks could kill, Jeff would be an extra from *The Walking Dead*.

"What is it? Do you have a girlfriend you failed to mention?"

"No, it's nothing like that."

"Then who is it?" She crossed her arms.

Jeff rose from the Futon, placed his hands on his hips, and hung his head. "It's my friend, Kurt–the goofy kid that works here in the afternoon?" He saw her indifference and took it as uncertainty. "The guy with the fro of blonde hair? Sings while he works?"

"What about him?"

"He had to be taken to the hospital today after–" Jeff hesitated, not sure he should tell her about the couple that had died in the hallway "–after he started his shift. He fainted. One of my co-workers went to the hospital to check on him. She's supposed to stop in on her way back."

"Well, then I guess I'll just go back upstairs." Meghan stood and headed past him, going straight to the door.

"Meghan, wait."

She stopped and glanced back at him. "Promise me one thing," she said.

"Sure, what is it?"

"Promise you'll come and check on me later?" Her eyes flashed to black, then back to normal. It happened so fast, Jeff convinced himself he'd not seen it.

"I promise." He walked her out of the back office and handed her the ice pack.

"Thank you for taking care of me," she said, planting a kiss on his lips before he could respond.

He watched her walk away before returning to his nightly post behind the desk. Waiting to for Rhiannon, he noticed that the odd couple, Kenneth and the big guy, had vanished. His bad feeling returned in spades.

CHAPTER FIVE

Eric stood behind the door to the stairwell, waiting for Meghan to step through. Before she could scream, he clamped one large hand over her mouth and clenched the other around the back of her neck; her ice pack fell to the floor with a soft thud. Dragging her up the stairs while she kicked and struggled, he sneered.

When they reached the top of the stairs, he flung her into the wall next to the door, covering her mouth and easily pinning her in place as he glanced down the hall for other guests. The corridor was clear.

Without a word, he hauled her back down to room 209.

***

Meghan's mind felt corrupted. Strange currencies of offsetting emotions fought for control over her senses. One moment she feared for her life, horrible thoughts of why this man had been waiting for her and what he planned to do. The next, while still quivering on the outside, inside she was cool as a winter's night on the verge of a storm; calm and ready for the forthcoming surge of power.

The timid half of her psyche regained control as the big guy shoved her inside the doorway to her room.

I must have left the door open.

There was a smaller but creepier man–naked and waiting–at the edge of her bed.

"Oh no...no, no, no..." she cried. The big guy's hands wrapped around her throat. Spots danced before her tear-filled eyes. When she was thirteen, she'd nearly been raped by her cousin's best friend. Back then she had managed to claw her way from his grasp before he could force himself inside of her—running all the way home in just a t-shirt. Up until now, that moment had easily been the most traumatic experience of her life. She had a feeling this would be worse.

CHAPTER SIX

In the arms of the girl who called herself Sarah, Timothy Laymon was reborn. His mind tingled, his skin–tight and slick with sweat and the scent of sex–felt brand new. He wanted to conquer the world, just like that old Bad Religion song, but before he could open his mouth to share these feelings of renewed vigor with her, she placed a cold hand to his chest; calmness settled over him. He was asleep within seconds. He dreamed, or rather, *remembered* the death of his ex-girlfriend, Shannon Huber.

August 22, 2007

Shannon had been acting strange the last week or so, but he just figured it had something to do with her new job at the little bookstore downtown, Burt's Book Nook. She had only been working there for three weeks when her boss, some queer from California, decided that Shannon could handle running the place by herself while he and his boyfriend ran off on vacation. She had to do all the deposits, handle all the orders, and work from open to close the entire week. She stayed late each night, slinking through the door to their trailer after ten o'clock, looking exhausted and heading to take a shower, then straight to bed.

Today, he was going to surprise her. Her boss had finally returned from his trip, and she had the next three days off. Timothy had planned out a whole evening for them to chill out and relax. He rented a room at the Hampton Inn in Freeport figuring a romantic walk along the quaint little streets filled with mom and pop shops snuggled in among the multitude of outlet stores would offer them a nice getaway. Maybe they would grab a lobster dinner at the Muddy Rudder before heading to Helena Park to stare up at the stars. The night would conclude with them making love.

In order to execute the surprise, he pretended to leave for work at eight in the morning as usual, when in fact he needed to pick up a couple of last minute gifts. Upon his return, he was surprised and confused to see the little red Jeep in his driveway.

Timothy walked up the steps gazing back over his shoulder as he reached for the door knob. It was locked. A sick feeling swirled to life in his stomach. He fumbled his keys out from his jean pockets struggling to unlock the door with his shaking hands. Upon entering, he instantly heard the unmistakable sounds; skin slapping skin, grunts and moans–Shannon and someone else's. His mind went red. He dropped the bag of gifts by the boots that were not his, grabbed his autographed Mo Vaughn baseball bat from his Red Sox shrine behind the TV, and stormed toward the heartbreaking, anger-inducing soundtrack coming from his bedroom.

He kicked the half-closed door open and confirmed what he already knew to be true. Shannon had her palms on the bed and her ass to the short, moustache-wearing motherfucker standing behind her.

"Timothy? Oh my God, Timothy–this, I'm–" she sputtered as she drew herself from the naked, sweaty loser behind her, trying to cover her filthy whore ways with the sheet, his sheet.

"Hey man," the naked moustache offered up, backing away, covering his throbbing cock with one hand and reaching down to the floor for his underwear with the other. "I don't want any trouble, man. I'll leave—I-I'll fuckin' leave."

Timothy gripped the bat in both hands holding the solid stick of ash out before him like a katana blade, ready to slay his enemy and exact his revenge. He turned his gaze to Shannon, the blood in his veins boiled at her pathetic look. She should have been sorry, she should have been apologizing over and over, instead, she looked like a teenage slut caught having sex with some boy; shameful, but with a hint of a smile waiting to return. He no longer gave a shit about the loser with the moustache.

"Get your shit and get the fuck out of my house."

"Yes, sir," the moustache said, without even glancing at Shannon. He had his pants on in seconds. Timothy stepped aside to allow him passage to the narrow hallway. He waited until he heard the front door close. He listened as the Jeep out front started and pulled away. Then, he turned his full attention to her.

"Timothy, I–"

"Shut the fuck up," he said.

"Tim…" Shannon reached out a trembling hand to him.□

Timothy went cold–the last two years, a lie, a sham, wasted. Before Shannon's filthy paw could reach him he had the bat cocked behind him. He swung as hard as he could at the extended appendage. He heard the bone snap and saw the broken arm aiming in the wrong direction. Shannon screamed. He brought his second swing down over the top of her skull, silencing her. Eternally.

Chapter Seven

Lee Buhl lit the smudge stick and a Lucky Strike. Despite the modest wealth provided by his publisher and his "special" clients, he liked to slum it in the budget hotels whenever he was outside the big cities. The smaller, economy brand motels offered a more interesting cast of characters, and more importantly–smoking rooms. The Hollis Oaks Motel 6 was his home for the next week. He was originally only booked for the two nights, but after discovering the strange stories about a place called The Bruton Inn, he'd extended through the next week.

Lee didn't usually make a habit of bringing his basket of shaman goodies into his rooms, let alone waste his supply of sages and Mugwort, but he couldn't shake the feeling there was something here with him. Whether it was his tired mind and his hyper-sensitive imagination conspiring to unnerve him or the fact that something knew he was here, he couldn't tell. Not at the moment anyway. He decided to burn the smudge either way.

After the quick cleansing, too tired to actually fall asleep, he decided to haul out his laptop and do a little more digging on the Bruton Inn. His search produced a number of additional bizarre tales and rumors about the out-of-the-way hotel.

The original owner, a businessman by the name of Nathan Ford, had been murdered during the inn's inaugural year. He'd been the victim of a violent home invasion that left his live-in girlfriend an invalid and his young daughter to the wolves of foster care. According to the article on the website, both Mr. Ford and his girlfriend, Kerry Anders, had suffered multiple stab wounds before being mutilated and sodomized. Ford was pronounced dead when the ambulance arrived. Ms. Anders was taken to Mercy Hospital in Portland arriving in critical condition, suffering from major blood loss and brain trauma. Another search told Lee that Ms. Anders had died four years later while still tied to machines. Nathan Ford's daughter disappeared off the grid altogether after the age of twelve. A Canadian by the name of Francois La Roux had snatched up the Bruton Inn shortly after the tragedies and reportedly still owned the property to this day.

Another tidbit he uncovered was the quiet fact that in 1983–the same year the two girls died in the swimming pool and the man whose room they'd stayed in went missing–another guest turned up reported as a missing person. Jason Perry was reported missing by his wife, Janet, that same fall. Mrs. Perry said her husband had gone out to have drinks with an old friend and never returned.

He kept searching and found the hum dinger of them all. In an article from March of 1984, it was discovered that the room the two girls–one Christina La Roza, a runaway from Colorado, and one Sarah Ford, the orphaned daughter of the original owner, Nathaniel Ford–occupied prior to their drowning's had been the scene of multiple murders. The article went on to say that the investigation had been kept quiet per request by hotel management until the case was closed. In total, it was presumed the two girls had lured and killed at least two men–Gordon McDonough and Jason Perry. Massive amounts of blood from both men and some from each of the girls were found all through the room.

Lee lit another smoke and poured three fingers of Jameson in his glass. He punched Christina La Roza into the search. It came up with a few articles rehashing the same story he'd just read, plus one featuring an interview with her mother. He knocked back the drink and then typed in Sarah Ford. A number of articles popped up about the death of her father and his girlfriend, most of them linking the brutal attacks to Sarah. There was no proof in any of the accusations, but dots could easily be connected considering her actions six-years later.

He sat back in his chair, staring at a picture of a young girl with long brown curls, and eyes as dark as night. The notion of a biography on this girl scrolled across his thoughts followed by a bag of cash and fantasies of a *New York Times* bestseller.

He jotted down the idea on a notepad, closed the laptop, and poked out his cigarette. He got up to stretch and noticed the room was cold, much cooler than it had been when he came in from the storm. He walked to the little smoke-stained thermometer on the wall. It read seventy degrees. He tapped its side and watched the orange needle slowly drop, stopping at fifty-eight. A bad feeling slipped past his whiskey buzz. In his mind, he saw the face of the younger Sarah Ford and those dark, dark eyes.

Chapter Eight

Kenneth's virginity had died a wonderful death at the will of his rescuer, the Ice Queen. He didn't count having his man-pussy ravaged by "Uncle" Wes as his official first time. He no longer cared about that, *she* had given him this beautiful girl as a reward for his dirty work in the woods. This girl had cried and fought for the first couple of minutes, but a few hard shots to the face had subdued her. He was about to explode his gift into Meghan Murphy when he was rudely snatched from behind and thrown to the far side of the room. His sweaty back slammed against the far wall, his hard on, slick with the girl's fluids, firing cum into the cold air. Eric had robbed him of his moment. Kenneth's eyes narrowed at the sight of the big guy moving in and out of their latest recruit. He imagined himself walking up behind the dumb lug, putting a blade in his spine, and watching him bleed all over the floor, but he knew *she* would not be pleased with such an action. Imagining the vengeful act would have to do, for now.

***

Meghan felt a change spiral through her. Her body betrayed her. Looking into the eyes of this larger man, there was a sense of desire coursing through her veins and a wetness between her legs. He entered her, fast and hard, driving into her sex–a Mack truck barreling down a steep hill with no breaks and no cares. More confusion, more impossible thoughts attacked her mind while he attacked her body. Her hatred faded, replaced with hunger. Her grunts came louder and with more ferocity at each powerful thrust. She sunk her long black nails into his broad back drawing blood as she dragged them down to his ass, pulling him closer, begging him to drive deeper. She moaned and growled until she felt herself racing toward climax. The moans turned to shrills of ecstasy. The anticipation was near unbearable. She began to whimper, began to cry. "Now! Now! Now!" she said. She felt his release; an electrical current blazed through her womanhood and up through her entire body. Her mind was slammed with a white heat as a dark red vision slipped over her sight. Images of a river of crimson pleasures, splashing across her own naked form buried the last shred of evidence that Meghan Murphy had ever been.

***

Eric had done as *she* had told him. This girl was now theirs. He finished his part and then pulled himself free and watched the spell take hold. The pretty girl's eyes rolled up into the back of her skull, her hands pawing at every inch of her body following the new energy moving through her. Her legs twitched, toes curled. One second she was laughing, the next she was crying. The scream that signaled the end of her transformation ripped through the room bringing a dark grin to his face. As the scream died out, her body fell still.

***

Kenneth McGowan needed a release, and not just the wasted jism he had decorated the floor in room 209 with. There was a monster inside of him that wanted out. He left Eric and the changing girl in the room, and walked down to the room he'd seen the man and the boy with the Red Sox raincoat earlier come from. He thought about them whispering about him.

I'll teach you to keep your mouths shut.

Kenneth knocked on the door and waited. After a minute, the man opened the door.

"Yes?" the man said. His eyes drop to Kenneth's nakedness. "What the hell?"

The man tried to close the door in Kenneth's face, but with the new gifts given to him by her, Kenneth pushed his way into the room. He grabbed the man who was almost half a foot taller than him and threw him to the ground. He slammed the door shut.

"What do you want? Money? I haven't got much, but I could–"

Kenneth slammed the heel of his bare foot into the man's mouth, feeling a surge of power and excitement at the sight of the blood. It was as if each act under her command gave him a little more strength; he liked it. He liked it a lot. Before the man could plead his benign case for mercy, Kenneth smashed his bleeding heel down again. He continued the violent act until the man's face was ruined.

"Daddy," the boy said, waking up from his slumber.

Kenneth McGowan limped over the broken body on the floor, stepping up to the cowering boy on the bed.

"You're Daddy's gone. I'm here to take care of you now." He raised a blood-splattered hand to the boys head, petting his blond crop of hair.

"Wh-wh-who are you?"

"You can call me Uncle Kenny."

CHAPTER NINE

The lights of the Bruton Inn came into view as Rhiannon turned the corner. Emotionally wiped, she'd already decided she would be staying the night; no way was she going back to her empty apartment. She needed to sit down and try to wrap her head around what the hell was happening.

She pulled into the parking lot of the inn. The pavement was wet. She hadn't seen a drop of rain in Hollis Oaks. The building stood silent. Room windows were lit up sporadically across the front side. For the amount of cars in the front lot, there should have been more signs of life. It was quiet. *Oh stop it*, she told herself. The nervous part of her brain wondered if she'd been wrong about the middle-aged quitters who believed in what? *Ghosts? Demons? Something* or *someone* had been in Kurt's room at the hospital. She wasn't fucking crazy. Whatever it was had chased her into town and that old man into the intersection.

She pulled around to the back lot. It wasn't nearly as full as the front. *See, there really aren't that many guests tonight. No ghosts, no goblins.* The thought was comforting, but there was still no way she was walking around out here in the dark. She turned around near the back corner, and drove back around to the front rolling up and parking beside a red mini-van. She shut the car off, got out, and walked into the lobby of the well-lit hotel. The front desk was deserted. She saw the *Be Right Back* sign sitting next to the little round silver bell and the *Ring Bell for Service* sign and decided to grab some coffee while she waited for Jeff.

***

Jeff ascended the stairs with caution certain that someone or something was going to jump out at him and send him plummeting down the stairs like Meghan. *Maybe I should quit reading so many horror comics.* He reached the top step and glanced down the hall. Kenneth McGowan came charging out of a room buck naked. Jeff stood quietly in the stairwell as Kenneth McGowan hobbled across the hall and knocked on the door.

What are you up to?

The door opened and Kenneth disappeared into the room; the lights along the hall flickered and then steadied. Jeff's mouth went dry.

Chapter Ten

Kenneth knocked on the door for room 225. A man opened the door. Kenneth walked in and pushed him backward. He closed the door, shutting the couple off from their only way out.

The woman on the bed in the sexy negligée covered herself at the sight of him. With one quick strike, Kenneth knocked the nose of the man between them up into his brain, dropping him to the floor

"Jonathan," she cried. Kenneth charged at her. She held her hands up in a weak attempt to defend herself. He picked up the phone from the nightstand beside the bed, yanking it free from the wall, and with the hard plastic base, smashed the shocked woman over the head. He was flooded with a lifetime of weak moments. He thought of Uncle Wes and his violating touch (he smashed her head again), he thought of his mother's denial and betrayal, her outright choice of his stepfather over her own son, her abandonment (he smashed the bloody face again, a piece of flesh clung to the underside of the hard plastic base), he thought of the big guy, Eric, and his intrusion upon *her* reward (he grabbed the makeshift weapon with both hands, bringing it up over his head) he saw Eric pushing into the pretty girl in 209–with all of his newfound strength and every last bit of rage built from his 19 years of guilt, shame, and impotence, Kenneth bashed the sickly, bludgeoned human skull, separating the jaw from the rest of its brutalized face.

He wanted to smile, he wanted more than anything to feel better, but he didn't. He was drained, and beneath the exhaustion running like a river forever winding, the anger flowed. For now, he needed to rest, to recharge. There would be time to kill the rage inside. If not, then he would just kill.

He lied down on the bed placing an arm over the gory mess next to him that still looked like a woman from the neck down. He closed his eyes thinking of *her* and slipped into dream. *She* was waiting for him. In the vision he lied down beside her on a bed of dead roses, the smell of her pool water perfume stung his nose, but faded as she held him in her arctic embrace.

***

In room 209, Eric stood silent staring out at the night beyond the window–a sentry, waiting. He had done as she wished. He had grabbed the girl, fucked her, and changed her. For all of his loyalty, there was one thing he wanted that she had not given him since their first engagement. He wanted to be next to her. She had promised he would have his turn, but when? His thoughts turned to the other man. *Timothy.*

He wondered where Kenneth the Rat had vanished.

Eric turned, left the room, and walked two doors down to room 211. He could sense that she was weak from a day of testing her limits and pushing her powers. Lethargy settled over him. He too would need to rest, but first he wanted to see her, to gaze upon her perfect form, even if it meant seeing her chosen one lying next to her. He reached for the handle of room 211.

The handle turned. He could see the vapors of his breath as he entered the icy room–she's here. A single light, shining through the window from the parking lot, illuminated the shape of Timothy. At first glance, the other half of the bed appeared empty, but upon further inspection, he could see the depression in the mattress where she lay. He wasn't able to physically see her. Part of him was wounded by this, the other part swooned. Satisfied, he crept back out into the hall and moved on returning to the room he had shared with his original traveling companion.

Bloodstains and bits and pieces of the broken TV stand reminded him of the darker glory *she* had impressed upon him. He lay down on top of the sheets of his bed crossing his large hands over his waist. Eric closed his eyes. His dreams were only of death.

Chapter Eleven

Jeff flew through the door to the back office.

Rhiannon screamed, dropping her coffee to the floor.

"Jesus Christ, Rhiannon, you scared the shit out of me," Jeff said, clutching the doorframe.

"Oh my God, you have no idea." Rhiannon snatched a towel from the closet behind her and bent down to sop up the wet spot on the rug.

Jeff noticed her hands shook as she did this. "Forget about that," he said. "Come upstairs with me."

"Why?" She left the rag on the floor and followed him out to the front.

Jeff walked over to the stairwell. "Come on." He climbed the steps as carefully as he had earlier.

"Okay, what's going on? You're freaking me out," Rhiannon said.

"Shhh, just get moving." Jeff reached the top step of the second floor and snuck over to the doorway, held his hand out and signaled for her to wait. He peeked around the corner. Nothing was there. "Come on."

"Wait," Rhiannon whispered. "Are you going to tell me what we're doing?"

He stopped and turned to her. "Okay, this is probably going to sound stupid, but you know Kenneth McGowan?"

"Yeah, the weird guy who always hears people doing it in the room next to him. What about him?"

"He's registered to room 219, but I saw him come out of one farther down, 225, 226 maybe. I couldn't tell. I watched him from here like this."

"Okay?"

"He was naked."

"What? Are you serious?"

"Yes."

"All right," she threw her hands up in the air, "and now you're just fucking with me. Nice."

"Hey." Jeff grabbed her wrist. "Hey, look at me." Her bottom lip came up as she rolled her glistening eyes. In all of his excitement over Kenneth he'd acted impulsively. She'd been through enough today without him dragging her up here with tales of some naked weirdo. He waited for her to calm down. "Look, I'm sorry. I know you've been through a lot already. Maybe this is stupid. Let's go back downstairs."

"No, I just...I just need a minute."

He let go of her wrist. She looked tired, run down.

"So, he was really naked?" she said.

"Yeah."

"What the hell was he doing? Where is he now?"

"That's the even more fucked up part. When he came out of that room, he was limping. He hobbled across the hall and knocked on the door."

"What happened–" Rhiannon stopped talking at the unmistakable sound of a door opening.

Jeff moved back over to his vantage point, daring a glance down the hall, praying that it wasn't Kenneth McGowan. He slid his face out just enough to view where the door had opened. It wasn't Kenneth. It was the bigger guy; Eric something. Eric slogged out of a room that he wasn't registered to.

What the hell is going on here?

The big guy headed to the last room at the end of the hall and disappeared inside. Jeff turned back to Rhiannon.

"Was that him?" she said.

"No, it was that big guy, Eric, that I saw him hanging out with earlier. He came out of a room in the same area, maybe even the same one that our naked friend had been in."

"Did you say they were hanging out together? What, is there a party going on up here?" she said.

"I have no idea," Jeff said, pondering his next move.

He stepped out into the open; the thought of checking in on Meghan crossed his mind. He had promised her he would, but decided there were more pressing matters to tend to.

"Jeff," Rhiannon whispered from the stairwell.

He motioned for her to join him.

"What are we doing now?" She saddled up next to him.

"I just want to walk the hall and see if I hear anything," he said.

"And if we do hear something, or someone?"

He didn't answer.

Chapter Twelve

L ying next to the faint trace of an invisible form, Timothy was brought through another doorway in his mind that he thought was nailed shut for good. *Sarah* unlocked the gate and ushered him back to his darker past...

January, 2011

Beth Marston was his saving grace. The guilt that had haunted his daydreams since dumping the body of Shannon Huber at the Grayson Quarry had eaten him alive. He moved from Gilford, Colorado to Meadville, Pennsylvania two days after the act of rage. Nestled into this dull little town, he tried to find his way back to a normal life. It took nearly four years to do so. He met Beth at a party held by one of his co-workers from Big Lots.

They hit it off and dated for almost two years. In that time, she encouraged him to work on his horror blog. They were both into horror movies and other things of a macabre nature. They attended the *Bodies* cadaver art exhibit in Philadelphia and would often picnic in cemeteries. Beth was a darker type of girl and he felt she better suited the post-Shannon version of himself. He began to feel like he could tell her anything and finally, one night, he did.

They were enjoying a documentary on Charles Manson and had worked their way through half a bottle of whiskey, most of which he'd consumed. Beth took a swig and turned to him with a sly grin that usually meant she had something fun on her mind.

"Do you think you could ever kill somebody?" she said.

The question would have made him nervous if not for the booze in his system. "I don't know," he said.

"Come on, you have to answer." She handed him the liquor bottle.

"Could you?" He took the whiskey.

"Oh yeah, I'd kill somebody...for the right reason."

He took a pull from the bottle and smiled.

"What?"

"Nothing, I would too," he said.

""You would too? Kill someone for the right reason?"

"Yeah," he said, and for some reason added, "I already have."

He told her about how he had caught Shannon fucking another guy in their bed, and then how he had just lost it and smashed her head in.

"Very funny, Tim." She grabbed the whiskey back from him.

"Beth, I'm serious. I know it sounds fucked up, but I mean, you know me. You know I'm not some cold-blooded psychopath. I just couldn't stand to look at her lying face," he said.

"Okay, now you're starting to creep me out a little," she backed away from him and looked in his eyes. She saw the truth in them. "What the fuck are you saying–you *killed* your ex-girlfriend?"

"Beth, I thought you of all people would understand. I mean you said you wanted to kill Bryan after you caught him cheating."

"My God, Tim, I said I *wanted* to kill him. Jesus Christ, I was pissed, I was hurt. What the fuck did *you* do?" She moved farther away from him.

He reached out a hand to ease her worries. "Beth, come on, it's not like that."

She yanked her arms away from him, "Don't–don't touch me."

"Beth…"

She ran to the bed, grabbing her coat up off the edge.

"Beth, wait a minute." He grabbed her upper arm as she passed him on her way toward the door.

She pulled free, went to the door, and turned the knob.

As she began to open the door, he drove his forearm into the back of her head, smashing her, face first, into the heavy wood. She crumpled to the floor. He paced back and forth running his hands through his hair. She slowly turned around. Blood ran down from her upper lip where her front teeth had punctured the soft tissue.

"Uhhh…" she moaned, placing her hands on the floor. She was trying to get up.

"Fuck, fuck," he said, pacing back and forth. She struggled to get her feet under her.

"L-let me go," she said, her mouth painted in crimson.

"I thought you loved me," he said.

"Love you? I don't even know who you are." She lunged for the door.

"No!" Timothy backhanded her with a closed fist, spinning her around .She slid back down to the floor. Tears fell from his eyes as he walked over to the corner of the room. "I'm sorry." He grabbed the electric guitar she had bought him for Christmas.

"Tim…what…what are you going to do…no…no–" Her words were halted as the solid body of the Gibson Les Paul smashed into her face. On the second strike, she was dead. He dropped the instrument and fell to his knees, sobbing at the feet of the girl who had loved a killer.

***

Present Day

"I think this was the room Kenneth went in." Jeff stood before the door to room 230. Rhiannon stayed back as he stepped up and placed his ear to the door. The room was quiet, the hallway too. They continued down to the stairwell at the east end of the building. Satisfied that no one was partying or getting beaten, Jeff led Rhiannon back downstairs.

Once they were at the front desk they finally had a chance to catch each other up on their wild night of events. By the end of the conversation, both were at a loss for words.

"So, how much do you believe the old stories?" Rhiannon said.

"What stories?" Jeff leaned against the desk and scratched at an itch on the back of his neck. "You mean the ghost of the Bruton Inn or whatever?"

Rhiannon picked up her coffee cup with both hands. "Yeah, I mean, you've been here a lot longer than me. I remember when Kurt and I got hired, the maintenance guy mentioned how the other workers had quit because they were so afraid."

Jeff gazed at her. He'd heard all of the rumors, but waited for her to finish.

"I thought they were dumb broads who watched too many ghost hunter shows. Now..." her voice trailed off.

Jeff had never believed the ghost stories. He knew there had been some deaths at the hotel, but he never thought they were related in any way. This night, in all of its fucked up glory, had burrowed beneath his flesh. He looked to her and said, "And now?"

"Now," she said, "I'm starting to wonder."

CHAPTER THIRTEEN

Rhiannon slept, making uncomfortable faces against the soft pillow beneath her head. She had every right to whatever horrible dream she was probably having. She'd stayed with Jeff downstairs until his relief came on at six. Now, they were up in his room. She had the bed, he agreed to just take the couch. They could have grabbed a room with the beds, but he didn't want to have to move his things. Jeff grabbed his backpack of clothes and moved into the bathroom. He took off his hotel uniform and threw on his pajama bottoms and an old faded t-shirt. He looked at the tired, tested face staring at him from the mirror.

"Hey buddy," he said. "You look as strung out as I feel."

He looked at his blood shot eyes, hanging features, and tousled hair. This day had been way too long and way too fucked up for him to relax. He crept back out into the room, snagged a couple bottles of beer from the fridge, looked for something to read from his messenger bag– not in the mood for horror, he passed up *The Narrows* for a classic Heinlein–and took a seat at the room's desk. After a few pages, even *Stranger in a Strange Land* felt too close to the moment. He downed the beers, closed the book, cuddled up on the sofa under the extra blanket from the closet, and waited for the slight buzz to do its trick.

His last thoughts, silently spoken to the sandman, were from the last thing he read: *There is no safety this side of the grave.*

***

Lee Buhl saw her. He woke up clenching the figurine necklace his grandfather had given him. The little Native American wood carving was of a faceless Native capped in an intricate and detailed headdress, the tiny body held no characteristics save for the dark feather held between two small hands. Lee had always worn the piece, more for esthetics than any real spiritual purpose; his dream changed that.

In it, he was performing one of his cleansing ceremonies when the smudge stick in his hands burst into flames. He dropped the burning stick; its normal earthly scent was defiled into one of iron and rot. The flame exploded upward from the tile floor of the room. The pool beyond began filling before his eyes. A crimson puddle rose to the lip of the pool's concrete sides, overflowing and stretching out, threatening to flood the suddenly shrinking pool room. A naked woman with long dark curls hanging over a perfect form emerged from the red lake beckoning him to join her. He felt the hypnotic power of this thing–for it was not a woman. The eyes of the creature before him bled black from the emptying sockets. A scream, like nothing Lee had ever heard before, pierced the moment and knocked him from his feet. He fell backward into the knee deep room of blood. He caught a faint whiff of saline just before he opened his eyes.

Now, sitting up in the bed of his cheap motel room, clutching the wooden figurine hanging from his neck and drenched in sweat, Lee Buhl could still smell the awful pool from the vision.

***

The girl in room 209 opened her eyes to a new dawn. The eyes no longer belonged to Meghan Murphy. The Ice Queen had arrived in the flesh.

VOLUME IV

DREAM, GIRL, DREAM

Rhiannon walked down the corridor of the Bruton Inn. Dressed in a t-shirt and panties; the hallway before her like a tunnel without end. Black and white portraits hanging along the walls watched as she passed. She stopped before the likeness of Nathaniel Ford. This picture should be hung just past the front desk in the lobby, but instead was now mounted outside the pool room. Mr. Ford had built the Inn back in 1977. She'd been forced to endure a video regurgitation of the history of the inn during the training course. In the portrait, Mr. Ford was staring back at her with the eyes of a pedophile–lingering over her in all the right places, smirking like he could care less if he was caught.

"Rhiannon..."

She turned from the creepy portrait in time to catch a glimpse of Kurt through the pool room door. She walked over and turned the knob. Frost covered the plastic chairs and the little towel rack next to the door. There was no sign of Kurt. She turned to leave. Something splashed in the pool. Slowly, feeling her heart accelerate, she swiveled around to see who was there.

Bodies in various states of decay floated throughout the water. Some were grey and swollen, others nothing more than bloodless skin suits clinging to the bones beneath. She brought her numbed hand up to quivering lips. Something moved beneath the surface of dead and bloated forms. She backed away, horrified at the gruesome sight and what else was there.

A man emerged at the end closest to her–*Kurt*. "Rhiannon, wait for me."

She pulled on the door, but it refused to budge. "Let me out! Let me out!" her voice strained. A hand touched her shoulder. Beneath its touch, an incredible cold sunk into her body, numbing her lungs, her voice...

"Wait for me," Kurt repeated.

Tears rolled from her eyes, freezing on her cheek. The door opened and she fell through, spilling into the hallway. She rolled over expecting to see Kurt, but he was gone.

"Wait for me..."

"Leave me alone. You're dead," Rhiannon said.

"Wait for me."

Climbing to her feet, she ran toward the lobby, the carpet beneath her disappeared. The slapping of her bare feet against the cold, tiled floor echoed. And still, his voice:

"Wait for me."

She ran faster; her breath coming harder, her lungs burning. The doors to rooms that shouldn't have been there opened one by one as she approached. In the frames more dead bodies waited: A man and his son, a husband and wife, a young man she remembered checking in with a tall guy, one of the college girls. She ran. More doors, more bodies... the elderly couple that Kurt had been with when she found him, the man from the hospital with the bad arm and milky eye, and *Kurt*.

She stopped. Out of breath, low on will, and ready to give up. Kurt's eyes were closed; he was grey with death and dressed in his hospital johnnie. Rhiannon walked like a zombie–mindless, simply going forward–toward the body of her friend standing like a statue in the impossible doorway.

She reached out for him, tears falling again. She thought of their date and how she had left him standing in the theater lobby. He had been nothing but genuine with her and that had scared her.

"I'm so sorry," she said, her hand inches from his face.

His eyes shot open, startling her and sending her flailing backward.

"Wait for me," he said. Blood, thick and dark with death, drooled from the corners of his mouth and then his eyes, "Wait for me."

She hit the wall behind her as laughter erupted from the end of the corridor where the nightmare began.

She dared a glance at the awful sound of joy in this place of cold death. She recognized more faces...Kenneth–the weird kid that heard voices, the big guy–Aaron or Eric, a well-dressed gentleman she couldn't place, and a girl. The girl slipped behind the others before Rhiannon could identify her.

A voice spoke within Rhiannon's spinning mind, "The Ice Queen is here."

Chapter One

R hiannon woke from the horrible dream tangled in the sheets of the bed Jeff offered up to her. Jeff was curled up on the cramped couch to her right. She slid her legs out from beneath the heavy comforter. The nightmare was already receding from the shores of her mind, dimming behind her growing alertness. *Good,* she thought. Stepping over to the couch, she grabbed the thin blanket that had fallen from Jeff in the night and covered him. He made a snorting sound and fell silent again. Rubbing the sleep from her itchy eyes, pieces of the dream floated into places they didn't fit. Even with the brilliant sun bursting through the window, she shivered. Menacing clouds floated in the distance outside. A storm was coming. She gazed down at Jeff sleeping with his mouth hanging open–"catching flies" her mother would have said–and wondered what he would do when he woke up. Would he go home? Would he leave her here alone? She hoped not. He had mentioned wanting to head into Hollis Oakes to do some research on their situation. She wondered what that situation was. What they were dealing with and if they should they even bother trying to find out. Maybe those desk clerks who quit last June had the right idea.

Still fully dressed from the day before, Rhiannon slipped on her canvas sneakers and headed out the door feeling an icy trace of the dream. She needed a hot cup of coffee.

"Hey Rhiannon, I didn't see you come in?" Carla said.

"Hey Carla, I had a pretty rough night. Ended up staying here." Rhiannon poured herself a cup of regular. Carla Dunn was in her forties, thrice divorced, and a round mound of sweetness. She was the housekeeping manager and had worked at the Bruton Inn for almost ten years. Rhiannon normally found Carla's cheerfulness to be the perfect yin to her yang, but today seemed to be carrying a bitter taste too strong for even Carla's joyful glow.

"What's up, Hon? Boy trouble?" Carla said as she neatened up the coffee station behind Rhiannon.

"Can I ask you something?" Rhiannon set her coffee cup down and placed a hand on her hip.

"Sure, anything, Hon," Carla said.

"Have you cleaned any of the rooms on the second floor yet?"

"Sweetheart, I've been here since–" Carla checked her watch before continuing, "–7:30 this mornin'. I've been bustin' my rump all day."

"No, no, no. I was just wondering if maybe you found anything...-*strange*."

Carla set down her cleaning rag, stepped back, and looked Rhiannon over like she was a nutzoid. "Strange like what?"

"Nothing, forget I said anything. I'm not awake yet." Rhiannon grabbed a second coffee cup.

"Well if you ain't awake yet, maybe you *better* double-fist that caffeine." Carla grabbed her rag, threw it in the front pocket of her apron, and turned to leave.

"Carla?"

"What is it, Hon?"

"Do you believe any of those stories about this place being haunted?"

"You really must have had a bad night. You just drink that coffee and get yourself ready for your shift. You're on in half an hour, ain't cha?"

Rhiannon sighed. "Yep. Guess I should get ready."

Carla turned and waddled down to the housekeeping office singing an out of tune Stevie Wonder song that Rhiannon's mom used to listen to.

Rhiannon wasn't sure whether Carla had purposely ignored the question about the ghost stories or not. If anyone would know the truth behind the whispers it would be Carla, but Rhiannon didn't have time to worry about that at the moment. She did need to get ready for work. Standing before the elevator, stacked-up coffee cups in hand, she remembered her uniform was still in her car.

Damn it.

She set the drinks down on the coffee station, ran by the empty front desk, and stepped out through the lobby doors. The air was still cool from the wet night, but the sun's warmth felt good on her skin. She walked over to the Escort, glad she had slept in her clothes and had her keys tucked in her back pocket. She unlocked the door and almost freaked. Her heart skipped a beat at the sight of a green Subaru. An invisible weight pressed down upon her. She imagined the girl with the brown curls and the old man with the milky eye. A family of three stepped from the sidewalk and moved to the vehicle. The heaviness lifted. She shook her head.

Fucking ghosts.

***

Jeff was at the front desk staring into the fog outside the lobby doors, waiting for the parade of freaks and weirdoes from his last dream; waiting for something to emerge from the swirling ghost clouds behind the glass doors searching for a way in. The automatic doors rattled to life and drifted open. Uninvited, the mist rolled into the lobby. Jeff stared at the foggy apparition, certain it was scanning the open space for him. The room was perfect silence save for his hyperactive breathing.

The temperature had dropped. The mist rolling in and encircling the furnishings in the lobby took shape and began to crystallize into a shape before him. Jeff could see his breath as a flurry of small cracking and crunching sounds accompanied the formation of the icy sculpture. There was a body trapped within the ice. Climbing the front desk, reaching out, he swiped his hand over the frost and saw Meghan. She was standing perfectly still with her hands up before her shoulders, eyes closed. His mind conjured a vision of Han Solo frozen in carbonite.

"I'll get you out," he said, the words dying the second they hit the air. The cold, sucking the color from the room, slowed his thoughts. He'd never been in a meat locker before, but he imagined this was probably pretty close to how it felt. He needed to free Meghan. Making a fist, he pounded on the solid block of ice with the underside of his hand. After the first few strikes, her eyes flew open.

"Meghan! Hold on." He struck the ice again and again until pinkish smears appeared. Jeff stopped and looked at the side of the hand covered in crimson and trembling uncontrollably. The skin had split. Blood spilled from the open wound thick and slow like molasses from a tipped container. He watched an impossible amount of blood running down his wrist and to the floor. Meghan gazed at him from behind her icy cage, an odd grin stretched around her face.

Thup.

He glanced back at his palsied hand to find his pinky missing. A gaping hole gushed red onto the counter where his missing digit lay unattached, pointing away from him.

Thup, thup, thup.

One by one his other fingers followed, dropping like dead leaves from a maple tree. Crimson syrup flowed like sap to the tiles below. The lobby floor had become a pool of blood. *His blood.* Lightheaded, his stomach twirling like a washing machine on spin, the remaining warmth drained from his face.

"Jeffrey," a voice said.

He looked at the melting glacier now sitting in the red pool. Meghan was free from its grip from the waist up. He raised his bloody, fingerless hand toward her, his eyes flashing back and forth from the blood pool to where she stood. His twitching hand touched the skin of her cheek. Meghan's eyes turned dark–two black marbles glared back at him. Mesmerized, he fell forward face-first into the lake of blood.

"Nooo!" he said, screaming himself awake, hitting the floor with a thud.

Searching his arms for the open wounds, he realized it had been another nightmare. They were becoming more frequent. He turned on his side, propping himself up on an elbow. He was on the floor of his hotel room.

A vision of an ice angel flashed across his mind. He shivered remembering the dream. He recalled falling. He caught himself rubbing the sides of his hands where, in the dream, the skin had opened. There were no such wounds. "I need to get the fuck out of here." He stood up and ran his fingers through his disheveled mop of hair.

There were some books he wanted to find at Barnes and Noble. From the look of the bruised-looking sky outside, he knew he'd better get going.

***

"Hey," Rhiannon said as Jeff walked up to the front desk. She smiled.

"Hey," he said. "Did you sleep okay?"

"No. I had some crazy dreams."

"Me too." He hesitated long enough to let her know his probably weren't too pleasant either. "I did some research online last night after you passed out on the chair over there. I was looking up ghosts and what they are and what they can really do. A lot of the stuff I found was all movies or book related, pretty much a bunch of BS. The take that made some sense, at least to me, was one about ghosts who haunt places where they were murdered. It's like they're trapped. Like they didn't die right. "

Rhiannon lowered her voice. "Are you talking about the guy who drowned this summer?"

"Maybe, I don't know."

"But what about the hospital," Rhiannon said. "How the hell does that explain the girl," she looked around, "the thing that chased me last night?"

"I don't know. Like I said, it was the closest thing I could find." He sipped his coffee. "I'm not saying I believe any of it. Not yet anyway, but something's going on around here. Can't you feel it?"

"I wish I didn't."

"Maybe you can do some digging on this place while I'm gone," he said, zipping his sweatshirt.

"Where are you going?"

"I'm heading over to Hollis Oaks. There are some books I found on the Barnes and Noble website about local Maine folklore–ghost stories, haunted lighthouses shit like that. I want to see if they have any of them in the store."

"Well, I guess I'll be here," she said.

"I should be back in an hour or two. I'm on tonight, and I'd rather not go home to my hammerhead roommates, especially when we might have some action going on here."

"Yay," she mocked. This shit was not what she considered fun. She wondered if Jeff would be so cavalier about it if *he* had been chased by a ghost and a creepy old man. She didn't think so. "I'll see what I can dig up."

"Are you staying again tonight?"

She thought of her empty apartment. Aside from Mr. Mittens, there was no one there. No way did she want to be alone, even if it meant staying here. At least Jeff and the other guests were around if something happened like what she experienced last night with that bitch and the crazy old man. "Signs point to yes," she said.

"All right, I'll see you in a bit."

Rhiannon thought of last night's chase as Jeff strolled out of the lobby. For whatever reason, it felt like something that happened in a dream, so far away. Maybe it was the daylight holding back the fear that had gripped her so tight. Maybe it was something else.

CHAPTER TWO

Her boys were resting. They would need to be at full strength for the fun she had in mind. Sarah moved to the bathroom, the light turning on as she entered. Standing before the mirror, admiring the body that had belonged to Meghan Murphy, she grinned. Her breasts were a little bigger, her cheek bones more defined, but one thing was off. She watched the long black hair begin to scrunch up and curl into the ringlets she was used to.

"There," she said.

She walked out to the bed and found a gray piece of luggage tucked halfway beneath it. She reached down and hauled it out placing it upon the comforter. Undoing the clasps and the zipper, she opened the bag and found what she was looking for. From the girl's clothing, she chose a red plaid skirt, a t-shirt, and a pair of tall black boots.

"Team Edward?" she said, reading the front of the shirt aloud. She wasn't sure who or what Edward was, but she didn't care, the shirt was black—her favorite color.

She zipped the tall boots up to her knees. "Let's go for a little walk."

***

As the afternoon moved along, a number of guests asking how to get to Hollis Oaks in search of food, a movie theater, or just an actual city, kept Rhiannon busy. She made it through the first three hours of her shift without thinking about the night before. That changed as soon as the morning crew began to clear out for the day.

"Hey Rhiannon," Pauline said, sticking her head out from the back office. Pauline Walters was the general manager. She had stopped in to catch up on a few things and ask Rhiannon about what had happened with Kurt and the two elderly guests.

"Yeah."

"Can you come back here real quick so we can go over this before I head out?"

Rhiannon followed the rotund woman to her little office in the farthest corner of the back room. Pauline's waddle always made her think of penguins.

"So I got Jeff's version of what happened from his message." She sat down behind her desk, the chair squeaking in defiance. "But he said that you got here right after it happened."

"That's right," Rhiannon said, taking a seat beside Pauline's life-sized cardboard cutout of Steven Segal. Normally the ponytailed 80s action hero made her laugh, but she couldn't find her funny bone today if she had a PhD to do so. She turned her head back toward her boss and began to gnaw at the skin around her fingertips.

"So what did happen?"

Rhiannon sat in silence, replaying the sight of the old woman falling back into the wall and Kurt crumpling to the floor with the woman's husband in his arms. "I'm really not sure. I came in and saw them all lying on the floor in the hall. I started to dial 911 on my cell, but the EMT's came rushing in. The portable phone from the front desk was lying next to Kurt. He must have called for help before he...fainted or whatever." Rhiannon envisioned him in the hospital room, remembered the flat-lining drone of the machine he was hooked to, the doctors rushing in past her, just as the EMT's had, and the girl crossing the room.

"Are you all right?" Pauline said.

Rhiannon shook the memories away. "Huh? Yeah."

"You don't look so good. Here." Pauline reached down and brought up a bottle of water. Rhiannon took it, unscrewing the cap. "Are you going to be okay? I mean with working tonight. I know you and Kurt were friends."

"Yeah, I'll be okay."

"Carla is upstairs finishing up the rooms that checked-out late. She should almost be done. I'm only a phone call away if you need me."

"Thanks," Rhiannon said.

"Well, I think I have all that I need from you. I just have a couple phone calls to return, and then I have to get out of here."

Rhiannon stood and headed for the door. "Pauline," she said.

"Yes."

"Do you believe any of the ghost stories about this place?"

Pauline laughed. "Lord no. I've been here for the past two years as acting GM and I haven't seen anything. Don't go jumping out of your skin and quitting on me."

"I wouldn't do that. I like this job."

"Good. Is that all?"

Rhiannon looked at her gnawed off nails. "Yeah. Thanks."

When she returned to the front, a girl with dark curls was waiting at the desk.

"Hello, what can I do for you?" Rhiannon said, setting her water by the issue of Rolling Stone she'd already read.

"Hi, my name's Sarah, I was wondering if you could come up to my room and check something for me?"

Chapter Three

Jeff continued to check his hands for wounds that weren't there. He rolled down Route 5 cranking the local rock station, WKIT. Rumor was Stephen King actually owned it. As he headed toward Hollis Oaks, he thought of the first copy of *The Shining* that he'd ever read. He'd found it while doing a paper route down in Portland back when he was in his early-twenties.

One of his favorite stops on his route was the Franklin Towers, a sixteen floor apartment complex in the center of town. The Towers loomed over the sleeping city like a sentry. Each floor of the old building held ten apartments on either side of an open room that served as a lobby. These lobbies had either a couple old couches or some rocking chairs or recliners. There were always magazines and books strewn about on one piece of furniture or another. Jeff made sure to scan the paperbacks every morning, adding a couple Dean Koontz and Stephen King novels to his collection. In all the time spent doing the route, he had only ever seen two breathing people in the building. He was there before most people had a chance to grab their first cup of coffee, so it never seemed odd until he did bump into someone. One of those people, was Mrs. Shelby who lived in apartment 86 on the fifth floor. She waited for him Sunday mornings to give him his tip, usually five bucks. The other person he ran into was a one-time encounter that he would never forget.

Jeff was in the elevator, waiting to deliver his last six Sunday Telegrams, exhausted from a morning of heavy lifting—the Sunday paper was a monster in comparison to the daily editions. When the elevator door slid open to the sixteenth floor he was startled at the sight of the man sitting on the tan pleather couch in the community space. The guy was hunched over holding a hand to his bloody forehead and looking confused, lost. Conflicted on whether to ask the man if he was okay or to just mind his own business, Jeff's legs carried him away from the open room. He delivered all but one paper. The last copy went to an apartment on the other side of the floor. Approaching the lobby, he imagined the various ways the man on the couch had come to his current bloody state—they all involved someone getting attacked. He stopped shy of the open room, the last paper of the night in hand, and contemplated skipping it. He could just take the stairs and never look back. A blanket of dread—warranted or not—swaddled him like a baby.

"Uhhh…"

The moan from the man just out of sight startled him. Terrified over what was probably nothing, he forced his legs to carry him onward. He dared a glance toward the couch and wished he hadn't. The man, staring at his blood-covered hands and rocking back and forth, looked up letting out another moan and locking eyes with him. Jeff dropped his gaze and scurried across the floor to the next set of apartments. He hurried down the hallway fearing the lights would go out any second and leave him in the darkness with the moaning, bleeding man. He saw himself being chased to the end of the corridor only to find the staircase door locked. Jeff got to apartment 318, dropped the heavy paper with a loud thud in the quiet space, and darted for the staircase door. He slammed into it—it wouldn't budge. He thought he saw the lights flicker. There was a sign hanging on the handle of the stairwell door:

Temporarily closed. Sorry for any inconvenience. Please use the elevator.

He glanced back down the hallway that suddenly seemed more like a tunnel in a coal mine. His chest was tight, a cold sweat breaking out over his body as he tried to shake all of the wicked images being flung at him from the dark side of his brain. He started forward, chanting a prayer under his breath. *Please be gone, please be gone.*

When he reached the open room, it was empty. Relieved, he hit the down button for the elevator as he glanced around the room laughing at his cowardice. His good feelings died as his eyes landed on the droplets of blood scattered in a trail from the foot of the sofa to where he was now standing. He raised his hand to his face and saw blood on his finger. The elevator button was smeared red.

Bing

He jumped at the elevator's arrival. Part of his body clenched as the door slid open revealing an empty space. He stepped in and found himself scanning the interior for more blood. There was none. He rode down to the ground floor feeling like he'd imagined the whole thing; the blood he wiped on his pant leg assured him he had not. The ding of the elevator arriving at the bottom floor felt like a gunshot signaling the start of a race. He ran out of the elevator as it opened to his freedom, tripping and nearly falling on his face over a book lying on the floor. He picked it up. It was a hard cover copy of *The Shining*. There was a bloody print on the back cover. He looked around the lobby, making sure the man from the sixteenth floor wasn't waiting for him. He was alone, as usual. Tucking the book in his carrier bag, he got out to his van, and drove home.

That copy of the King classic, bloody print and all, was sitting on his backseat even now as he drove down Route 5 toward Hollis Oaks. He glanced in his rearview mirror and for a moment thought he saw someone smiling back at him. He rubbed his eyes and looked again. Nothing. The hair on his arms and neck raised like tiny antenna seeking out a signal. He passed the sign for Hollis Oaks and took his next right into town.

Entering Barnes and Noble, he followed the welcoming aroma of coffee to the sample-size Starbuck's café, grateful to have people around. With a fresh shot of caffeine in hand, he set out to find the books he'd seen online. He found the local section just beyond the magazines, and skimmed past a plethora of town-by-town histories, a series of Maine hunting books, and a lakes and campground book before finding what he was looking for. *Ghosts of Maine: Lighthouses, Ghosts on the Coast of Maine, Haunted Coast*. He spotted two that looked intriguing–*Ghost Legends of Vacationland*, and another in the *Ghosts of Maine* series: *Ghosts of Maine: Hotels, Inns, and Bed and Breakfasts*. Before he could reach them, the man he'd been quietly joined by grabbed both.

"Oh, sorry, were you looking at these," the man said.

"I was–" Jeff noticed a book display to the left featuring the man's likeness.

"Yeah, that's me. Lee Buhl, nice to meet you..."

"Oh, so it is. Jeff," he said, holding out his hand.

"Nice to meet you, Jeff. You're into ghosts I take it?"

"Not exactly. I'm just doing a little research."

"Same here. Say, I hope you don't mind me asking, but you wouldn't happen to be privy to any tales in this particular area would you?"

Jeff hesitated. "Not really. I mean, kind of–"

The man stepped back. "Are you're experiencing something now? Is that why you're looking for these books," he said, holding the books up.

Jeff looked into the man's eyes. "I think so."

"Well, I'm not sure if you're familiar with what it is I do, but maybe I can be of some assistance. How's about we grab a bite to eat."

"Sure," Jeff said. He felt compelled to grab a copy of the man's book while in his presence. Part of him hoped the guy would offer him a free copy–he didn't. Instead, the man handed him the two local ghost books they had both been interested in.

"How's about you meet me out front after you pay for these. I'm going to run to the restroom."

You've got to be kidding me.

Jeff wondered why a professional author was making him pay for the books—agreeing nonetheless. He waited in line, purchased the books, and met Lee Buhl out front.

"You know this area," Lee said. "Where can I get a good slice of pizza? I'm fucking sick of seafood."

"Matt's," Jeff said. "It's a couple streets over."

"Lead the way."

Jeff wanted to laugh at the way this guy was dressed: fancy button up shirt, pleated pants, and a ring on almost every finger. What kind of jerk wore so many rings?

Writers.

Lee talked mostly about his books and his travels while sucking down two cigarettes. Jeff nodded along, half-listening as he led the guy to the best pizza in town. They walked in the local joint, an Aerosmith song blaring from the speakers, the smell of fresh pizza and onions in the air. He saw the shop's proprietor, Matt Hilton, standing behind the counter talking with one of the new girls. He nodded, Matt waved, giving Jeff's company a second look. He led Lee to a booth near the KISS pinball machine in the back.

"So, Jeff, what's this current predicament you're in?" Lee said.

Chapter Four

Carla Dunn was singing an old Supremes song as she pushed her housekeeping cart down the corridor. Her singing was more for distraction than anything else. She knew the Bruton Inn shared a space with *something*, but over the years, she'd minded her own business and had been left alone in return. She'd felt the presence throughout the inn–pockets of cold, like you'd find in a lake. There was always a sense of being watched, something being in the room with you, but never any poltergeist-type activity. She'd yet to see a bed levitate or drawers flying across a room. Rhiannon's asking her about ghosts was like someone cleaning a fishbowl–stirring up all that nasty stuff you didn't usually see. Carla was feeling one of those cold pockets now.

The last couple of late check-outs needed cleaning and suddenly she wanted to get them done as quickly as possible. She noticed a number of the rooms on the second floor had *do not disturb* cards in the door–211 had not been touched in a week. It was hotel policy that she had to get into every room at least once every six days to change the blankets and vacuum, a number of the rooms were due tomorrow for the sixth day cleaning. 211 was due and had not been checked off today. The girls must have missed it.

She knocked on the door. "Housekeeping." Carla stood there giving the guest a chance to respond. Placing an ear to the door, fear snuggled up around her. Her mouth went dry. She fished the master key from her apron, removed the *do not disturb* card, slipped her key into the lock for 211, and turned the knob. She was welcomed by a blast of frigid air and an unexplainable sense of dread. She wanted to turn around and leave the room for tomorrow, maybe have a couple of the younger girls do it, but her feet carried her over the threshold. "Hello?" She propped open the door then grabbed her cleaning cart and shivered. Her arms busted out in goose pimples as she made her way in. Her eyes followed the naked mattress down to the bathing suit and skivvies crumpled at the foot of the bed. It was empty.

Someone had a good night. The thought usually produced a smirk from her, but instead she felt her flesh crawl, her stomach turn. She moved past the sick feeling building within and began to gather the discarded bedding when she heard the toilet flush from the bathroom across the room. "Housekeeping," she said again, her voice barely squeaking through her lips. More silence. She wished she had skipped this room and gone home for the day. "Hello?"

The door behind her slammed shut. She looked back and saw the rubber stopper—the one she'd used to hold it open—melted into the rug. She turned her head back and dropped the bedding she'd been clinging to. A naked man with long blonde hair and dark eyes stood before her. She wanted to scream, but couldn't catch her breath. He placed his hands on either side of her face and stared into her (*through her*) with pitch black eyes. She thought of her husband, John, and her son, Parker, before the naked man lifted her from the floor and tossed her across the room. There was a deep crack as she came down on the nightstand and fell to the floor in a broken heap.

"Please, Jesus–" she tried.

"Shh, shh, shh, come on now," the man said. Carla began to convulse as he smiled at her. *He* was doing this. "You came into *my* room," he said crouching down before her, stroking her hair. "Are you frightened?"

"Y-y-yes, please d-don't–" He placed a hand over her mouth.

"I will," he said. "I don't like strange people coming into my room unless I ask them to. Did you not see the card in the door? Don't answer that."

Tears bled from her eyes, snot dripped from her nose down onto his hand. He lifted his palm from her lips and glared at the mucus with a look of disgust.

"Why? Why are you doing this now?" she said. "I've known you were here for years, but you've never hurt any of us?"

"Ha, ha, ha," his laughter was awful. She closed her eyes and thought of her husband and son again. "You speak of my love," he said. "She's a fine piece of work. She tells me the staff is harmless, but I'm new here, and frankly, I don't like you." He placed his thumbs over her wet eyes.

Carla Dunn screamed as he pressed them in.

***

Timothy Laymon pulled his gore-soaked thumbs from the screaming woman's eyes. He snapped her head to the side, silencing her.

Standing up and stretching, he felt *her* power flowing through him. Killing had always come easy, all he had to do was unleash the rage; it was the guilt that came afterward that had kept his humanity. This was different. He felt a surge of power from taking the woman's life. He'd been born for this, just as *she* had said. The ecstasy purring through his veins felt like heaven and he wanted more.

CHAPTER FIVE

Jeff sat across from Lee wondering how to explain the events of the last twenty-four hours. The more he thought about them, the more he saw the dots connecting. Kurt and the elderly couple, that night with the bizarre love-fest in the pool room that was then suddenly wasn't, naked Kenneth McGowan and that tall buddy of his–*what had they been up to last night? Coincidences?* Or part of something bigger that he had somehow not put together? He didn't know, but maybe Mr. Buhl would. Looking across the table, Jeff had a few questions running through his head. Was this guy in the fancy clothes and jewelry the real deal? Was he a real ghost hunter or some fraud in it for the money? Jeff picked at the corner of his thumb. He glanced around to see who might be in listening range. He didn't need to be treated like a weirdo in a place he enjoyed frequenting.

"First off, let me clarify, I'm not sure what I believe right now," he said, looking over Lee's shoulders before continuing. "There's just a bunch of things that are kind of adding up, and truthfully, thinking about them right now, it's sort of...*freaky.*"

"Okay, that's all right. A lot of people in these situations are often confounded by what they're experiencing, afraid of sounding crazy or being ostracized by those they eventually confide in. I'm not going to judge you, hell, I don't even know you." Lee reached for his pack of cigarettes. "Shit, I always forget you guys don't allow smoking anywhere up here." He slid the smoke back into the pack, dropped the pack back on the table, and continued. "So, maybe you don't know what you're dealing with. Let's try starting with what's going on. What in particular is piquing your otherworldly senses?"

Just as he was about to begin, the rock station coming through Matt's speakers started playing Alice Cooper's "Welcome to my Nightmare." Jeff and Lee both glanced up toward the speakers, each giving out a nervous laugh. Jeff collected himself and began. "I think we might be dealing with something evil, maybe a ghost. I don't know."

"Go on," Lee said.

"Well, I'm not sure if I believe it's a ghost per se, but..." Jeff trailed off pondering his theories. "...but maybe it is."

"What exactly have you experienced?"

The grey world beyond the large glass pane separating them from its vampiric cold caught Jeff's attention. The bright sun that woke him this morning had been murdered by the coming storm. Folding his hands together on the tabletop he opened the can of worms he never wanted. "My friend said someone, or something, chased her from the hospital last night." He felt stupid saying it out loud, but then thought of the elderly couple they had found alongside Kurt. "And I think I believe her."

Sitting across the booth from him, Lee Buhl looked like a twelve-year-old at one of the Hollis Oaks Cineplex's Saturday Night-mare Matinees. Jeff thought of the time he'd gone to see the afternoon double feature of *The Gate* and *Prince of Darkness*. He'd been so engrossed he thought he'd fall into the seat in front of him. That was how Lee looked now.

"Go on," Lee said.

"There have been rumors, stories about something being there, but I never saw anything, I still haven't," Jeff said, raising his hands as if to claim some sort of innocence. "Outside of a couple nutjob veterans and a naked geek who roams the second floor."

"You said something being there. Where exactly is there?"

"At my work. There have been whispers about a ghost. A guy died in the pool a couple months ago and everyone–"

"A pool?" Lee looked ready to jump out of his seat.

"Yeah, a guy was found floating in the new pool one morning. The cops came and took pictures and everything."

"And this happened at your work?"

"Yeah, I work at a hotel–"

Lee held up his hand. "What hotel do you work at?"

"The Bruton Inn, off Route five."

CHAPTER SIX

Kenneth opened his eyes to the brutal scene he'd produced the night before. The small room reeked of iron and feces–the scents of death. He would have to drag the bodies out at some point. *She* demanded they be discarded, buried in the patch of woods beyond the back parking lot. The room was cloaked in shadows. The alarm clock next to him read 6:07. He rose from the blood-sodden mattress and moved to the window. Pushing the heavy curtain to the side, a grey world shivering beneath a darkness it had no idea was coming stared back at him. He would have to wait until the shrouded sun fell from the sky before moving the two ruined forms. He could at least get the graves ready. He glanced down at his naked form, and then toward the dead man by the door; the dead man's clothes would have to do.

He cinched the pants that were about three sizes too big in the waist with the nice leather belt hanging in the loops. He passed on the shirt–the blood splattered Rorschach dressing its front would draw more attention than his boney chest. He grabbed the man's socks to hide his wounded foot, smirking as he recalled the man and his son in the other room. He would have to take care of those bodies, as well. Quiet as a mouse, Kenneth cracked open the door and glanced out into the hall. He watched a family of four carrying enough luggage for an entire move rather than a few nights stay make their way toward the elevator. He remembered the college kids partying in the pool for the last few days and wondered if they were all heading home today.

That'd be a real shame. I'm just getting started.

As soon as the family disappeared, he placed the *do not disturb* sign in the door and headed for his own room. He liked wearing the mess his victims had made, but knew the big guy would have a shit fit if he saw him wandering around like he'd just stepped out of a slasher film. He'd had enough of Eric. First made or not, Kenneth had already decided he was going to make sure he put his lights out for good. The big guy would never see it coming. He felt confident that she would forgive him.

Entering his room–free from the tiny voices that had plagued him before she arrived–he made for the shower, curious where the rest of their little group were, especially the girl. Maybe he'd get another chance with her. No matter, there would be time for that when they were done. He had plenty of chores to keep him busy. Besides, she would let him know when he was needed. He showered, dressed in jeans and a sweatshirt, and headed back to his private graveyard.

Chapter Seven

She was in his arms again; tangled in a mess of sheets and sweat, her roars of ecstasy making him harder. Eric pinned his Ice Queen to the mattress and drilled into her, wanting to make her scream, demanding the pain, but she unleashed her own needles of death. Just as he came, she transformed before his eyes from the beauty that walked with a sultry sway to the demon that demanded revenge. He watched the skin bleed from her face, her arms, her chest—hollowed eyes suddenly aglow with the blood of their victims peered into him. He could no longer differentiate whether he was ejaculating or pissing, either way, he knew it made no difference to her. A shriek blasted through the darkness causing something warm and wet to seep from his ears. He tasted blood on his lips. His nose began to leak. The husk of a human form remained beneath his nakedness. He sat back on his feet watching as its damned soul rose to the ceiling, its crimson eyes staring back down at him. Eric wanted to look away, but couldn't. The eyes of the thing above him dropped at a break-neck speed, slamming into him, sending him flailing backward to the floor. Dust from the withering form upon the bed dispersed into the air of the electric room, sparkling, then fading and disappearing.

Eric awoke to the sound of thunder. He could still feel the power of the dream, the electrical current of the vision somehow following him into the real world. His sheets were soaked; strong with the scent of urine. He rose, dropping the wet sheet to the floor. The pitter-patter of rain tapped on the window before him. He walked over and split the heavy, green curtains. Lightning flashed beyond the sea of trees dressing the earth below. He spotted movement within the closest patch behind the back lot–*the Rat*. He was going to see what the little puke was up to. Maybe he'd put him into one of those holes he loved to dig so much. He wasn't sure what his dream had meant, if anything, but he couldn't feel her call for him at the moment. This temporary freedom carried with it a sense of abandonment–the hurt he'd felt as he tried to see her last night came around for a second swing, but this time, there was a budding rage there as well. He would take the anger with him down to the Rat's little play land.

***

The afternoon rain escalated from a soft hint to an unrelenting barrage without transition. Kenneth didn't mind, he preferred the rain–it softened the dirt and made his task easier. He emerged through the swaying trees to the small clearing that served as his burial ground. The soil had already sunken in above the plot he'd made the other night. No matter. He wasn't concerned with someone stumbling upon his bodies. They would never live to tell.

Stepping over the dead, he dropped to his knees twelve feet from his genesis grave and sunk his fingers into the earth feeling the already muddy particles packing beneath his fingernails. He hadn't bothered wearing a jacket; it would have soaked through in seconds just like the rest of him. He piled clump upon clump of mud off to his right, his progress filling with the downpour as he went. He continued on, undaunted, getting lost in his directive.

***

Eric moved through the trees, his presence hidden behind the powerful storm. Kenneth came into sight a few feet in. Eric watched from the tree cover as the scrawny geek clawed away at the ground. He wondered if the Ice Queen had already spoken to him. Had she sent the Rat on a mission and not him? Eric recalled his dream, the pain she had delivered, the mess he had made of himself. If she wasn't going to use his talents because of this rain-drenched buffoon, he would just have to slim down her options.

Eric stepped from the shadows. Kenneth kept on digging. He walked right up behind the Rat as the drenched excuse for a man carried on playing in the mud. The thunder roared through the darkening sky as Eric reached down and wrapped his hands around the Rat's neck.

***

Lee Buhl got up from the booth as Matt brought out the steaming hot pizza. "Sorry, can we get that boxed up?"

"Yeah, sorry, Matt. Something came up." Jeff's hands shook as he grabbed his sweatshirt.

"That's fine," Matt said. "You look a little pale, Jeff. You feeling okay?"

"Yeah, I'll be all right. I just didn't get much sleep last night."

"I don't know how you do those overnights, man. I'd be dead in a week. I'll go grab a box and meet you at the register?"

"Sure," Jeff said.

After Matt walked away, Lee could smell the lingering wave of cooked onions and green peppers. He looked over to Jeff. "Hey, I hate to do this to ya, but I left my wallet back in my car. Can you get this?"

He watched Jeff's brow furrow, if only for a second, then relax again as if he caught himself doing it.

"Yeah, I can pick it up," Jeff said.

"Great. I need a smoke. Meet you outside?"

"Sure."

Lee stepped out under the darkening sky; he thought the day looked infected like something had settled in and soiled it.

That would sound good in my next book.

No sooner than he got the cigarette lit, the rain began to fall. "Shit."

Jeff came out holding the pizza box. "What's up?"

"Nothing. We better get moving," Lee said. The clouds let go all at once.

"Holy shit." Jeff carried the large box over his head. He could already feel the warmth of the delicious pie trying to escape the bad weather. The rain came hard and fast.

"Come on. Let's get the hell out of here," Lee said. He pushed Jeff ahead of him.

"Where to?"

"Back to the bookstore. Back to my car. Go, go go." He followed Jeff as they crossed the street and headed down another little road. Jeff stopped under the awning of a store with mannequins dressed in hippy garb in the window. "Go, go, and don't stop," Lee said, raising his voice above the rapid-fire deluge pelting everything beneath it.

They rounded the corner; Lee saw the Barnes and Noble across the street. He took the lead as they scooted between cars on Bell Street. His car was in the closest corner. He unlocked the doors and stopped. He watched Jeff surveying the soggy pizza box. "Ditch it. I don't want that thing in my car," he said. Jeff tossed the wilted cardboard to the ground and got in.

"Sorry I'm getting your seat wet," Jeff said.

The thought of his leather seats cracking and looking like crap spilled over into his delivery. "Not much we can do about that now, is there?" He started the car, threw the wipers on high–though they were hardly able to keep up with the rain–and headed for the exit.

"Shit, wait."

"What is it?"

"I left the books back at the pizza place."

Of fucking course you did.

"Where are we going?" Jeff said.

"I gotta go back to my hotel and grab some stuff. We can dry out a little while you tell me everything you've heard about your hotel."

"What about the books?"

"Don't need 'em," he said, looking over at Jeff. "We've got you."

***

The moment the large mitts wrapped around his throat, Kenneth couldn't breathe. He couldn't yet see his attacker, but had a good idea who it was. He tried pulling free and only wound up helping close off his airway.

"No you don't," the big guy said through the storm. "I don't know why she chose you, but right now, I don't really care."

Kenneth was seeing dots. He felt his eyes trying to fight their way from their sockets. He tried clawing at Eric with his dirt-filled nails, but the rain made it difficult to puncture through the big goon's slick skin.

How is this happening? Where are you?

He managed to donkey kick the big guy in the shin, but still couldn't break his grasp. Instead, Eric flung him backward slamming his head into the ground. A ringing resonated through his ears. The world began to drift from his sight and the rain threatened to drown him. His mind slowed as the world closed in upon itself.

***

Eric continued squeezing long after the Rat stopped fighting. He finally let go when the puddle of water he was holding Kenneth's head in was up to his wrists. His hands shook as the thought of what he'd just done and the ramifications it might have for him, crossed his dizzying mind. His world began to spin. He closed his eyes, placed his fists in the mud, leaned over, and took some deep breaths. After a minute, the feeling passed.

He grabbed the Rat and dragged his still body to the shallow grave the fool had managed to scratch out before meeting his fate. Eric considered pushing the sloppy mound sitting next to the hole over the ugly face staring back at him. "Fuck it. You're not even worth a half-proper burial," he said. He hacked up a glob of phlegm and spat. The yellowy wad landed just under the Rats left eye, the rain washed it away immediately. Nonetheless, Eric's grin returned.

He tried the back door before realizing he'd forgotten his room key. He would have to go around to the front lobby. Soaking wet from head-to-toe, he lumbered around the side of the building. He watched a group of teen girls pile into a large van, their parents struggled behind them with a luggage cart. They paid him no mind as he passed them by. As the lobby doors opened, all of the residual giddiness from choking out the Rat dissolved, instantly replaced by a sense of dread at the sight of the girl they'd changed last night. The Ice Queen had stolen the body. Her hair was different, and her eyes–Eric tried to think of something to say. A voice screamed through his mind.

Shut your mouth, you look like a fool. Get up to your Goddamn room.

***

Rhiannon stared at the big guy. He was the one Jeff had said was with Kenneth. He stood dripping wet, looking like he'd just been caught doing something he wasn't supposed to. Before she could ask him if he was all right, he bowed his head and took off for the stairs.

"Wow, that was weird. I bet you guys get a lot of that, huh?" the girl said.

Rhiannon wondered what the hell he had been doing out in the storm.

"Hey, are you okay?" the girl asked.

Rhiannon slowly came back around. "Yeah, uh...did...you still want me to come up to your room?"

"Actually, I forgot about something I had to take care of first. I'll call you when I finish cleaning things up."

Rhiannon didn't say a word as the girl, Sarah, crossed the lobby and disappeared into the stairwell.

Ring, ring ring.

"Thank you for calling the Bruton Inn, this is Rhiannon speaking–"

"Hey, hey." It was Jeff.

"Hey, what's up? Where are you?"

"I'm at the Motel 6 in Hollis Oakes. Are you okay?"

"I'm...yeah, so far it's been pretty quiet. Why are you at the Motel 6?"

"I met someone who's interested in our...situation. We'll be there in a bit."

"Okay, see you in a few." Rhiannon's thoughts shot back to the girl, Sarah. She seemed familiar. She figured it was the girl's A/C unit that was on the fritz, but she liked to at least make an effort to check things out before just switching her guests to another room. Sometimes they tipped you for going that extra mile. She wondered if Sarah would give her a tip.

Chapter Eight

"I haven't read any of your books," Jeff said. "What is it exactly that you do?" This guy seemed like a grade A prick so far, but if he was legit, they might need him.

"I'm an urban shaman."

"Like a magic man or an Indian voodoo guy?" Jeff cringed, realizing how stupid he sounded.

"Not exactly, but sort of. We're healers, for the most part. Defenders of the mind, body, and spirit," Lee said as he buttoned up a dry shirt. In his first real act of kindness, the guy threw Jeff sweatpants and a t-shirt. "Put those on. They're the only non-dressy clothes I have with me."

"Thanks." Jeff peeled off his soaked sweatshirt and undershirt. The t-shirt Lee had thrown him had the words *One of these days I'm gonna get organezized* scrawled across the front. Jeff recognized it instantly. "*Taxi Driver*, right?"

"Sure. I guess. A fan left it in my room in Denver a few weeks ago." Lee sat on the edge of the bed, replacing his socks. When he was finished he shook another smoke free from the pack on his bed and lit it.

That figures. He doesn't seem cool enough to know who Travis Bickle is anyway. He held the sweatpants Lee threw him and considered how he was soaked all the way through. "Uh, I don't have any dry underwear," Jeff said.

"Keep 'em," Lee said, waving his hand at the sweats. "You go commando in 'em, they're yours."

"Thanks," he said. He shuffled by Lee and went into the bathroom. The guy must have been the cheapest bastard Jeff had ever encountered, and working in the hotel business, you run into more than your share of tightwads. This guy took the cake, no doubt. Jeff wondered what the girls would think about the guy. They'd probably think he was attractive. For the first time today, he thought about Kurt. What if this, whatever it was, had affected Kurt?

Kurt's dead.

He still couldn't believe it, but Rhiannon had said she heard him flat lining before she was chased out of the room by...something. Maybe it was possible that they had saved him. Maybe he was–

Bang, bang, bang

"Hey, what are you doing? Jerking off in there? Come on."

Jeff regained his composure, and opened the door. "Sorry, I was thinking about someone."

"That's usually how it works," Lee said, lighting another smoke.

Jeff ignored the comment, moving toward the kitty-cornered desk. There was a wicker basket sitting on top. He reached for the lid.

"Don't touch that!" Lee said.

Jeff jumped, startled by the sudden outburst. "I... I wasn't. What's in it?"

Lee placed himself between Jeff and the basket. "Those are my tools of the trade, so to speak."

"Sorry," Jeff said.

"Here, hold this." Lee handed him the cigarette. Jeff took hold of it, not quite sure how to handle it. He'd never smoked cigarettes. He went with the pinching technique, holding it between his thumb and forefinger like a joint. They hadn't allowed smoking at the Bruton Inn since the early nineties. These rundown, side of the road motels always had a handful of ashtray smelling rooms. It finally dawned on him why Lee would choose the dump.

"Let's talk a little more about that inn of yours." Lee carried the basket over to the bed. Setting it down, he lifted the lid and produced a bundle of green stuff. Jeff thought it looked like a bundle of grass and weeds. Lee slipped his lighter back out of his pocket and flicked the wheel. A flame burst to life. Lee watched it burn for a few seconds before blowing it out. The earthly aroma immediately began to search its way through the room.

"Is that incense?" Jeff said, feeling less stupid, but having a feeling he was wrong again.

"It's a smudge stick." Lee watched the trail of smoke pirouetting up into the air. "It's a collection of herbs–sage, mugwort, and some others."

"What's it supposed to do?"

"It's not what it's *supposed* to do. It's what it does," Lee said. Jeff sensed he had stepped on the guys feelings again. "Since I arrived here for the book signing, I've felt something trying to get to me." This got Jeff's attention. "I haven't determined whether it is good or evil, but there's definitely something that knows I'm here. Either way, this is my protection."

Jeff wasn't sure if it was the collective of incidents or all the shaman mumbo jumbo, but at the moment he felt something bad, too. He thought of the dead guy in the new swimming pool, the elderly couple from the other day...*Kurt*. He thought of Rhiannon and Meghan alone at the hotel. "We have to go," rushing over to the phone by the bed.

"What are you doing?" Lee said.

"I have to call Rhiannon. I have to tell her to get her and Meghan out of that place."

"Hold on," Lee grabbed his arm. "Settle down. Breathe. How far is it from here?"

"It's only like half an hour or so, maybe longer in this weather." Jeff pulled his arm free.

"Listen to me," Lee said, grabbing him again before he could pick up the phone. "You're panicking, you're not thinking straight. You need to clear your mind."

"I *need* to warn my friends."

"They'll be all right."

"You don't know that," Jeff said.

"We need to be prepared. If the presence I've been feeling around me is there, it's powerful. For me to be picking it up this far away, it may well take all that we can manage to stop it. You called her, your friend, when we got here. You told her we were coming."

"Yeah, but I wasn't...I wasn't convinced we were really up against something. I mean, I thought–"

Lee gripped his shoulders tighter and shook him, staring into his eyes. "You are walking the right path. There is something supernatural going on at your hotel. Okay? What I need to know from you right now, this very minute, is what you intend to do."

Jeff felt dizzy. Thinking of the rumors, the ghosts, the shadows housekeepers whispered about seeing in the corners of rooms, guests complaining about knocking and voices from rooms next to them that were supposed to be empty...

"Jeff, are you willing to stand up to this, or are you going to run."

"I...want to help Rhiannon and Meghan."

"I'm going to need more than that."

Jeff's stomach was twisting in a swell of anxiety and fear. Horror books were one thing, dealing with this shit in real life... He broke free from Lee's grasp, making it to the toilet just in time to watch his morning coffee splash into the white bowl. He'd been scared plenty of times in his life, but he'd never considered himself a coward. Part of him wanted to go home and just start searching for a new job on Monday. There was a tiny voice in his head just below that one saying that he didn't really know Rhiannon and Meghan all that well. That he should just call them, warn them, and let them decide what they wanted to do for themselves.

"Jeff, I'm going to need your help," Lee said from the doorway behind him.

Jeff stared into the brown pool of coffee and stomach fluids. He wanted to run. He knew it was wrong, but he didn't want to go back there.

"I know it's hard to believe, but there are things that are *not* of this world. Whatever resides at that hotel has been around for a while. I've read up on some things. The Bruton Inn has been cursed since it first opened.

Jeff wondered how this was supposed to sway him.

"You are already stronger than most. You have accepted its reality. You know it is there. Some of these spirits prey upon nonbelievers, the ones who lie to themselves even in the face of such things. That weakness is what feeds these spirits. I sensed in you an inner strength. I can feel it now. Come with me. Stand with me."

Jeff closed his eyes, took a deep breath and stood up. "What do we have to do?"

CHAPTER NINE

Eric hurried up the stairs and down to his room. He saw the look on her face. He couldn't tell if she knew what he'd done or not, just that his Ice Queen was not pleased to see him drenched to the bone, dripping all over the lobby. Her stare had been one of intent. She would be coming to see him. As much as he'd been longing for and dreaming about it, he had a feeling this would not be a pleasant visit.

Just as he finished the thought, there was a knock at his door. He knew it was her. Outside his window, beneath the violent thunderstorm, the day was dying. For the first time since his change, Eric wondered about his own mortality.

He opened the door. Kenneth the Rat stood dripping water and mud all over the floor. His eyes were nothing but black orbs. He grinned behind a dirt-covered face. Eric wasn't sure how the weakling was standing before him and not buried in the grave he had made, but he was damn sure going to put him back in it.

"You can try," Kenneth said, stepping forward. "But I wouldn't if I were you."

How he had just read his thoughts, Eric wasn't sure, but he didn't like that he couldn't do the same.

"You're services are no longer needed," Kenneth said.

"What the fuck do you think you're going to–"

Kenneth grabbed Eric's wet shirt and threw him backward, taking the big guy off his feet, and sending him sailing into the far wall.

"How...what..." Eric tried to say. Kenneth stepped aside as a man in a dress shirt and slacks with shoulder length blond hair entered the room. The temperature dropped as if *she* were here. Something erupted inside Eric that he hadn't felt in years–*fear*.

"Who the hell are...?" It took a second for Eric to recognize him. It was the guy with the shaved head from the pool, the one that *she* was toying with. Timothy.

"As young, obedient Kenneth stated, you're services are no longer needed."

In a blur of movement, the chosen one was at his throat. Eric felt a strange and painful sensation rush through him. He watched the room go red and then fade back to normal. His chest hurt, his eyes burned, his muscles went numb. He knew he was no longer one of them. "I'm sorry," he said. "I'll do whatever She wants. I'll–"

"Too late," Timothy said.

He pulled Eric to his feet and threw him. Eric's body smashed through the window. He thought of Jimmy and knew he had this coming. The pavement below rushed to meet his face. His neck snapped on impact.

"Should I put him with the rest of the bodies?" Kenneth said.

"Just drag him out of sight," Sarah said from the doorway. Both of her boys turned to her from the shattered window now being assaulted by the torrents of rain whipping in from the storm. "After tonight, there will be no one left but us."

VOLUME V

AWAKENING

Rain thrashed the building like a thousand angry insects crashing against an unseen force. The hallway, as dangerously quiet as a path through woods almost remembered, stretched outward. Tan walls, holding portraits perched like gathering crows on a telephone line, waited in silence along the corridor. At the far end, an EXIT sign glowed like a welcoming threat. Voices came to life:

"Should I keep him with the rest?" a male voice said.

"It doesn't matter. After tonight, there will be no one left but us," the female responded.

Unsure of who or what any of them were–*Ghosts? Spirits? More? Less?*–and only now cognizant of its own existence, the entity floated down the unattractive hallway. It was, or had been, alive. Now, it was again, in some manner of speaking.

Longing for warmth and communion with someone, something, she–*yes, she, it remembered*– Christina moved toward the others.

"It doesn't matter. After tonight, there will be no one left but us."

The words were clear. The ominous message spewed poison into the air. *That voice...*she knew that voice. Something reached out–something dark. The young spirit, suddenly frightened, moved away, knowing there was something rotten among the group. The hum of a soda machine momentarily stole her attention, its steady drone broken only by a door opening down the hall and then slamming shut. A raggedy looking man appeared, covered in mud, dripping wet from head-to-toe. He paid her no mind as he turned the other direction and vanished through the doorway beneath the EXIT sign.

The smell of chlorine stung her burgeoning senses. Something like a nightmare crossed her waking mind–something with swimming pools and sirens... If a spirit can shiver, she did. Fearful of being discovered by the familiar one, she slipped farther away.

Thunder boomed on the other side of the walls. A wicked night was saying hello.

CHAPTER ONE

Kenneth's blood was alive, pumping through a vengeful heart with an excitement previously unknown. He stared out into the rain. Lightning sparking across the sky lit the lot below. The motionless body of the goon who tried to kill him lay sprawled in an awkward display. Eric had landed face first on the paved lot with the rest of his body flopping over, nearly decapitating him. He lay still–dead and broken.

"What shall we do next?" Timothy said, stepping to her side.

"Why don't you tend to those left up here, while young Kenneth heads down to my room to wait for his new girlfriend," she said. "I'm going to go have a little fun with Jeffrey and his spiritual guru."

Kenneth felt like his moment had arrived. He had managed to topple Eric in their battle for her affection. There was still Timothy, but he liked Tim. He could sense something special behind the man's eyes, under his skin, something just beyond. There was an admiration, a respect, he felt toward her *chosen one* that validated the man's presence. Kenneth stepped next to Timothy, who looked amazing and menacing dressed all in black.

"Kenneth," Sarah said. "Before you get your prize, I want you to scrape up that mess in lot, but don't worry about laying him to rest with the others. Just get him off the blacktop. When you're finished with that, you may go wait in my room. I'll send your angel right along."

"I'll be ready," he said.

She moved to him, gently sweeping his wet bangs across his forehead. He gazed into her eyes as she said, "I know you will, dear. I am so proud of you." She kissed him on the lips, arousing every sense in his body. He wanted to weep, even more, he wanted to destroy. For her, *all for her*.

He pulled away, slipped into the hallway, closing the door behind him, and left to clean up the mess in the parking lot.

Descending the stairs, his thoughts were held hostage by the cute girl from the front desk. The one *she* would be sending to him. He knew her name was Rhiannon. He could tell she was one of those cute, but tough kinds of girls. He'd been timid in his limited conversations with her throughout his stay, but tonight, tonight would be different. He was different. Everything was different. Shy, pathetic Kenneth was gone. The loser she'd thrown annoyed looks at and given the cold shoulder to was about to make her squeal and squirm. Maybe she would beg for mercy. Maybe she would beg for death. Maybe he would make her like him and she would just beg.

***

"Where will you be–" Timothy said.

"Shh..." Sarah placed a finger to his cold lips. For a moment, she felt...*movement*. "Try not to have too much fun without me, my love."

Taking her hand from his lips, she went into the light of the hallway and closed her eyes. There had been something... Was it the half-hearted shaman? Maybe, but it felt more familiar. No matter–it was gone. Timothy was watching her.

"What is it?" he said, standing in the doorway.

She walked up to him, kissed his open mouth and smiled. "I have things to tend to, and so do you." She moved toward the stairwell, stopped and gestured to the tunnel of doors, giving one last look for the disturbance. "When you finish whoever remains up here, finish off the rest."

***

Timothy wasn't sure what had just happened, but he could tell something had bothered her. Having not seen an ounce of weakness slip from her since they met, whatever it was she wasn't telling him had broken through her defenses. Before he could think on it any further, two women emerged from a room two doors down holding towels and beers.

Time for him to earn his keep.

CHAPTER TWO

"Hello," Timothy said. The two girls smiled.

"Hi," the redhead on the left said. The brunette beside her, giggled as they stopped.

"My name's Tim. Weren't you at the pool yesterday?" He looked at the redhead.

"Ah, I don't think so. We just got here. Sorry."

"Oh, well it must have been another beautiful girl who looked like you."

"Yeah, must have been." She smirked to her friend. "Well, we were on our way down to the pool for a dip. Care to join us?"

"No, no. I had something else in mind." He gazed at the brunette next to her like she was welcoming him into her bed. He watched the shorter, dark-haired girl go from smiling to tightlipped and fidgety.

"Okay, well we're going down, so if you change your mind–" Red began.

"No," he interrupted. "You're not. You're not going anywhere."

The redhead pulled her towel up over her chest. "Sorry, Tim, but yeah, we are."

He stepped in their path placing his hand on the wall, blocking their route.

"What the fuck do you think you're doing?" Red said.

"Come on, let's go." The brunette yanked on her friend's arm and pulled her back the way they came.

Timothy reached out and grabbed Red's other arm. "Hey," he smiled at the brunette and flashed his charcoal eyes, "let's see who gets to get their wish."

"Hey," Red screamed. Timothy punched her in the face, dropping her to the floor unconscious. The brunette took off running.

The lights in the hallway flickered like strobe lights at a rock concert as the whimpering girl stumbled down the corridor. Just before reaching the elevators, a picture of the Maine State House flew free from the wall, smashing her over the head and knocking her feet out from under her. Timothy watched her face bounce off the floor.

He dragged Red into Eric's room and then retrieved the brunette.

The rain was still blowing into the room from the broken window he'd thrown Eric through as the brunette opened her eyes. "Good morning, Sunshine," Timothy said. He watched from the room's second bed as she looked around the room. Her eyes went wide. "You scream and I'll tear pretty little Red over here's eyes out." Red sat slumped against the bed from her spot on the floor; the bruise next to her eye was already purple. Timothy stroked the unconscious girl's hair.

The brunette cried as she shook her head. "What do you want?"

He rose up from the corner of the other bed, smacking Red's cheek with the back of his hand. Red blinked her eyes, raising a hand to protect her from his. He looked over the brunette's bikini-clad body and said, "I can think of a couple things."

***

Sarah stalked down the first floor hall glancing around, searching for something. She stopped by the pool room. A couple and their two children splashed around inside. The two little blond kids played in the shallow end while the adults treaded water in the deep. Sarah placed a hand against the glass. Frost quickly formed beneath her touch. She drifted back to a memory of her own childhood. If only she could have had such enjoyment. Her past was tarnished by an egocentric, perverted father and his filthy whore of a fiancée.

"Hey," a voice said, bringing her back to the pool room window. "Did you still need me to come up and check that A/C unit?" It was the girl, Rhiannon, from the front desk. Sarah pulled her hand from the frosty glass, placing her back against the cool surface.

"Actually, yeah, I have some errands to run right now. Do you need me in the room to check it out?"

"Not if you don't mind me being in there when you're not," Rhiannon said.

"Great, why don't you go ahead and do that."

"Are you sure?"

"Absolutely, I'm not the type of girl who gets all freaked out about her possessions. I'll check in with you at the desk when I get back." Sarah wore her best normal person smile.

"Okay, I'm not promising results," Rhiannon said, "but I'll see if it's something I've dealt with before or if we just need to switch you to another room."

Sarah's smile came easy as she thought of Kenneth. "Whatever you need to do to get it resolved is fine by me. I'll see you in a bit?"

"Sure."

Sarah glanced over her shoulder; the ice was gone. She nodded at the front desk girl and walked toward the lobby pretending she had someplace else to be. She heard the stairwell door close behind her and thought of Kenneth awaiting his prize.

CHAPTER THREE

Kenneth stepped into the downpour, letting it wash over him. He glanced over at the broken body of his nemesis–just as he thought *she* had not cared. Quite the contrary actually, she seemed pleased with his act of revenge. His smile faded as he wondered what her plans were for him. After tonight, would he too become expendable? He shook the thought from his head and ran to clean up Eric's crooked carcass.

After dragging the body behind the trees, following her orders not to bother with burying it, he brushed his hands on his pant legs and headed back inside–his reward for being a good boy would be waiting for him.

***

Rhiannon reached the top of the stairs and turned down the hallway. The corridor, finally calm and peaceful–no naked people running from room to room, no crying babies, no odd complaints about voices coming from unoccupied rooms–offered Rhiannon a moment of quiet, welcomed solace. Gone, at least for the moment, were the various fears induced by the last thirty or so hours.

Approaching the door to room 209, she noticed something–the picture of the State House was gone. A cursory glance around the hall and the little area before the elevator told her what she already knew–college kid shenanigans. Happened every weekend they stayed. Two weeks ago, a group of eighteen and nineteen-year-old camp counselors stayed. The hotel had to replace the portrait of famed Maine adventurer (she still wasn't sure what an "adventurer" was) Tom Frost that had been hanging in the hall for years–someone had drawn a semen-spewing dick in front of his mouth. They also had to throw out the plant that used to sit next to the Pepsi machine–a guest told her and Kurt that she'd seen one of the boys stumble over and urinate in it. They usually fucked with things on the second floor where there was less of a chance of being caught by one of the desk agents. Typical crap. Most of the college kids had departed this morning; the few remaining stragglers were due out tomorrow.

Tomorrow. For some reason the thought felt empty. She was at the door to room 209 before she could ponder the depressing feeling further. The girl, Sarah, had said to go in. She couldn't recall whether she said she was alone or not. Rhiannon knocked. "Front desk?"

No answer. She pulled her master key and opened the door.

***

Kenneth watched his prize walk down the hall.

Shit.

He didn't want to fuck this up, didn't want to end up like the big guy. He moved like a ninja, coming up on her swift and silent, ducking in the space by the elevators as she reached the room. He watched her, waited for her to crack the door and then...

***

Cold air rushed out from within the room just as wet hands grabbed and shoved Rhiannon from behind. She spun around to find Kenneth McGowan leering at her from the doorway. "What the hell do you think you're doing?" she said, holding back the fear tracing her spine like the tip of a blade. "You can't be in here."

"I can be in here. In fact, I was told to come here by the girl staying in this room."

"I don't think so. If you don't get out of here, I'm going to call the police."

"Oh no..." He held his hands up to his mouth feigning cowardice. His pale skin dripped mud to the floor of the freezing room. The hungry look in his beady eyes covered her flesh with invisible maggots. She watched him turn and twist the bolt on the door. He turned back toward her and said, "Now, I want you to know that I won't kill you if you don't make me."

Rhiannon backed away trying to think of a way out. She glanced at the window over her shoulder.

"I don't think that's a very good idea," he said, beginning his approach.

"Stay the fuck away from me!" She eyeballed the phone by the bed.

"Ah yes, you were going to call the police..." He nodded toward the phone. "Go on." It was like he was reading her thoughts. A bad feeling crept over her already anxious mood–this wasn't the same quiet guy that checked-in [however many] days ago. He was different. "You have no idea," he said. "I want you to meet her. I think she'll give you to me if I ask."

"Who?"

"The Ice Queen. She's been waiting for us, for this moment. You're going to be a part of something special."

Rhiannon needed to get out, and fast. Trying to act, not think, she rushed him.

He grabbed her as she plowed into him and they fell to the floor. He wrapped his arms around her legs. With his nose inches from her crotch, he started sniffing at her like a dog as she struggled against his clammy grasp.

"I can play rough, too," he said.

"Fuck you." She sat up and cracked her boney fists in a flurry of quick strikes to his face. Blood seeped from a cut beside his eye, but he continued to smile through the barrage of her tiny fists. She wailed away even harder, ignoring the pain in her knuckles, letting the urgency open fire. The sting of her knuckle splitting open as she made contact with one of his front teeth caused her to pull her hand back. Blood flowed from the wound.

He laughed, releasing her and rising to his feet.

"Why don't you go ahead and start screaming," he said, touching the gash she had made on his face and spitting out the tooth she had knocked loose. "I think I'd like to hear that pretty mouth of yours roar."

She scrambled back to the door, spinning and grabbing for the knob. His foot caught her square in the back. Sliding down the door, gritting her teeth, she refused to give this fuck-hole the satisfaction of her cries–she feared what might lie ahead. He stepped closer and she launched at him again, driving her bloody fist up into his balls.

"Oomph." He clutched his crotch and dropped to his knees.

She turned for the door again. She screamed, surprised and pissed as he yanked her hair. She spiraled back into the room as he flung her away from the exit. Hitting the corner of the bed, she bounced off the mattress and hit the floor.

"I knew you'd be feisty," he said, grinning from ear to ear. "I'd be lying if I said I wasn't turned on–" His speech was cut off by the lamp from the TV stand nailing him between the eyes. Stumbling backward, reaching for his face, she launched the lamp from the desk at him.

"Fuck!"

"You wanna hear me scream?" Rhiannon grabbed the microwave from the corner of the desk and charged at him. "Arrrgghhh!" She unleashed, rushing and swinging the appliance at his face.

"Not this time, bitch." He grabbed the microwave and pulled it from her grip. Before she could react, he swung back around and nailed her between the shoulders, dropping her to the floor. She reached a hand behind her, moaning as she rolled on the ground. She knew she'd fucked up.

Kenneth threw the appliance down and kneeled next to her, grabbed a fistful of her hair and yanked her head back until they were face-to-face. His breath was a mix of rotten hamburger and shit. "I know you think I'm ugly and you would rather be dead than lie down with me, but if you give me a chance, I bet I can fuck my way into your heart."

She spit into his face. "Eat shit, you fucking faggot."

He let the spittle slowly crawl down his cheek then shook his head. "You shouldn't have called me that." Yanking her head back farther, he slammed her, face-first, into the floor. Her nose exploded on impact, her head swam to stay above the flood of stars swirling behind her eyes.

Kenneth stroked Rhiannon's dark locks. In spite of a valiant effort put forth from the rebellious girl, he was enjoying his small victory. Gazing over the softer edges of the tough little thing, he moaned thinking of what he was about to do. Turning her over, he scooped her up, cradling her in his arms. She was his promised reward, and this time, there was no Eric, no Uncle Wes, and no son of a bitch step-father to ruin his moment. Laying her down on the bed, he pressed his lips to hers. She tasted like mint and honey. Slowly undoing her button-up work shirt, and gently spreading the fabric to expose a pink bra patterned with black roses, he kissed between what little cleavage she had. He moved to her slacks, unfastening them and pulling the dark polyester down over her thighs and slipping them over her sneakers. He ripped his damp t-shirt off, tossing it behind him and began unbuttoning his jeans. A fever burned within him as he grew hard. The TV at his back suddenly came to life. The sound of white noise filled the room.

CHAPTER FOUR

With a hand under his jaw, fingers tapping his bristled cheeks, legs shaking like an unstable washing machine, Jeff stared out the window as Lee drove down Route 5. All the books, all the movies he'd either read or seen; nothing had prepared him for this. He felt like an idiot that would fit perfectly into a Wes Craven film. He told Lee he would help him; he was only going in to check on Meghan, and if she was all right, he would make sure he got her and Rhiannon out. This jerk could use his untouchable basket of voodoo if he was up for it, but Jeff wasn't fucking stupid. He was more on the get in and get, and get as far away as possible plan.

"Do you see that?" Lee's voice broke through Jeff's thoughts. He couldn't see much of anything past the hammering rain pounding the windshield.

"What? I don't see–"

Lee slowed the vehicle.

"What are you doing?"

"There's something in the road."

Jeff saw her, but could not believe his straining eyes. Meghan Murphy stood in the middle of the road, soaked to the bone, wearing nothing but a t-shirt and panties. Lee brought the car to a full stop twenty feet from her. Jeff reached for the door.

Lee grabbed his arm. "Where the hell do you think you're going?"

"I know her. That's one of the girls I was telling you about that's staying at the hotel."

"No. Wait."

"She could be hurt. The hotel's only a couple miles from here." Jeff grabbed for the door again. Lee grabbed him by the collar of his t-shirt, jerking him to a halt. Rage boiled up within Jeff's veins. He'd had just about enough of this prick's grabbing at him and condescending attitude. "Get your fucking hands off me."

"That's not who you think it is."

Jeff looked out the windshield and watched. His jaw dropped. Meghan pulled off her shirt and then slipped out of her underwear. Her eyes flashed red as she raised her panties over her head and swayed her hips in a dance that under any other circumstances would have had him salivating. Lee let go of his shirt and revved the engine. "What are you doing? Shouldn't you be rummaging through the basket for something?" Jeff said, staring at the supposed shaman.

"Some things fucking die easier if you just run them down." Lee buried the gas pedal, shooting the Shinari at Meghan.

"Wait! Wait," was all Jeff had a chance to spit out holding on for dear life as the car smashed into the girl he'd kissed the night before. Instead of being pulled under the vehicle's wheels or sent flying up over the car, the body splattered on contact. Blood and flesh splashed the windshield, obscuring their view of the road. Lee stamped the brakes; the car screeching to a halt. The wipers took a second to move, under the weight of the gore covering them.

"What the hell was that?" Jeff said, still clinging with one white-knuckled hand on the seat and the other gripping the door so tight he was sure the handle would pull free.

"A taste of what's waiting for us."

Jeff thought of Meghan. Between Kenneth McGowan's nude stroll the other night, and his adventures with Lee, he didn't know what the hell to make of this. "Was that her?"

"Her who?" Lee said, reaching for his pack of cigarettes.

"That girl, *that thing*...in the road. Was that Meghan?"

"I don't think so. Here." Lee held out a cigarette for him. A sickening feeling crawled through Jeff's already tense stomach. "Smoke 'em if you got 'em is something I've learned to live by," Lee said.

Jeff hadn't smoked since he was twenty-two, giving up the habit after his Grandmother passed from emphysema. He wondered if Meghan, the real Meghan, was okay. He thought of their kiss, his promise to check on her... He had thought of her as the girl of empty promises, but now he was the one coming up short. The flash of guilt mixed with his ever growing pile of anxieties, pushed his nerves to their frayed limits. "Yeah, I think I could go for that." He reached a trembling hand out and took the cigarette as Lee pushed the car's lighter in.

"I've never smoked in this car before, never used this lighter before," Lee said. "But I think we're both in for a night of firsts." The lighter popped out and Lee handed it over. Jeff sparked the cancer stick to life. Lee lit his own, cracked both windows, and hit the CD button on the car's stereo. Jeff recognized the song as it drifted out of the speakers in perfect clarity.

Riders on the storm... riders on the storm...into this world we're born, into this world we're thrown...

Jeff took a long drag from the cigarette—his lungs surprisingly acting like it was old hat—and glanced up into the dark, cloud-covered sky.

God, if you're up there, we sure could use a hand.

Thunder cracked.

CHAPTER FIVE

Timothy watched the brunette and the redhead lay motionless on the bed, eyes staring blankly at the ceiling, chests rising and falling. He considered his words carefully. While his counterparts may have enjoyed the quick kill, he preferred to play the spider to the fly, or flies, in this case.

"Would you believe me if I confessed my sins?" he said, though neither could answer until he allowed them. He was standing with his back to the bed, staring out at the night. The rain was letting up and the fog was rolling in. Gazing down at the lot he thought the few remaining cars looked like gravestones; the fog, creeping around them, holding mass among the dead. In essence, the empty vehicles would serve as exactly that–markers for the fallen. "I killed two girls I loved very much... Just like I'm going to kill both of you." He listened to the soft patter of rain, the whispering wind through the trees across the lot. "I was destined to be what I have become from the very beginning. You are both here with me now as it was meant to be." He turned to them, watched as the wide-eyed pretty things began thrashing on the bed. "Ah...now, now, shh-shh," he whispered.

Timothy saw his new face, the Ice Queen's gift, reflecting off the framed portrait depicting a generic beach setting, hung over the bed. His eyes were like burning embers–pure black surrounded by a fiery, red glow. The skin around his mouth pulled taught revealing an army of canines. His skin—pale and cold—revealing the thick blue veins beneath. He reached out a clawed hand and scraped a set of sharp yellowing nails down the length of Red's leg; a thin trail of blood seeping in its wake.

"I can tell you want to scream, and believe me, there's nothing I would love to hear more. However, due to the sensitivity of our surroundings, I think your blood and tears will have to suffice."

He lifted the clawed hand up, resting it just between Red's bikini top. Saliva, drooling from his jagged teeth, dripped down onto her flesh as he looked into her eyes. Her emerald greens went wild as he punctured her flesh, ripping his hand down the length of her torso. Blood, spraying like a fountain, covered his face as he tore through the rest of her. The brunette, thrashed madly, waiting her turn.

Chapter Six

The spirit watched the one called Kenneth. She had seen him attack the girl from behind and followed them into the room. The room...she knew this room. Phantoms of her past pulsed behind a hazy curtain. There was something there, something she needed to remember, but she couldn't. Not yet. She watched the girl fight off this thing, all the while seeing bits and pieces of a forgotten past. The girl was strong, but not strong enough. The spirit needed to figure out a way to help her. The hotel clerk was unconscious on the bed, defenseless to this dark creature's whim. And he was a creature. She wasn't sure what exactly. He wasn't dead, but he wasn't alive either. The evil one had done this. Somehow, it had made this one and the other. They had to be stopped. All of them.

Watching him undress the girl, she looked at the broken television on the floor. Without touching the device, she made the static screen come to life.

Chapter Seven

"What the–" The hairs on Kenneth's neck tingled in the charged air. *Eric?* A hint of the old Kenneth, the weak Kenneth, and his penchant for paranoia slipped through. If *she* could bring him back after the big guy's earlier attack, she could do the same for Eric, but why? "Where are you?" He scooted off the bed, walked to the TV, and hit the power button. The white noise continued. Kenneth grabbed the TV from the stand, ripped it from the wall, and threw it to the floor. Though muffled against the rug, the white noise continued. Gripping his hair in frustration, he brought his knee up. "Shut. The. Fuck. Up!" His foot came down with each seething word.

The room fell silent.

Knock, knock, knock.

"All right, you big dumb fuck," he said. "Come back for more, huh?" Kenneth walked to the door, undid the lock, and yanked it open. Complete darkness. He stepped out into a black pocket of cold that felt *alive*.

"Sarah?" his voice called, shrinking with his libido.

There was no answer. A light farther down the hall flickered to life, and then grew to an amazing brightness, causing him to block its brilliance with his hand as he moved forward. The bulb shattered in a splash of sparks and glass and the door behind him slammed shut.

Stumbling through the black, seeing spots as he went, he reached out for the door knob and heard the lock click back into place.

"Arrrhh," he yelled, pounding his fists on the door. The light from within, barely registering in the darkened hallway via a sliver at the foot of the door, caught his eye. Resting his forehead against the barrier, he laughed. "Heh, heh, heh, you think you can keep me out?" Stepping back, he ran and kicked the door. The hinges buckled. "Huh? You think you can lock me out, bitch?" He made a second run at the door, landing with another solid kick. The hinges gave a little more. "I'd step back if I were you," he said, before lunging again. This time, the door gave way, crashing into the room. "Now," he said.

The girl still lay unconscious on the bed where he'd left her. Kenneth started huffing, the rage building steam. He thought of Timothy. *Maybe he's fucking with me now, just like Eric.* "No! She's mine, you hear me? She said this one was mine. And I'm taking her right fucking now."

Stalking toward the bed, Kenneth stepped over the discarded microwave. The broken TV on the floor came back to life. The static hit his ears like some terrible metal band with a bad drummer, out of place and out of time. "Fuck you," he said, dropping his pants to the floor. The hallway lights suddenly sparked back to life flashing back and forth between light and dark, life and death. Undeterred, Kenneth mounted the now moaning girl. Reaching down for her panties, he felt something cold shoot through his back.

"Uhhh..." he gasped. He felt a freezing cold sensation penetrate him like he'd been harpooned by an icicle the size of a broad sword. He couldn't move, the crippling cold holding him hostage.

"Arr...arrr.." His voice was a whisper as the piercing frigidness sapped his strength. His eyes fluttered into the back of his head. Convulsing, he fell from the bed.

***

Rhiannon opened her eyes and caught a faint blue shadow looming at the edge of the bed. The vision was gone in the blink of an eye. Sitting up, she slipped her butt back against the headboard and gazed down at her exposed flesh.

Her attention was stolen by the stirring, pantless body on the floor. "I don't fucking think so," she said as she climbed from the bed. Scanning the floor for a weapon, she spotted the microwave. Kenneth's arms reached for her as she stepped over him, bent down, and picked up the kitchen appliance. Raising the small microwave over her head, her muscles strained, her arms and lips trembled. She sucked in a quick breath as his eyes blinked open. Onyx orbs glared up at her. Without a word, she slammed the hefty metal machine down onto her attacker's angry features, the contact sounding like a pumpkin being smashed. Kenneth's appendages twitched and then stopped.

Rhiannon hacked up a glob of snot and spit it to the floor. It was dark red, a result of her busted nose. She had no idea what the hell happened to Kenneth, or what had stopped him, what had made him cry out at the edge of the bed, but she didn't care. She was safe, he was dead. She was getting the fuck out of here.

***

Down the corridor, Timothy Laymon rose from the crimson mess on the mattress. Stepping from the bed, covered from head to toe in the gore of his two victims, he felt electric. He moved from the parade of tattered flesh and bone, running his hands through his hair. All traces of their blood upon him disappeared. The door opened without being touched as he walked on through. He stepped out into the open corridor just as another door slammed shut. Someone had just taken off down the stairwell at the opposite end of the hall.

Run, run little girl.

Two rooms down, a stalky Mexican with a tattoo of a skull sprouting red and black wings across his bare chest came into view. "What in the hell is going on out here?"

Timothy waited as the inebriated man turned to face him. "What the fuck you lookin' at?" the man said.

His bloodshot eyes, staring into Timothy's true face, reflected the burning pits of hell. "M-m-m-Mr..." the man mumbled as a bottle of liquor slipped from his grasp, falling to the floor. In a matter of seconds, his throat landed next to the draining alcohol followed by his heavy body.

Stepping over the carcass, and pushing the door open, Timothy gazed upon the sexy Latina lying naked upon the bed. Her perfect ass up and swaying from side to side as she chirped soft little moans watching the skin flick on the TV at the foot of the bed.

"What are you doing Enrique? Come back in here and–"

Timothy didn't even have to say a word to make her shut her trap. Walking into the room, the TV died; she screamed until he sent her decapitated head smashing through the window.

CHAPTER EIGHT

Jeff cradled his third cigarette between trembling thumb and index fingers. Partly from the anxiety over the Meghan-thing they had encountered in the road, partly because of the nicotine. He and Lee were both chain-smoking their way back to the Bruton Inn. He didn't have a very good feeling about Meghan Murphy, and from Lee's response, it didn't seem as though he should.

His eyes itched from the smoke refusing to go out the window. He stared at a piece of the thing they'd hit in the road caught on the edge of the windshield and flapping against the car. The rain, now just a drizzle, hadn't been able to wash all the gore away.

The last few miles on Route 5 were quiet save for the slapping chunk of flesh and the thumping of the wipers. Jeff tried not to think about what was ahead, but Lee's shaking left leg kept waving like a flag of nerves in his peripherals. He thought of Rhiannon, alone and ignorant of the gravity of their situation. *Maybe it's a good thing; at least she won't have chewed her fingers down to nubs. Then again, she could be in trouble if whatever's there wants to fuck with her.* The fight or flight conflict arm-wrestled for supremacy within his heart as the Bruton Inn came into sight, standing against a darkness that had settled in for the evening. There was no turning back.

***

Lee pulled the car around the front, glancing through the lobby doors; he couldn't see whether anyone was at the front desk or not. He forced the beast of a car to a crawl, purring around the corner of the building, following the parking lot to the back of the property.

"You see that," he said.

"What?" Jeff tried to find what Lee was looking at.

"Up there, second floor," he said, pointing with the cigarette between his index and middle fingers. "There's a broken window."

"Where? Oh yeah, oh shit. And look, another one."

Splotch

Whatever they had just run over made the car thump. Lee stopped the vehicle.

"What was that?" Jeff said.

"Hold on." Lee stuck his half-done smoke between his lips, shifted the car in reverse, and backed up. There was a second, less-messy noise as the wheels rolled over whatever they'd squashed beneath the tires once more.

"What the hell is that?" Jeff said.

Lee stared hard through the windshield, and despite the fog now covering the ground, he could see the hair in the headlamp beams. "That's what they call, a bad sign." He put the car in drive and drove forward, being sure to steer clear of the severed (and now flattened) head in the lot. He didn't think Jeff's mind allowed him to see what the road kill was, and he didn't say any more of it. He didn't need the guy freaking out before they even had a chance to get inside.

A great weight was pressing against Lee's spirit. *Something cold, something dark.* His own spine was threatening to come undone. Two shattered windows and a decapitated head bordered on too much in his book. Clutching at the wooden figure hanging from his neck, he prayed for the spirits to guide his heart.

Lee pulled the car to the far end of the property, killing the engine. "Open the glove compartment." Jeff struggled with the latch.

"You have to press the button and pull at the same time."

The guy fumbled a second longer before the compartment fell open.

"Grab a pack out of that carton."

"Hope you're this prepared with your voodoo, too," Jeff said, handing Lee the cigarettes.

Little shit.

"Yeah, this is sort of what I do. You just try not to piss your pants when we get in there." Jeff's lips tightened and his nostrils flared.

Good, get mad. I'm going to need someone with balls, Lee thought. "It's in there," he said.

"You can feel it?"

"Yes, and so can you." Lee opened the pack and drew out two more cancer sticks.

"So," Jeff started, taking the offered cigarette. "What do we do now?"

"First, we need to get in the proper headspace. Get our spirits right" Lee reached over the seat, pulled out the smudge stick and a piece of white chalk from his basket. "Light this," he said, handing the green bundle to Jeff.

Jeff did as he was told, then went to blow out the flame.

"Not yet!" Lee said. "Let it burn a minute."

"What's the chalk for?"

"We all have spirit animals. Power animals—mine's the wolf. We need to find yours."

"How do we do that?" Jeff said, waving the burning smudge back and forth, watching the smoke drift up.

Lee pulled a CD from the basket in the back and slipped it into the stereo. The familiar, comforting sounds of Zamfir and his flute filled the air within the car, joining the smoke of the smudge stick. "Blow it out." Jeff did. Lee took the stick from him and squeezed it into the space between his cup holder and leather seat. "Sit back and do as I tell you."

"What the hell are we doing?" Jeff said.

"Trust me. Lean back and try to relax."

Lee closed his eyes and lay back, letting his muscles rest. He peeked to make sure Jeff was following his lead–he was. With the guy's wavering attitude, Lee knew he had to stay on top of him.

"Now, I want you to take some deep breaths. Try not to think of anything." He knew it was a hell of a lot easier said than done under normal circumstances. As Jeff's breathing began to slow–a good sign–Lee pushed on. "Now, steady your breathing, and try to think of the moon. See it in your mind, bright, full, and sitting high in the sky." He waited giving his apprentice a chance to form the vision. "Do you see it?"

"Yes." Jeff sounded neither surprised, nor condescending.

"Now, feel the cold..."

"I, I feel it."

"Now, lower your vision from the moon. There's a mountain..."

"Yes," Jeff said.

"Now gaze upon the mountain, there, on the cliff..."

"I see it."

"What do you see?"

"It, it looks like a ....like a fox."

"Okay, you're on the cliff. The fox is now in front of you. There's a clearing..."

"Yes."

"Tell me what you see beyond the clearing."

"Woods... a forest."

"Go into the forest."

"No... no... I'm not going in there." Fear bled through Jeff's voice.

"You must."

"I can't."

"Follow your spirit animal. It will protect you."

"No. There's, there's something in there...I see it...I see...her...a girl...with red eyes..."

"Go on," Lee said.

"She's...she's..."

"Yes?"

"She's going to peel your flesh and drag your skin over your fraud of a Grandfather's grave."

Lee sat up, gooseflesh covering him. Jeff was lying perfectly still, in the trance, in the vision. "Who are you? What is your name?"

"S-s-s....uhhhh."

Lee slammed backward against his door as Jeff, eyes closed, vomited down the front of himself. The smell of curdled milk trumped the earthy smudge for superiority.

Jeff coughed, hacking up more puke. His eyes shot open as he threw his hands out, grabbing at the door, and the middle console, trying to get his bearings.

"It's okay," Lee said, trying to sound calmer than he felt, placing a hand on Jeff's shoulder. "You're okay. Can you hear me?"

"Yeah, yeah...what the hell just happened? Uh... gross..." Jeff turned away at the sight of the bile. He grabbed the door handle and pushed.

Lee considered stopping him. The preparation ceremony wasn't complete yet, but he couldn't blame the guy for wanting to get out and get some fresh air. The first journey into the spirit world can be a real mind-fuck, especially when something evil finds its way in. He wasn't sure what Jeff had seen or if he would even remember, but he knew they couldn't wait any longer. They had to get inside.

"Suck it up," Lee said, holding out another smoke.

Jeff took it, letting Lee light it for him.

"Do you remember what you saw?"

Jeff shook his head. "Yeah, it was...do you see that?"

Lee turned around not sure he wanted to be enlightened. The lights on the second floor were flickering on and off. Lee searched the two windows on the end of the building, there was nothing–"There," he blurted out. The face in the window of the door disappeared.

Lee looked at Jeff–the man looked white as a ghost–and said, "It's time."

CHAPTER NINE

Standing in the hallway, Timothy raised his arms out to his sides and struck his best Jesus Christ pose. He'd never felt so powerful, so perfect, so right. There were more warm bodies to ruin and release to her salvation, but the one he desired most had vanished down the stairwell. Flexing his powers, the lights flickering at his command, he moved forward, admiring his trick and feeling an immense gratitude for his true love. Before Sarah, he lived a lie. Denying his urges, constantly thinking those near him could see the truth, could see Shannon and Beth–dead, broken, and buried. All the years of trying to fit in, conforming to the drones walking blindly through painfully hopeless lives, hiding his razor-sharp longing to become more, his desire to live uninhibited, free to feed his darker urges, but fearing the status quo and their condemnation of things they did not understand. Those days led to this–liberation from all the trappings of the dying world outside. Sarah had opened the door to his cellar of crimson dreams. It was time to realize his potential.

The eyes of men and women in the black and white photographs hanging like silent sentries along the pulsing lights of the hall began to fill with blood. Walking down the corridor, Timothy's thoughts were of blood too–the blood of numerous victims of his Ice Queen. She showed him all the death she had produced. Through her, he *knew* the blood reigning down now and where it came from; the blood of her father and his bimbo; of Gordon McDonough; of Jason Perry; the blood of the last two days...so much life, gone. Timothy inhaled the intoxicating scent of so many fallen, his eyes rolling back, a wave of black ecstasy trickling through his veins.

Placing one leather dress shoe before the other, he followed the path of the pretty young thing who had danced to the death with Kenneth. He stopped before room 209, glancing in at the boy's dead body. He wasn't sure how she was able to kill Kenneth; the obedient servant's death was unfortunate, but at least this little girl was proving to be fun. He sensed her strength, and could feel a mild sympathy that such an undaunted soul should be snuffed out.

She will run, but she will not get far. Her swan song, like all great curtain calls, will be one of legend.

He would make certain of it.

Chapter Ten

Rhiannon stood at the bottom of the stairs, her heart hammering, thoughts glazing over, body swinging into shock. She collapsed in a heap into the corner of the stairwell, afraid, ashamed even, to step into the lobby. She tried to urge her body to get up and move, to get the fuck out of this madhouse. She trembled. Her cousin Jack had told her about the time he hydroplaned completely horizontal on the interstate in a heavy rain storm. She remembered him saying that after the car straightened out, he pulled over and cried while his body shivered uncontrollably for fifteen minutes. The aftermath of her encounter with Kenneth McGowan had slipped deep under skin. Something had inhabited his body. She knew with her heart of hearts that he was not the same shoelace-staring, frail, and awkward guy that had been living here for the past month. His eyes...she saw the black orbs that flashed with sinister glee before she smashed his skull in.

"Hello? Is anyone here?"

The male voice from around the corner called out, bringing her back from the ledge of sanity. She grabbed the railing above her head and pulled herself back to her feet. The lights in the staircase died. The fine hairs covering her body stood at attention, her stomach dropping.

"Hello?" the man in the lobby said again.

Rhiannon ran into the lit area.

"Oh, hi, I was wondering if anyone–" the man said.

"Get out," she said.

"Excuse me?" The man in the green t-shirt and Bermuda hat looked her over. She was still half-naked. "Ma'am, are you in some kind of trouble?"

Before she could answer, his pale blue eyes looked behind her. The sliver of dread worming its way inside her like a parasite told her all she needed to know.

Rhiannon ran toward the guest in the Bermuda hat, shoved him, and said, "Go! We need to get out of here!"

The guy attempted to grab her by the arms. She swatted him off, moving past him. She turned to find the man with long blond hair, dressed all in black, standing by the lobby doors with his hands behind his back. He was leering at her. She suddenly felt faint, like her thoughts were being stirred.

Bermuda Hat stepped forward, putting one arm out as if to block the man in black from her. "Is this the man who attacked you?" he said. She couldn't answer. "Sir," Bermuda Hat said, taking another step toward the man. "I think you and the miss here are done for the night. Why don't you–"

The man in black's eyes released her and turned to Bermuda Hat. Rhiannon felt the swimming feeling in her head sweep away.

She grabbed Bermuda Hat by his t-shirt. "Never mind, we need to get out of here. Come on." She pulled at him.

"He's not going anywhere, Ms. Jenner–"

He knows my name.

"I know many things," he said. "This chivalrous gentleman is not leaving, and neither are you."

Bermuda Hat made a gurgling sound.

"Come here, sir," the man in black said.

Bermuda Hat moved forward. Rhiannon backed away, watching in horror as darkness swallowed the whites of the man in black's eyes. Bermuda Hat stopped in front of him. The man in black glanced at Rhiannon, his black eyes exuding a coldness that sunk into her marrow. Not wanting to see what was coming, she turned and fled. A series of sickly wet sounds like the ones her old dog, Wolf, would make when he ate a can of Alpo were followed by something that sounded like jelly slapping on the floor, and then a thud. She didn't have to look behind her to know it was Bermuda Hat hitting the floor.

She ran down the hall reaching the halfway point of the first floor. The girl, Sarah, who had sent her to the room with Kenneth, stood at the end of the corridor, smiling, the light of the Exit sign above her shadowing her pale face in red. The elevator was on Rhiannon's right. She had no choice. She hit the up arrow, watched the door slide open and ducked inside tapping the number two with her fingers like a woodpecker on speed. Footfalls clicked down the hall, closing in. The chrome door slid before her, the elevator began its ascent.

VOLUME VI

DAYS GONE BY

The girl had finished him and fled the room. The darkness inside the one called Kenneth faded into nothing. It was gone, and so was he. Christina moved over his empty vessel. So young... just like... just like... Looking around the room, she was hit by a feed from days gone by.

The haze lifted, the memories began rolling back. The hotel...they were at the hotel, *this* hotel. She remembered the room—big bed, color TV, the mini-fridge full of drinks. Laughter, smiling eyes...and then the horrors. She saw the men—one had tried to hurt her, the other.... She saw the blood and remembered the lies, the death. She saw the girl...she saw *her*. Sarah.

The pool...

Back in the room, she sensed something else—one of *them*—was approaching. The cold was coming closer like an awful blackness closing in, devouring all of the light in its wake. She moved into the bathroom and hid out of sight. Hoping it would pass.

The deathly entity stopped. She felt a heavy presence just outside the door, and then, it moved on.

Something bad was happening. And it was only just beginning. She had to find a way to help. Find a way to stop it. To stop her. She had failed once, long ago, but she had to be here for a reason. She'd been given another chance to put an end to Sarah's lust for death and destruction.

Chapter One

"Stop," Lee said. He pulled Jeff to the side, their backs facing the building. Another hard rain had begun to fall.

"What is it?" Jeff said, raising his voice over the deluge. Lee turned his head, wicker basket in hand, and peeked in the window of the inn's back entrance.

"I saw a girl," Lee said. "It was the girl from the vision I had the other night–the one haunting my spirit." He turned back to Jeff. "And I suspect the one you saw in yours."

Jeff swallowed hard and held his hand to his brow shielding his eyes from the rain. "She's the ghost?"

"Yes, but I think she's something more than that."

Jeff didn't respond. A ghost was bad enough. He didn't want to think about something worse.

The night howled as the angry storm whipped the trees behind the inn from side to side.

Lee moved his face back to the window. "She's gone, come on." He reached for the door handle.

"That's not going to work. We need a key to–" Jeff said, stopping as the door opened.

Lee looked over his shoulder, "Looks like we're expected."

Jeff shivered in the cold, but it wasn't the storm freezing the blood in his veins, he knew whatever was waiting for them was not going to be so welcoming once they found it.

"Stay behind me," Lee said.

"Holy shit, it's cold in here." Jeff tried to will the warmth back into his arms by rubbing them. He and Lee were drenched.

"It's the spirit," Lee said.

"Did you see where it went?"

"No, it was just there, walking away," Lee pointed down the hallway. "Then, it was gone."

"We have to find Rhiannon and Meghan. Can't you project yourself, like a spirit or something," Jeff said, stepping past Lee. He wanted to get in and get the fuck out.

"Not so fast," Lee said, grabbing him by the sleeve. "It's watching us."

"Well, can you?"

"Can I what?"

Jeff jerked his arm free and said, "Can you do that power animal stuff, and I don't know what they call it...put your spirit out, like a lookout?"

"I think what you're referring to is astral projection. I have the ability, but I'd rather not expose myself to our friend here. It's dangerous, especially when you're not sure what you're dealing with."

"Then how do you know it's watching us?"

"It left the door open. It wants us here. Think about it."

Jeff didn't want to think about it. Thinking about this whole fucked up situation was giving him an ulcer.

"Where would your friend be, the one that works here. At the front desk?" Lee said.

"Yeah, down at the other end." Jeff pointed ahead.

"And the other one?"

"She should be up in her room. I hope." Jeff glanced up the stairwell to his right.

"Okay, first we need to do something." Lee crouched down next to his wicker basket (the outside of which was dripping wet). He pulled the lid off. Jeff expected the contents to be soggy and ruined, but they seemed to be perfectly dry. Lee hauled out another smudge stick and a fat piece of chalk.

"What's that for?"

"We have to block this exit. We're going to bind it within this building."

"Bind it? You mean lock it in here...with us?" Another icy wave went through Jeff's stomach.

"That's exactly what I mean. This is its home. More than likely, it won't want to leave, but in the scenario where we're running like hell for our lives, I don't want the fucking thing following me. Plus..." Lee looked down the hallway. The lights along the corridor dimmed. "I don't think we have much time."

***

Sarah watched the half-hearted magic man draw his useless little lines. He was right about one thing, this was her home. This was her heritage. She wouldn't be going anywhere and neither would they. It was time to have a little fun.

She pulled back within the body of Meghan Murphy and opened her eyes. Standing before the mirror hanging over the bathroom sink, she watched her reflection. Her hair went limp–the bouncy brown curls returning to Meghan Murphy's perfectly straight, black locks. She wondered if Jeff had missed her. She would have to get him alone and find out.

***

"Help," yelled the voice.

Jeff recognized it instantly. "Meghan?" He rose from his dripping perch next to Lee.

"*Jeff? Is that you?* Thank God."

"Meghan–"

"That's not her," Lee said from behind him. Jeff was already on the move, but stopped a few feet away, and turned back to Lee.

"You don't know that. You said so yourself." Doubts about Lee's abilities suddenly flooded his thoughts, washing over the small amount of trust built on the ride over.

"I'm telling you, that's not her," Lee said, replacing the lid on his basket and standing up.

"*Jeff?*" She sounded much closer.

Jeff spun around and saw Meghan Murphy hobbling toward him, using the wall for support. His heart made the choice. "Meghan, stay right there."

"Jeff!" Lee said.

Jeff ran toward her, no longer listening to what Lee had to say. He scanned her body for injuries. Outside of the wounded expression on her face and the slumped shoulders, she looked amazing. Her brown eyes met his, filling his head with water, his thoughts swimming accordingly. Faint footfalls approached as if from a dream. The world around him shrank–Meghan was in his arms.

"Are you all right?"

Her eyes flashed from red to black, then back to brown, the visual display nearly knocking him from his trance. She laid her freezing head upon his shoulder.

Lee shouted from the outskirts of the dream, "Jeff, get the fuck away from her."

"You were supposed to come back to check on me," she whispered in his ear.

Jeff tried to turn his head back, tried to look at her again, but couldn't. The door to the room behind her flew open and she pulled him inside.

"Jeff, don't-" Lee's voice was silenced as the heavy door slammed shut.

***

Lee tried the handle. To his surprise, it opened. Only the light from the dimmed hallway penetrated the darkness within. Cold air wrapped around him. His nostril hairs threatened to freeze. Lee slipped his hand inside, searching the wall for the light switch and pulling back at the touch of frost in its place.

"Why don't you come in and join us," the demon spoke.

"Jeff, are you all right?"

"He's just fine. Come see for yourself."

Lee peered inside trying to spot them. There was a closed door to the right, maybe the bathroom, maybe a closet. The black beyond was impenetrable. He stepped back glancing down the hall and cursed himself for leaving his basket at the back entrance. If he could get to his tools he could-

"You could try, but do you really want to leave your friend alone with me?"

It could read his mind.

"Yes, I can. I can also taste your fear."

His grandfather had taught him exorcises for such spirits. He only hoped he could remember the techniques. Lee hung his head, clenched his fists, and cleared his thoughts. The hallway was relatively warm-the cold was in the room with this thing and Jeff.

"What have you done to my friend?"

"I told you to come in and find out."

The TV in the room came to life, illuminating the form sitting on the bed. Lee gasped. The thing dressed in the girl's body held a ball in its arm. Lee's eyes dropped to the body lying motionless on the floor. He looked back up at her. Two blood-red orbs stared back.

"Jeffrey should have listened to you." It rose to its feet. Lee watched, clutching at the wooden pendent around his neck. Praying his grandmother's gift would protect him. The thing inside rolled the prize in its arms toward the doorway.

After what he'd seen in the parking lot when they arrived, Lee was afraid he knew what was coming.

Jeff's dead eyes stared up at him from the severed head. Lee stumbled backward, his lips trembling as he hit the wall. He looked away unwilling to believe the horror at his feet, unable to accept the evil. After a few quick breaths, he dared a glance back into the TV-lit room for the monster responsible–it was gone, and so was Jeff.

CHAPTER TWO

R hiannon stood in the corner of the elevator clinging to the chrome rail within. Her heart hammered so hard and fast it hurt. She wanted to scream but couldn't find the breath to do so. Instead, she wondered where the hell Jeff and his friend were. How dare they leave her here in this fucking hotel hell to face these monsters alone? She would kill them both...if she got the chance.

Bing.

She prayed for an empty hallway. The doors crawled open with all the ambition of a blue hair on the interstate. She bit her lip so hard she tasted copper. Watching the door slide open was akin to witnessing the live reveal of the winner on American Idol. She could hear Ryan Seacrest now: *"All the votes are tallied...for one of these two, a dream of a lifetime is about to come true. This is it, America. And your. 2014. American Idol. Is ...we'll find out, right after this break."* Rhiannon stepped out of the elevator and slipped in something thick and wet. She fell backward, landing half inside the elevator squirming as though covered with roaches. The carpet was spongy with a dark fluid. She looked down at her hands–blood. It was everywhere. The whole damned floor must've been flooded with it. She propped up on her elbows and then turned to reach for the chrome rail she had been clutching on the way up.

Bing

The elevator jerked, threatening to descend even with the door ajar.

"Nooo!" she cried moving forward. The elevator floor dropped two inches. "Arrgghhh!"

The whole contraption convulsed, dropping half a foot, and then another. She lost her balance and slid back into the death trap.

"Noo!" she cried again as she got to her feet. The elevator bucked and clanged. *I'm going to die right here, right now,* she thought watching more important inches give way. She jumped up grasping at the second floor, her fingers slipping through the blood. The crimson swamp began to pour into the elevator. She jumped up, trying again, but was still unable to gain any traction from the slick rug above.

I'm going to die here, I, I...

Bing.

"No, No, No!" she said, her voice reclaiming its resolve. She backed up, gaining a little space for momentum, targeted the edge of the door—the door began to close.

"No," she grunted. She took two full strides and propelled her body upward, catching the unmoving edge and the closing chrome door. It was going to close on her. "Ahh!" She pulled her skinny frame up and through, her sneakered feet clearing the door just before it shut. Her exposed flesh and work shirt were covered in crimson. She looked like a survivor at the end of those gory B movies.

Nice thought, Rhiannon.

Getting up and creeping to the corridor, the spongy floor squished beneath her sneakered feet. She tried not to think of what she was stepping in. The lights up here were dim, like the pale-yellow of a full moon behind gray clouds. Her eyes moved to the stairwell she'd stumbled down earlier. She couldn't help but wonder if either the man or the woman chasing her were waiting for the elevator to drop or if they had taken the stairs and were on their way to capture her. Maybe they were already up here. Fear crawled up her spine like a thousand creepy crawlies in the dark.

Rhiannon's heart seized its incessant pounding at the sight moving across the blood-drenched floor. A tarantula scuttled across the open space no more than five feet from where she stood. Another played in the corner of the room where she spied a web large enough to capture a grown human being–set, ready and waiting for its prey. *Waiting for her.* The carpeting was slick and made squelching noises as she crossed her arms over her chest and shuffled away from the spiders. Another appeared farther down the hall. Then another one. The arachnids were multiplying by the second. She moved her foot backward, stepped on a thick cord, and jumped.

Snake!

"Ew," Her voice trembled. She felt the ghost of her skin molt from its gooseflesh covering. The floor at one end of the hall now lay blanketed with tons of slithering, and hissing serpents. She did an odd running-in-place/tap dance motion and lost her footing landing on her ass with a thump. Something fuzzy scuttled across her right hand; something small landed on her head–she could feel it creeping through her hair. Another thing fluttered down the side of her face, passed her neck and fell between her breasts, landing on her bare thigh.

Cockroach!

A number of the crawling bugs began pelting her head from above, like an insectophobic's worst nightmare. When the hallway lights died, Rhiannon screamed.

***

Timothy stood cloaked in the darkness (he'd invited) at the end of the corridor. The girl's screams were delicious, spilling terror into the world. Along the hall, doors began to open, voices–confused and frightened–filled the spaces between the girl's shrill cries. Under the cover of total blackness, Timothy stepped forward, salivating over the carnage he had in mind.

"Hello, *ma'am?*" One male voice said.

The inquiring guest was followed by more.

"Hey, what the hell? Anyone know what's going on?"

"Hello? Who's there?"

Timothy planned to deal with each of them accordingly.

"Eeek! I think there's a snake in the hall," a woman screamed.

His manifestations served their courage-crippling purpose. With an unmatched grace and swiftness he stepped to the first open door. The man inside stood there wielding an ironing board like a weapon; his eyes squinted above a large, prominent nose. Timothy grabbed the edge of the full-sized board and slammed it through the man's neck. Before the man could yelp, his decapitated head rolled down the board and thudded against the door frame. His body fell back into the room. A woman with a smoker's rasp, shouted about calling the cops. She barely had time to register his frozen presence–her throat was slit in one quick swipe from Timothy's razor sharp fingernails. He continued toward Rhiannon–his scream queen. Timothy gripped his bone thin fingers in the mop of a man's hair asking what was going on. He tore the scalp from the jostling guy and sent him back into his room screaming then slammed the door shut. The man's pain and terror continued behind the closed door. The woman who had scrambled out into the hallway squawking about the snake was lifted inches off the ground and smacked like a ragdoll from one wall to the other–her neck snapped on the second hit. One woman fell in the blackness, knocking herself unconscious on a luggage holder. A young gentleman ran for the stairwell and directly into Timothy–his neck twisted in milliseconds, his body, tossed aside. At the height of confusion, Timothy re-lit the corridor, landing a spotlight upon his sixty-second massacre. Bodies lay in various states of murder. The spiders, roaches, and snakes were no longer there. The front desk girl was on her feet and rushing away from him. He took a deep breath and used his powers to pull another portrait from the opposite end of the hall. He smiled as it flew at her head.

***

Rhiannon caught a portrait out of her peripheral vision, and instinctively raised her left arm to cushion the blow. The frame stopped in mid-air, sat suspended, inches from her arm, and fell to the floor. Rhiannon reached the stairwell door, too frazzled to try to comprehend what the hell had just happened. She bolted down the stairs with visions of bugs and blood crawling through her mind.

CHAPTER THREE

Lee rushed into the room, found the light switch where it should have been, and flicked it on. The room was spotless, untouched. He searched for the body, for signs of a struggle, for blood, but found none.

"Christ," he said, placing his hands on his hips. Movement in the floor length mirror on the closet door to his right caught his eye. He spun around, shocked to find the images in the mirror moving with a noticeable fluidity, like the tide coming in. The demon was still here, but it was not as strong. *Maybe it's farther away, maybe...it's weakened,* he thought. The sliver of hope was grabbed by the throat–the mirror's reflection brought him back to his twelfth birthday....

Lee's grandfather had come early in the morning to take him out for his present. Lee loved his grandfather, but had been annoyed with being taken away from his Saturday morning cartoons, especially to be dragged out into the cold. His grandfather brought him to the old abandoned family home two towns over. His grandfather still owned the three-story house, though after Lee's grandmother's passing, the old man left, claiming there were too many ghosts there to live with. On the drive over, he confessed to Lee that there were indeed spirits residing in and around the property and that he wanted to share a special part of his life with his grandson. In the basement of the abandoned family home, Lee's grandfather introduced him to the ways of the shaman. It was there that Lee reconnected with the spirit of his deceased grandmother. That was the first time he felt the power stir to life within him. Delivering him the wooden pendent, his grandmother's spirit spoke words he never forgot: *This is pure love, the liberation from one's concepts of this world, and the introduction to another...*

Standing before the perversion reflecting back at him from the hotel room mirror, Lee felt his stomach turn. He thought of his books, his gigs, and the Hollywood-version of shamanism he'd sold to pad his bank account. A shroud of guilt and shame weighed on him like stones at the bottom of a lake over what he'd done with his grandparent's gift.

Lee stood, shoulders slumped, listening to the rotten flesh-covered version of his grandfather in the mirror. The old man's eyes were black holes filled with despair and regret. His mouth spewed crawling worms, his words hitting Lee like body shots from a heavyweight fighter.

"You are a disgrace to the Buhl shaman who came before you. You are a disappointment to these old eyes, to this old spirit," the image said.

"I, I..." Lee began.

"*You* are empty," his grandfather said. Worms, tumbled from his disintegrating jaw and fell down to the ice-covered pond beneath his feet. One of the old man's hands detached from his arm with a soft tearing, like an old piece of fabric being pulled apart. An ear came loose next, falling to his grandfather's wrinkled, bare chest, before slapping the ice at his feet with a wet thud. Two red eyes, surrounded by a head of dark, curly hair, appeared over the shoulder of his grandfather's crumbling spirit. A skeletal hand reached out from the red-eyed demon, touched the glass, causing a rippling effect before passing through the barrier and into the hotel room.

Lee felt the penetrating cold return; his heart–bruised and quiet, like an abused child–wanted to give in. He couldn't take his eyes from his grandfather–the perversion of the man he'd loved broke apart and fell like ashes in the night. Something singed his chest. Lee looked down expecting to see the death-touch of the thing left standing where his grandfather's spirit had been, but found the figurine he kept on his necklace throbbing with life. He heard his grandmother repeat what she told him on his twelfth birthday in the basement of the old house: *"This is pure love, the liberation from one's concepts of this world, and the introduction to another. You must be of the light, and through this light, through this love, defeat all evil before you."*

Lee wrapped his hands around the wooden pendent. "Come to light, demon spirit. Come to light, and be absolved of your burdens. Come to light, demon spirit, and be redeemed in love." Lee spoke the words he declared to many an empty home, empty hotel, time and time again, but with a spiritual resonance exiled since his youth. His ancestral calling beat within.

The mirror with the red-eyed creature splintered. The demon in retreat departed with a final blast of arctic air, lifting Lee from the floor and casting him backward. The back of his head slammed against the wall, his hands fell from the pendent and everything went black.

***

Sarah had underestimated the shaman's power. Not her fault—even the fool had been oblivious to the strengths he possessed. No matter. She would arrange a meeting between him and her Timothy. She had another reunion of sorts in store for the blood-covered girl from the front desk racing down the stairs.

The Ice Queen slammed the door behind her, locking the shaman in to await his fate.

Chapter Four

Rhiannon slipped down the final steps on blood-covered sneakers, grasping the rail in time to counter her body's lack of balance. She wasn't about to become easy prey for the creep pursuing her. She crept forward, hunched over, her hair heavy with the coppery perfume of death and matted to her cheeks. Eyes darting left to right, lips trembling, hands shaking, she moved through the doorframe–an EXIT sign screamed of salvation, like the old neon Jesus Saves sign that hung over shelters in the dystopian films she used to watch with her cousin Jeanann. She reached out and shoved the chrome push bar on the door–it wouldn't budge.

Broken by the moment, Rhiannon laid her crimson-painted forehead to the glass and cried. Some part of her knew she had to move to survive; another part of her acknowledged the emotional break and found something in her sorrow cathartic. All her years of playing the tough girl, staying in control, maintaining the shield of a once-wounded child, all wanted to follow and flow through this invisible opening. She knew she should try to find another way out, but she could not pull herself away from the locked door.

A voice down the corridor did it for her.

"Rhiannon..."

"*Kurt?*" she said, stepping into the hallway. She felt stupid saying his name out loud, but couldn't deny the voice. Her bewildered mind demanded she be open to anything.

"Rhiannon," he said again. His voice was muffled. Moving down the hallway glancing at the carpet for any signs of the blood from the upper floor, she heard movement behind the closest door.

"*Kurt?*" There was no answer. She reached for the door handle.

What if he really is here? Impossible. But what if...

Her hand was inches from the handle when the door opened. On the other side was the hospital room where she'd abandoned her friend. Kurt lay perfectly still on the hospital bed, his skin pale and bloodless. Rhiannon's feet carried her inside. A grey tiled floor–cold and somehow threatening–led her to his bedside. The inner voice trying to shout about impossibilities was drowned by the hope in her heart. His eyes were closed. She reached out and placed her bloody hand on his face. His skin was cold.

"What happened to you?" she said.

Kurt's baby blue eyes opened, swimming with a hollow mix of what was and all that would never be. Her lips quivered as tears leaked from the corners of his eyes. Her heart had only felt this bruised the day her deadbeat father gave up his parental rights. She leaned forward, placed her head on Kurt's chest and sobbed on his hospital jonnie. Worried she might make him more uncomfortable she rose, ready to wipe the tears from her cheeks. A hand–cold as Death's–clenched her wrist.

The door behind her slammed shut.

***

Jeff opened his eyes to find himself right where he thought he would–in the pool room. The lights were brighter than they should be or he was suffering from a concussion. He found a large lump on the back of his head, pulled away his fingers and saw blood. He remembered entering the room, chasing after Meghan, and then, nothing. *Lee?* Where was Lee? He remembered Lee yelling not to follow her.

Jeff climbed to his feet, his balance unsteady. His head throbbed as he worked his way to the door. A bout of nausea gripped him, dropping him down on one knee. The vomit splashed the floor adding another not-so-pleasant odor to the room. After a moment, he got back up and continued forward.

Someone passed behind the glass in the door, heading down the hallway. He could have sworn it was Meghan. He got to the door and tried the handle. It wouldn't move.

Just great. Lee, where the hell are you?

"Jeffrey," the voice said.

He turned around faster than his aching head could appreciate and stumbled to the right using the wall for support. Meghan stood in the water, naked, beckoning to him.

"*That's not her,*" Lee's voice screamed in his mind.

"I've been waiting for this moment," she said. "And besides, I'm not sure how many more opportunities we're going to get."

He couldn't find his tongue. His eyes, straining from the sharp lights around the pool, couldn't resist her body. The tops of her breasts were peaking up from the water, calling to part of him in their own come-and-get-it kind of way.

No. It can't be her. None of this is right.

"We've both made a lot of promises, spoken or otherwise, that we've not kept. I'm probably the worst of the two of us, but I'm hoping you'll let me make things up to you," she said, swimming toward him.

"I can't, I, I have to work–"

"I don't think so." She reached the edge of the pool. "I think after tonight you're probably going to need a new job...you and that little friend of yours."

Rhiannon.

He moved back toward the door watching as the Meghan-thing placed her hands on the concrete lip of the pool and pulled her nude form into full view. His hand searching the door behind him found a frozen handle.

"I want you, Jeffrey." Her hands rubbed her breasts, moved to her pale brown areolas and pinched her nipples before sliding down the rest of her tight body. "Take me, right here, right now."

He watched her hands with the awe of a kid half his thirty-five years. He tried to pull his hand from the frozen knob, but couldn't.

"You really don't have much of a choice in the matter." She stepped up to him, her breasts pressing into his chest. She grabbed his crotch and placed her lips to his neck. "You might as well make the most of this night," she whispered moving up to his ear, "it's your last."

Ignoring her groping hand and soft lips against his skin, he tried to turn the handle again to no avail. He was trapped in here with this thing, this ghost.

"Oh, Jeffrey, sweet Jeffrey," she said, stroking his hair. "I'm much more than that."

Her grip on him tightened. "Ahhh," he cried, his voice echoing in the great acoustic room.

"Now, I told you to join me in the pool, and I expect nothing less."

The flesh of his palm tore from his hand as the Meghan-thing ripped him free and dragged him by the front of his pants to the water's edge. Her mouth locked onto his, her tongue entering like a snake, dancing with his own in some hypnotic embrace. His mind and body were sluggish, his thoughts slow. Everything became perfectly clear as her teeth bit through his tongue and the awful taste of iron filled his mouth. He pulled a way, managing a couple steps back. His screams brought a smile across her bloody maw. She spit his tongue onto the floor then reached out and tossed him into the pool.

CHAPTER FIVE

Lee Buhl (his body lying unconscious on the hotel room floor) moved through a world of shadows. He knew it was a dream, but felt it was more. He was here for help, for guidance. He saw a wolf and a fox, instantly recognizing the power animals of his grandparents. He moved to them, bowed down, and planted one knee in the unseen earth at his feet. Fog rolled across all that he could see.

The eyes of the two power animals gazed at him, acknowledging his presence, his desperation. They took turns speaking with him telepathically:

"You seek counsel. Welcome, Grandson," the wolf said.

"You have drifted from us, from your heritage. You are not lost," spoke the fox.

"I'm sorry for the way I have used this gift. I'm–"

"There is no time for apologies. What's done is done. You must listen," said the wolf.

The fox sat before him. Lee bowed his head.

"Look at me," the fox said.

He raised his eyes.

"This spirit is powerful, but not unbreakable. You must light up its place of rest. You must burn the evil from its well. The demon must come to light."

"How can I–"

"It has underestimated your faith, your strength. You must believe. You must be of the light. You must act now. Go." The fox turned away, vanishing in the foggy shadows. The wolf stared at him. The twinkle of his grandfather's eyes flashed and then the wolf joined the fox in the place beyond his dream.

Lee's eyes flew open. The shattered mirror across from him reflected half of his face. For a moment, the eye he saw was the same as the wolf's. He stood up and searched the room for any sign of the thing he'd confronted. Satisfied it was elsewhere he turned to the door. He knew the doorway was bound before he touched the knob. He grasped the silver knob in his hand, closed his eyes, and began the breathing exercises his grandfather had taught him. "This way shall open for the light. This way shall open to the light," he spoke the words, not knowing where they came from, but trusting they were right. The knob turned. He moved into the hallway ready to rush to the rescue, but refrained. He would need his basket of supplies to attempt to thwart this demon.

He spotted the wicker container down the hall where he'd left it before chasing after Jeff.

Jeff.

The demon had shown him lies.

Jeff's screams erupted from somewhere down the hall. Lee hurried back to his basket, gathered the few items which had fallen out, and spotted the bloody footprints and the crimson smudge on the chrome bar of the Exit door. A pounding from the room closest to him stole his attention. Lee set the basket down, slid to his knees, placed his fists on the floor and closed his eyes. He took three deep breaths and reached beyond his physical self. He projected himself through the wall and saw her. The girl, Jeff's co-worker–she wasn't alone.

***

Rhiannon tried to break free from the Kurt-thing's icy grasp, but it just continued to mock her with its Kurt-face–blue eyes turned into black pools swimming in from a world beyond. Rhiannon's fear gave way to rage. She lashed out at the perversion. "Let. Me. Go." She swung wildly at the appendage holding her hostage. Still, it held on. Done fucking around, she unloaded a barrage of punches from her clenched fist, pummeling the Kurt-thing's twisting face. Urgency spurred her on as she thought of the man in black. Surely he was down here with her already. She looked around the room, combing the shadows in the corners for any sign of the man, all the while continuing to wail away at the face lying on the hospital bed. The hand around her wrist finally let go. She turned to see the damage she had inflicted and brought her hands up to her mouth. The face had caved in under her assault. She began to retreat back the way she'd come in rubbing the purpling spot around her wrist from the thing's grip. She looked back to the bed–it was gone, the Kurt-thing with it. The room returned to normal. She was standing next to a large mahogany desk. Before she could breathe easy, her second floor nightmares returned.

Spiders, cockroaches, and serpents of all sizes emerged from every dark possibility in the room. They were crawling up the edges of the desk, slithering over her feet below. Her raging bravery was extinguished immediately. She wasn't sitting like some helpless girl through this mess again. Rhiannon ran to the door. When it refused to let her out, she pounded against it and screamed for help.

"Hello, *Rhiannon?*" a male voice asked.

"Yes. Who's there?"

"My name's Lee. I came here with Jeff."

"Is Jeff out there with you?"

"No. Can you open the door, or is it stuck?"

She tried again. "It won't open. It won't open. You have to get me out of here."

"Okay, okay, give me a minute."

So far the bugs crawling on her and the snakes sliding over her shoes weren't causing her any physical ailments, but her psyche was under full attack. "Please hurry," she said. She closed her eyes trying to shut out the army of nightmares.

The man spoke in a low tone, "This way shall open for the light. This way shall open to the light."

The door pushed inward, Rhiannon maneuvered around it and into the hallway swatting off the things that were crawling over her arms and face.

"Hey, hey, stop." The man followed her. He had high cheek bones, soft brown eyes, and a strong jaw. Part of her acknowledged his good looks; the rest of her urged caution.

"You're Lee, the guy Jeff met." She was still searching her skin for the bugs that were never there. She was standing half-naked before this total stranger. Feeling a warmth flood her cheeks. "Where's Jeff?"

"I think he's with the dark spirit." He looked away as she buttoned the front of her shirt.

"Which one?"

"What do you mean?"

"The guy or the girl?" she said. "There's more than one thing haunting this hotel."

Chapter Six

"There you are," Timothy said, stepping from the room the girl had just escaped. He stood with his hands behind his back, moving his eyes from the half-naked girl to the young man with the shining soul. "And who is this?"

"Run!" the girl shouted, grabbing her new friend.

Timothy smiled as they headed in the direction of his Queen. His lust for death had been quenched tenfold, but he had a special feeling about these two. He started after them, stopping as something cold passed through him. He looked down at his chest, searching for the source of this foreign touch. A shape moved in the hall ahead of him. His smile fell. He thought of Kenneth, lying broken on the floor in room 209, and wondered if this presence had anything to do with the girl's escape from the Ice Queen's young friend. He thought of the portrait that should have rendered the girl unconscious and how it had instead, stopped in mid-air. He thought she had caught it, but now knew better. Whatever was helping her was weak, but present enough to interfere. No matter. He would put a swift end to its meddling.

***

"Come on," Rhiannon said, pulling at Lee. She hoped Jeff was all right, but wasn't about to confront the man in black. She'd gotten away from him twice already and wasn't going to push her luck. She stared straight ahead at the Lobby exit ready to bust out of this damned place and try to figure out a way to find Jeff.

Halfway down the hall, Lee tugged on her. "Wait, we need–"

"We need to get the fuck out of here," she said, stopping near the entrance to the pool room. Visions of her dream (the waters filled with bodies and Kurt emerging from them) flashed across her mind. She shook the nightmare away and said, "Forget about it, come on. We need to get out." She pulled at him, but Lee resisted.

"You should listen to your little friend," the man down the corridor said. "There's nothing left here but death."

Rhiannon glanced back at the man in black, taking his time, hands behind his back as if casually strolling through the streets of Paris. "Come on." She glanced down at the basket in Lee's hand. "Or you can go have your picnic with him."

"We need to get to a room," Lee said. "I can keep him out."

"What? No, no fucking way. We're leaving." A rush of cold air surrounded them. "Shit."

"No. It's not one of them," Lee said. He glanced back at their pursuer then pushed Rhiannon forward. "To that last door, go."

"No, we can't–"

"We can't leave your friend. He came back for you. We cannot leave this place until I bring it to light."

Thinking of Jeff risking his neck to come back for her, sickened at the realization of her cowardice, Rhiannon relented. "Let's go." She could still feel the cool presence around them.

They ran to the door. "I don't have a key," she said.

"This way shall open for the light. This way shall open to the light," Lee said. The door opened.

"What did you? How did–"

Lee shoved her inside. "No time." He closed the door behind them then reached into the wicker basket in his hand. He pulled out a piece of chalk and began drawing a line around the entrance. "No darkness shall penetrate this passage. No darkness shall pass."

She was freezing. The cold had come with them.

"I think you're too late," she said. "There's something in here with us."

"It's okay. It's on our side." He reached back into the basket and hauled out a handful of candles, a bunched up thing of long grassy-looking stuff, and a small vile of dark liquid.

"What's all that for?"

He set up the candles in little tin holders, placing two behind him, one to his right, one to the left, and handed her the last one. "Here, place this behind you. Line it up so that it completes the pentagram."

She noticed the star pattern and thought about asking him if he was a devil worshipper. Instead, she did as she was told. She put the candle in place and waited for him to hand over the lighter. He finished lighting the last one to their left and then the bundle of grassy stuff. The earthy smell it gave off was somehow calming. He handed her the lighter.

"Light the candles," he said, picking the chalk back up from the floor and placing it by her feet. "Then draw a circle around us with the chalk. Quickly, we're running out of time."

She did as he instructed, lighting the candles, spinning around for the chalk and drawing the circle around them. She stepped back to her spot waiting to see what happened next. Lee blew out the burning grass and waved it around them. After a few seconds, he pulled out a small ceramic plate from the basket and placed the smoking bundle in the center. He grabbed the glass vile, popped the top, and drank it down.

"Take my hands," he said. She did. A thousand questions demanded answers, but there was no time. She watched him close his eyes, raise his head, and begin.

"I am already given to the power that rules my fate. I cling to nothing, so I have nothing to defend. I have no thoughts, so I will see.

I fear nothing, so I will remember my name. Show me the light where there is none. Show me the truth," Lee said.

An energy, a vibration tingled through their connection. Rhiannon closed her eyes and was someplace else. The hotel room was gone. She could hear the sound of rushing water and a crackling, like a fire burning in the woods. She opened her eyes and looked across from her–a wolf stared back. She was not afraid. It was him, it was Lee. And she could hear him.

"Who are you?" the wolf asked.

A girl's voice answered, "My name is Christina."

"Do you know what haunts this place?"

"Yes."

"Can you tell us what it is?"

"It was somebody that I used to know. Somebody dark. Somebody who did wicked things."

"What is her name?"

"Sarah," the voice said.

"Christina, will you help us to rid this place of Sarah's presence?"

"Yes."

There was the sound of thunder somewhere beyond them. Rhiannon could hear a series of booms.

"Where is Sarah's home?" he said.

"The pool."

"There is another. Do you know him?"

"No, but he is not as strong."

"We need safe passage to her home."

"I can help."

"Thank you, spirit. May you come to light when all is through."

Rhiannon felt Lee's hands in hers again. She opened eyes that she hadn't realized she'd closed. Lee let go and began collecting the candles, blowing each out. "Help me gather my things."

Bang, bang, bang.

The thunder she'd heard in the dream, or whatever had just happened, was the man in black banging at the door. He hadn't been able to get through. Not yet anyway. She felt a small burst of confidence. They might make it through the night after all.

Chapter Seven

J eff grasped at the Meghan look-alike, the sharp pain from his severed tongue was like nothing he'd ever felt before. He flew backward into the pool water. Submerged, he realized this wasn't water at all. It was thicker, slimier. He tried to swim, his head throbbing, his body betraying him. He kicked his legs as best he could to combat the resisting liquid. Waving his hand out before him he made contact with something and tried to wrap his hand around it. He grasped onto an arm, *her arm?* And pulled his body up, bumping into something or a bunch of something's as he did. He got his head out of the pool gasping for air.

"Sorry about that Jeffrey, I was just having a little fun. You're not mad at me are you?" The devil's voice came from somewhere in the room.

Wherever she was, she wasn't who he was clinging to. He opened his eyes and prayed it wasn't Rhiannon and found himself surrounded by bodies in varying stages of decay. They filled the pool, floating in a bath of blood. He could see things squirming in the mouths and open flesh of the bodies closest to him. He was too shocked to scream. He wanted to wake up, but knew this wasn't another bad dream.

"No. This isn't a dream, Jeffrey. You have a promise to fulfill."

He looked up. Her face was moving; the skin– pulsating, her eyes dancing from one luminous color to another. Her hair seemed alive, reaching out to the room of dead things. Her nudity no longer registered. He looked into her eyes and stared, mesmerized. She moved down the length of the pool. His only thought was of the sweet welcoming arms of death. He followed her, wading through the bodies, using some to pull himself along.

"Come to me, Jeffrey." She moved down the stairs at the shallow end, holding out a hand for him to join her. And he did.

***

"I see her," Rhiannon said.

Lee reared back in time to see the shape of a girl up in the corner by the door, her hands dim-blue and pointing toward the door.

"What's she doing?" Rhiannon said.

Lee finished putting the last pieces of his collection back in the basket, stood up, and said, "She wants me to blur the binding line and let the demon in."

"*What?*"

"I think she has a plan. We have to trust her," he said. "I trust her." Lee knew although she was trapped here like the others she was different. He'd seen glimpses in his vision. She was brought here by this devil and she was here now to help stop it. "Back up. We need to make some room. This demon may not be as powerful, but that doesn't mean it's not dangerous." Lee placed the basket on top of the bed and pulled out a few more tricks.

"That guy, that thing out there. I saw what it can do. There's no fucking way we can let it in here," she said. Lee watched Rhiannon backing away, shaking her head, looking at him like he was throwing her to the wolves. "He can read your thoughts; he can make you see things; he killed all those people..."

"Trust. You must trust the light. Whatever is happening or has been happening in this hotel, it's all born of darkness. The only way to rid this place of its grip is to stand up, trust in good and have faith in the light." Lee grabbed her by the arms and stared into her brown eyes. "Do you trust me?" His faith had been strengthened in the last few hours, but he couldn't deny that the river of deceit he'd been living off for most of his adult life twisted below the surface. He needed her to believe. Their fate depended on it.

"I, I..." She looked past his shoulder.

"Rhiannon," he said.

The door behind them was buckling, the pounding growing louder.

"You can't hide in there all night," the demon said. "You'll give in, and I'll be waiting. Do you hear me?"

Lee shook her, "Look at me," he said. "Listen. We are not in this alone. But we are the only ones here who can stop it. Right now. I need you to believe."

"I," she began then dropped her head. "I don't. I'm sorry, but I don't. You don't know what I've been through."

Lee looked the girl over; the blood on her hands and feet, covering her shirt, her hair.

"Are you kidding? How do you think you've made it this far? How do you think all the others are gone, and yet, you're still standing here? Breathing, fighting...you're stronger than you give yourself credit for. Look at me." She brought her blood and tear-stained face up. "I believe that you are the reason I'm here. You are the light that led me to this shadow." He knew he had to confess it all.

Bang, bang, bang.

"Open this goddamn door or I'll rip it the fuck off," the man in black said.

Lee continued. "I've been nothing but a magician, a boy with a few tricks up his sleeve, a guy using his heritage, his gift, to make a living. I forgot the truths my grandfather had shown me. I had forsaken who I was, what I was supposed to be."

The barrier can no longer hold him, the spirit said inside Lee's mind.

"I know who I am. I am where I'm supposed to be. We are here to end this darkness."

The frame around the door began to crack and splinter.

He's coming in, the spirit said.

"Do you trust me?"

Rhiannon's eyes met his. "Yes."

"Do you trust in the light?"

"Yes."

The door crashed inward slamming against the wall. Lee looked over and saw the man in black with burning coal for eyes–his smile was no longer playful.

"Give me the bitch and I'll let you run," the demon said.

Lee got up, placed himself in front of Rhiannon. "You will not take this girl, demon. You will not take one more soul."

The man in black stepped forward. "You just missed your chance to get out of this alive."

Lee reached in the basket, pulling out a large knife and another vile.

"Is that the good stuff?" The demon smirked.

Rhiannon stepped out from behind Lee, taking the knife from his hand.

"Oh, this one likes to play so rough," the demon said, staring at Rhiannon.

Lee grabbed the blade back from her. "No. Let me," he said.

"But I believe you."

"I know, but it must be me," he said.

***

Rhiannon let go and moved behind Lee.

The blue shadow on the ceiling behind the demon moved into action. Before the demon could turn, the shadow exploded into him.

Lee placed himself between the demon and Rhiannon. Holding out the knife he flipped the top off the vile. "Bless this blade that it may cut the darkness. Bless this weapon against the evils of the world." He dumped the contents of the vile upon the eight-inch blade and then watched the bright white light illuminate the knife.

The demon screamed.

The blue shadow sailed through the man in black, flying straight up before them; the man in black, arms spread, chest out, head back, reeled forward.

Rhiannon collapsed to the floor behind Lee.

She watched him step toward the screaming thing, gripping the handle of the knife with both hands, thrusting it forward, sinking the bright white blade into the heart of the demon.

"Ahhhh!" Lee screamed in its distorting face.

Rhiannon sat transfixed on what was happening. Light spread like fire through the convulsing body of the demon before them. Its mouth, nose, eyes burst with the blinding luminance. The cries of a thousand beasts torn to pieces in the night ripped from its throat. A blast of energy exploded out from its form sending Lee off his feet and flying backward. She heard the shattering glass above her as Lee was sent smashing through the hotel window.

The room was left in blackness. The man in black was gone. Lee had done it. Lee and Christina.

Rhiannon stumbled up to her feet.

"Oh my God," she said, staring at Lee's body lying motionless on the lawn outside the hotel.

***

Lee couldn't open his eyes. He knew he'd sent the first demon into the light, but something bad had happened to his body. He concentrated, focused on Rhiannon and pushed himself forward. He saw his body below, dotted with bloodspots where the shards of glass from the hotel window had penetrated. There was a sliver of blood drooling from his busted lip, which was never a good sign. He had no time to worry about his own well-being. He could see Rhiannon, and the spirit, Christina, watching from the room. He would have to communicate to Rhiannon through the spirit.

***

"Rhiannon," the spirit said.

Rhiannon turned to the girl–eyes meeting hers, hands formed and held out toward her–waiting.

"Christina?" Rhiannon said.

"Yes, listen, your friend, Lee. He's with me," she said.

"Oh my God, is he, is he..." Rhiannon brought her hands to her mouth.

"No. He's not dead. He's weak, but his body is still alive."

Rhiannon looked out at his body, and then back to the spirit. "He's with you?"

"He says Jeff is with Sarah. You have to stop her."

"What? How? What about you?"

"He says *you* have to do this. *You* have to bring her dark resting place to light," Christina said.

"What do I do?"

"He says to follow the spell with the candles in the pentagram, the smudge-stick in the plate, when it reveals itself, read the vanquishing incantation from the notebook, Burning Darkness. He says to wait until she's in the center of the pentagram."

"Lee, how do I–?"

"He's gone. His spirit is very weak. Listen to me. I feel responsible for what Sarah has become. I, I tried to stop her once before, when we were alive. I failed." Christina's luminescent blue gaze bloomed before Rhiannon's eyes. "I will help you destroy her."

CHAPTER EIGHT

Rhiannon grabbed Lee's wicker basket of supplies and moved back down the hall toward the pool room, knocking on doors along the way–no one answered. Christina said she had to get things rolling, and that the spirit would make sure Sarah was where she was supposed to be. Rhiannon wondered what life with the real Sarah must have been like. She shuddered. Two doors from the pool room, she found the maintenance office. She tried the knob–it was locked.

Of course it is.

She wanted to check on Jeff, but didn't think she'd get more than one crack at what she had planned. She hurried back down the hall to the front desk, went into the back office and moved to the big red box where they kept all the hotel keys. She found the maintenance key and grabbed it. The lost and found box by the housekeeping office caught her attention. She fished out some jogging shorts and a raggedy, red hooded sweatshirt. The clothing helped to ease her sense of vulnerability. She also grabbed what looked like a reusable shopping bag from Jenner's Grocery and threw it over her shoulder. She slipped the maintenance key in the sweatshirt's pocket and was ready to run down the hall when an idea struck her. She moved to the fire security panel and scanned the system's operating menu on the inside of the small grey door. She found the alarm silence button and pressed it. The system functioning indicator turned from green to red. The curtains hanging in each window of the back office gave her another idea. She reached into Lee's basket for his lighter, crouched at one curtain, zippo in hand, then the next, setting fire to each of them one by one. She left the room–already filling with smoke and flames–and hurried down the hallway looking like Red Riding Hood.

Steve, the maintenance manager, had an amazingly organized office. Tools, signs, ladders, and spare parts all labeled and neatly tucked in their own spaces. She found the bright yellow cabinet that read "flammable liquids" tucked away next to his small, black desk in the back. She opened it to find more than enough fuel to do the job. She grabbed soda-sized bottles of white-labeled green and black liquids. Their labels read: *Total Alkalinity Indicator, Silver Nitrate Regent,* and *Sulfuric Acid.* She also grabbed a metal canister of something called Handi-Strip and a couple small cans of enamel. The smells assaulted her nose, promising to do the deed. She used a screwdriver to pop the tops off the cans of enamel, and exited the room. Smoke filled the lobby toward the east end of the floor.

It had begun.

She sat the wicker basket at the start of the carpeting and tilted the small cans, one in each hand, making her way down the corridor, pouring out their contents. When they emptied, she started with the Handi-Strip. She reached the exit door at the far end of the hall, satisfied that this would do the trick then ran back to the wicker basket and pulled the Zippo out. The pool room was diagonal from the maintenance room; she dared a glance, and noticed the frosted glass pane to its entrance. It was in there, and so was Jeff. She wondered where Christina had gone. She hoped the spirit was ready.

She flicked the wheel, igniting the lighter, and held it to the carpet. The blue flames came to life, racing down the cold hallway. She tucked the Zippo in her pocket, picked up the basket, and moved to the pool room door.

No turning back.

The thought crossed her mind with an air of finality. She grasped the frozen silver handle and opened the door. What she saw tilted her universe.

The pool was filled with blood and decaying bodies, lots of them. Her stomach turned threatening to cripple her. She followed the blood-soaked corpses with her eyes to the opposite end of the pool and then forgot all about them. Jeff, eyes open and staring off into another dimension, lay naked, slumped against the far wall, his mouth, neck, chest, and exposed manhood covered in blood. The girl next to him looked dead, too. Dark hair covered her face, but Rhiannon recognized her as the girl with the broken air conditioner.

She had called herself Sarah. If the dark presence was no longer making her home in the young girl, then where the hell was it? Rhiannon glanced around the room, the hairs on her body reaching out in terror, pleading with her to run the other way. Lee had told her what she had to do. She opened the basket and pulled out the candles, the smudge-stick, its plate, and the notebook he had told her to read from. She lit the smudge and let it burn a few seconds before blowing it out and letting its positive aroma spread up into the air dancing with the trail of smoke. She carefully laid it on the plate and began to light the other candles. With each one lit, she stood and placed them around the pool remembering to align them in the shape of a star, or pentagram, as Lee had referred to it.

Fight fire with fire.

She sat two at this end, one to the left of the pool, and then circled back around, not quite ready to step near Jeff's body. Then she placed one on the right side. As she approached her co-worker's slumped and bloody form, she noticed a stirring among the floating cadavers in the pool. She hurried the candle to its place between Jeff and the girl. With the pentagram complete, she moved back around the way she came, keeping an eye on the movement below the lake of blood and death. She reached into the grocery bag for the other chemicals from the maintenance office. She twisted the tops open and scurried to the moving pool water, emptying the contents and throwing the containers in as well before she returned to the basket. Finally, she grabbed the notebook. A head emerged from the sea of corpses. Rhiannon stood, trembling before the evil that brought this night to a head. Her fingers refused to flip through the pages of the notebook, the thought that she couldn't do this slammed into the front of her mind.

The girl who emerged from the pool reminded her of the girl from that Stephen King movie. Blood-soaked hair matted to her face; a few dying curls stubbornly hanging down over bare breasts. Her eyes were two hot coals with an orange fire blazing behind them. Her lips curled at the corners in a sinister grin that made Rhiannon want to hide. The girl, the thing called Sarah, stood fifteen feet away, dripping blood into the small puddle of crimson at her feet.

"So," Sarah said, glancing around at the candles surrounding her home. "Did our magic man put you up to this?"

Rhiannon stood silent. Fear pummeled her courage into complete submission.

"You two managed to stop my sweet Kenneth and my Timothy. I should say that makes me want to tear you to pieces, but truthfully, I'm more impressed than anything. It's a pity to lose such devoted hands, but they were only the first. My powers are only beginning to reach their full potential."

"What are you?" Rhiannon asked.

"To be totally honest with you, I don't really know."

"You're a demon."

"Maybe," the thing said. "My father built this hotel. This was his *real* baby," the demon's voice sent a chill through Rhiannon. "He was in love with his–"

Sarah looked up as if something was there.

Rhiannon, seizing the moment, focused on the pages before her.

Burning Darkness; the incantation that Lee had instructed her to read once the demon revealed itself and moved into place. She read the words in her mind, trying to commit them to memory.

Sarah's dead eyes turned back to her. "Sorry about your boyfriends." She looked over her shoulder at Jeff. "Jeffrey was the most fun." Her eyes latched back onto Rhiannon's. "He had one last good fuck before he went. He tried to think about helping you, but I wouldn't have that. I needed his full attention." She stopped and looked down toward the notebook in Rhiannon's hand. "Why don't you hand that to me?"

Before Rhiannon could reply the notebook flew from her hands, into the air, and landed in the blood pool behind Sarah.

"No," Rhiannon cried. Her voice sounded even more desperate bouncing back at her from across the room.

"I can't have any more of these little hiccups." Sarah looked to her left. Rhiannon followed her gaze; the frost on the door had melted, the conflagration on the other side blazing against it as if hell had come knocking.

Sarah's eyebrows furrowed as she glared back at Rhiannon, her eyes now matching the orange glow outside the room.

Didn't see that one coming, did you?

"You little bitch," Sarah said, her voice doubled, sounding like a chorus of evil. She took a step toward Rhiannon and stopped. The grin from her lips dissolved into a sneer. "You," the voices said. Sarah's blazing eyes stared past Rhiannon.

Rhiannon circled to find Christina behind her. The ghost was more solid now. She had short black hair, soft features, and black eyes that had locked onto Sarah's like a sniper eyeing its mark. Rhiannon stepped aside.

"Little Tina, come back to try and finish what you fucked up before?"

The shadow—Tina—didn't answer.

"I knew these fucks couldn't stop my boys without some kind of help." Sarah stepped forward, her skin crawling, stretching and ripping from her body. "You're nothing. I helped you become something."

Tina didn't respond, or move.

"I gave you freedom. I gave you *this*. Can't you feel the power? What a waste."

The form beneath Sarah's skin was rotten, her blood-darkened hair turned grey and rose around her skeletal features. Patches of skin clung to bones and the browned tissue of her face, her voices taking on a shrill edge. Rhiannon remembered what Lee had said. *You must wait until the demon reveals itself.* She tried to recall the chant.

"This time, it's my turn to snuff you out," the demon said.

Christina's features blurred. The blue luminance around her intensified.

"Come here you fucking bitch and take your goddamn medicine," the Sarah-thing screamed and launched at the blue shadow.

They tangled, resembling a throbbing, dark cancer attempting to attach itself to a healthy cell. Rhiannon ducked down as they flew up and shot around the room from side to side. Unintelligible shrieks burst in quick audible strikes making her cringe and cover her ears. She recalled the chant, but needed to wait. The dark spirit had to be in the center of the star.

They bounced from one wall to another, to the floor, to the ceiling, knocking down lighting fixtures and the rack of towels before dropping into the pool of bodies. A splash of crimson shot up like a geyser, and covered the area surrounding the pool in blood. Rhiannon didn't hesitate:

"Bind thee, dark spirit, to rest. Let darkness burn and come to light. Let darkness burn and come to light..." she stalled.

Oh my God, what's the rest of it?

A charge went off in the pool. Waves of blood rose over the concrete lip and spread out onto the floor. Rhiannon raised her hands to her temple trying to block out the activity and concentrate on the missing line. The thing that tangled with Christina began to rise from its lake of blood. Its eyes—now red and brimming with hatred—zeroed in on her.

Rhiannon was ready to curl up into a ball as the light went off inside her head. She spit it out: "Bind thee, dark spirit, to rest. Let darkness burn and come to light–"

The demon let loose a howl of rage reaching out its skeletal claws in Rhiannon's direction.

"–Let darkness burn and come to light. Give into the power that rules your fate. Demon, burn, and come to light."

The demon was at the pool's edge when the blood ignited into flames. Howls of anguish and defeat filled the room; the cries of a tortured soul. Rhiannon covered her ears, and watched the magnificent flame engulf the demon and pull it back within the pit of fire. Rhiannon stole one last glance at Jeff–sadness sliding in behind her exhausted mind–and lunged for the door. More flames met her as she realized she was trapped. She dropped down on her hands and knees, positioning herself between the red hot door, and the burning pool.

Across the room she saw the changing area. There were windows in the stalls. She got up, ran over and threw the door open, not bothering to watch the shamanic fire morphing from orange and red to purple and green. The demon's cries had faded. Rhiannon burst through the door of the first stall and saw the open window above the toilet. She climbed the porcelain god, and punched at the screen that blocked her exit. It came free after a couple of whacks. She grabbed the window sill and the side of the stall and pulled herself up. Grasping at the wet grass and clawing her fingers into the mud, she pushed her body through, clearing the window and liberating herself from the inferno.

CHAPTER NINE

Lee's body lay motionless farther down the lawn. Rhiannon climbed to her feet and ran to see if he was still alive, praying he'd made it, but not thinking it likely. The entire hotel was ablaze. Flames and smoke billowed out from almost every window. Crackling, loud pops, and shattering glass replaced the serene night that otherwise surrounded the inn. From ten steps away, she could tell he was dead.

Rhiannon dropped to her knees. Lee's death, a final cheap shot from this God-awful night, landed the hardest blow of them all, sapping the last of her will to fight.

The building sizzled and popped giving off a nonstop, high-pitched whistle that sounded like a scream.

The building's dying.

The thought would have made her smile if she could. Instead, she got back up (one more time) and stumbled away from Lee and the burning hotel.

"Uhhh…"

Was that?

Rhiannon spun around to find the shaman slowly lifting his head from the ground. "Lee!" She dropped to her knees by his side. His eyes opened.

"Did we, did you…"

"Yes, we did it–me, you and Christina."

"What about...what about Jeff?" he said, turning his eyes to hers.

Her tears pelted his shoulder as she shook her head and squeezed his hand. "I thought you were dead, too."

"I had a little trouble getting back to my body," he said. "Help me up?

"Are you sure you can?"

"No, but it seems we haven't let that stop us yet." He tried to smile.

She helped him to his knees, then to his feet. Together, they limped their way across the lawn. With the blazing hellfire at their backs, they watched their shadows limp along as well, stopping at the road. Lee–one arm clutched around his ribs—Rhiannon was sure some were broken–let go of her shoulder, then slid down onto his ass in the dirt. Rhiannon put a hand behind him and helped him lay back. She dropped down beside him.

Waiting for anyone to pass by, she stayed next to him, silent, bruised, alive and staring up at the starry sky watching the old inn burn into the night. Rhiannon prayed that no one would call the fire department until it was too late. She wanted the whole place to burn to the ground.

She thought of Jeff, of Kurt, of a blue shadow named Christina.

We did it.

EPILOGUE

Lee Buhl sat at his laptop smoking a cigarette in a crummy Econo Lodge outside his hometown of Malden, Massachusetts. It had been nearly a year since the incident at the Bruton Inn and his father's subsequent passing from a sudden stroke two days afterward. He'd finally come back home to visit his father and his grandparents' graves and see about putting a claim in on the old family ghost house. His mother, grateful to have her boy home again, wanted nothing to do with the haunted relic and said it would just be a matter of paperwork to get him the keys and the deed. He should be in by week's end.

In his meditations following the happenings at the Bruton Inn, he'd made a promise to his grandparents to stay on the path of his heritage. Roots were important. Family was important; not to be forgotten or taken for granted. His days as Lee Buhl, "Urban Shaman," were done. No more working lonely old crows for their savings; no more novelty merchandising or crappy volumes of half-believed haunting books. The true shaman practiced love and respect and harmony on a daily basis, on his own and out of the spotlight.

He'd not gone back to the scorched land off Route 5 that once held the foundation of the Bruton Inn. He did not care to.

Rhiannon had kept in touch on Facebook. He was proud to have made such a great friend and extremely impressed with the way she had entered the battlefield, slayed the demon, and pulled through what would have crippled many. Via email, Facebook messaging, an occasional phone call, and Skype, per her request, Lee had shown her the path to Shamanism. She was a willing and open receptor taking his teachings and–with an amazing grace–applying them to a life in progress. She was attending school at Oswego in upper New York with a friend of hers. She studied Zoology, trying to put all of her focus on animals. She'd joked that she'd had enough of humans–too many skeletons in the closet, too many ghosts. She'd encouraged Lee to write the book of all books and tell their story–so long as he promised to change her name to Alana or Crystal and pass it off as fictional.

He felt dirty even considering the book, especially in the wake of his spiritual rebirth. But eventually, through Rhiannon's constant support, he finally put pen to paper and crafted his most honest and cathartic piece of writing to date. And his first official work of "fiction."

For once, he was going low key, choosing a small horror press to release *their* story, changing the names and places in the book as he'd promised Rhiannon (though he did cave to the will of his publisher who pushed for the "based off true events" tagline for the back jacket). *Burning Darkness* was set for an October 2015 release.

Lee finished typing his message to Rhiannon filling her in on the details of the release. He sent it off on the wings of the web, closed the laptop and crushed out his last cigarette. He stood and stared out at the perfect clear night beyond the window of his hotel room. Even calm nights like this made him shiver if he stared into the darkness for too long. He stripped off his shirt and ran his fingers over the row of ribs that had taken nearly six months to fully heal.

After a moment, he lowered himself down onto another lumpy mattress, dropped his head to the pillow, and clenched the wooden pendent around his neck. He kissed the head of the Native figure, whispered a prayer of love and light, and closed his eyes.

His dreams were filled with blood-bathed mermaids and a lake of fire–a small penance for redemption.

THE END

Also By Glenn Rolfe

Novels:
Blood and Rain
Becoming
The Window
Until Summer Comes Around
August's Eyes

Novellas:
Abram's Bridge
Things We Fear
Something in the Groove

Collections:
Slush
Land of Bones
Nocturnal Pursuits

ABOUT THE AUTHOR

Glenn Rolfe is an author from the haunted woods of New England. He has studied creative writing at Southern New Hampshire University and continues his education in the world of horror by devouring the novels of Stephen King, Richard Laymon, Brian Keene, Jack Ketchum, and many others. He has three children, Ruby, Ramona, and Axl. He is grateful to be loved despite his weirdness.

He is a Splatterpunk Award nominee and the author of *August's Eyes, Until Summer Comes Around, Blood and Rain, The Window, Becoming, The Haunted Halls, Chasing Ghosts, Adam's Bridge, Things We Fear, Boom Town,* and the collections: *Slush, Land of Bones,* and *Nocturnal Pursuits.*